# A Letter to Keep You Safe

Also by Rachaele Hambleton

*Part-time Working Mummy: A Patchwork Life*

*A Different Kind of Happy*

*The Patchwork Family: Toddlers,
Teenagers and Everything in Between*

*The Power in You: How to Live and Love Your Life*

# A Letter to Keep You Safe

**RACHAELE HAMBLETON**
PART-TIME WORKING MUMMY

ROBINSON

ROBINSON

First published in Great Britain in 2026 by Robinson

Copyright © Rachaele Hambleton, 2026

1 3 5 7 9 10 8 6 4 2

The moral rights of the author have been asserted.

*All characters and events in this publication, other than those clearly in the public domain, are fictitious and any resemblance to real persons, living or dead, is purely coincidental.*

All rights reserved.
No part of this publication may be reproduced, stored in a retrieval system, or transmitted, in any form, or by any means, without the prior permission in writing of the publisher, nor be otherwise circulated in any form of binding or cover other than that in which it is published and without a similar condition including this condition being imposed on the subsequent purchaser.

A CIP catalogue record for this book
is available from the British Library.

ISBN: 978-1-47214-926-8 (hardback)
ISBN: 978-1-47214-925-1 (trade paperback)

Typeset in Adobe Garamond by Hewer Text UK Ltd, Edinburgh
Printed and bound in Great Britain by Clays Ltd, Elcograf S.p.A.

Papers used by Robinson are from well-managed forests and other responsible sources.

Robinson
An imprint of
Little, Brown Book Group
Carmelite House
50 Victoria Embankment
London EC4Y 0DZ

The authorised representative
in the EEA is
Hachette Ireland
8 Castlecourt Centre
Dublin 15, D15 XTP3, Ireland
(email: info@hbgi.ie)

An Hachette UK Company
www.hachette.co.uk

www.littlebrown.co.uk

*To Joshua, thank you for making all of this possible.
ILYSM x*

# MONDAY

Dear Martha,

I heard what happened just before 9 a.m. today. I was pulling up to your house to drop off Woody's teddy and sun cream when Jen called.

She was at work when you arrived in the ambulance – she was the first person to see you. She said when you got to the hospital it was obvious immediately that things were bad. Your right eye was totally closed over and swollen, and you had blood coming out of your ear. They wheeled you in on the bed and you vomited. You were making sense at times, but then not so much, and your voice was slurred. When you were making sense, you were scared. Of course you were scared.

Jen said she could see you were fading away as you waited on the hospital trolley, and they wasted no time getting your head scanned.

You were taken straight from the CT scanner to surgery.

They said you would have died if they hadn't operated. The bleed from your brain was so bad that your brain was being pushed over to one side. They removed the blood that was trapped between your brain and skull, and are hopeful that there won't be any more bleeding. You're lucky to have survived . . . or are you?

Is it bad that I think that? Does it make me a horrid person, to wonder if you'd have been better off not making it? But I remember the attacks that I survived, the ones I woke from ... And I know you, I know how our brains work – you're one of my best friends, we've had these conversations a million times – and I know when you wake from this, the chances are you might wish you weren't here.

My manager – you know, Mags – was incredible. I sat outside your empty house and called her straight away. I could hear she was trying to hold it together. She's grown to care so much about you, Martha – from that first risk assessment she did when you were originally referred to us for domestic abuse support, to the help she and the team have given you over the last few months. I could hear from her voice that this is going to affect her – but not just her, our whole team. The work all of them, and you, have done, the progress you'd made ... This is going to be heartbreaking for everyone.

I returned home at 10.15 a.m. I don't know why it took me so long to make the ten-minute car journey back, but it did. I sat in the car and cried. I screamed, I gripped the steering wheel, wanting to punch it. I rested my forehead against it and just let out fat, loud sobs whilst the tears splashed onto my bare legs – sobs for you, for Woody, for me, for all the women and children like us. Tears for all of us, for the fact that so many lives look like this, because these fucking men continue to hurt and kill us, every single day.

I don't understand. No, I do. I get it, all of it – because I led your life for so long when I was married to David. The secrets, the lies. My desperation to believe he would change. The way I listened every time he promised me he would do better, try harder, get help. The guilt I felt when he would cry about losing the boys if I left, when he told me I was ripping our family apart.

I understand all of it. It fucks me off that I understand it so well. I wish I didn't.

Jen assumed he had attacked you randomly on your way back from the nursery run, but from the sounds of it now, it was a planned meeting. I keep going back over the last few weeks. I know you'd had some down days, but nothing that would massively red flag to me that you were missing him to the point of meeting him. You were relieved when he got those bail conditions, and you fought so hard to get the non-molestation order in place . . . But the police are suggesting that you planned to meet him. I feel like I should have checked in with you more, asked you if you were OK – actually OK, not just pretending to be.

I wish you'd have told me, Jen, Meg or Jo – or all of us, last week when we were having dinner and things felt OK. You seemed OK. Seeing as the four of us have been best friends for over two years, I feel annoyed at myself – especially given where I've come from – that I didn't see this coming. I'm so devastated that you didn't tell any of us that you were planning to meet him – but I also get it. I can't help but wonder whether, if I'd shared more of my story with you before this, you wouldn't have gone. And right now we would both be on our way to work as we are every Monday morning, chatting on the phone about everything and nothing whilst you beg Woody to get his shoes on and George sorts his Pokémon cards in the back of the car. And tomorrow we would still be going to the zoo with Jo and Megan and all the kids as we'd arranged – something you were so excited about doing with Woody, as he loves animals and you said this was going to be his first ever zoo trip.

Instead, you're in a coma after Craig attacked you with a brick, and I don't know what the future looks like now for you or Woody.

Mags was already at my house when I arrived back. She stayed for most of the morning. We drank tea, curled up at either end of my sofa. We went between total silence and non-stop talking.

I feel lucky to have Mags as a manager. She's such a decent human – passionate about women's rights and domestic abuse. The way she treats the women and children we support is incredible. I'll never forget when she first interviewed me for the position of support worker a year after I'd left David. Her knowledge and experience, teamed with her warmth and gentleness, made me really want the job. It made me want to be like her, to support women at the worst times in their lives. I was excited to work for someone who made me feel safe and supported within spending less than an hour in their company – something that, in those days, was almost impossible for me.

She wasn't surprised you'd arranged to meet Craig this morning. In fact, it was kind of like she'd expected it to happen – but she's been in this line of work for over two decades and, in that time, she's seen and heard things that you or I probably couldn't imagine. She's into double figures now, with the number of women she's lost to suicide – suicide due to the effects of domestic abuse. Most of those women's former partners, the perpetrators of that abuse, continue to roam the streets. Some even have the full custody of the children they created together – free to go on and destroy more lives. So I suppose after supporting so many damaged, vulnerable and broken women, it takes a lot to shock Mags. But even though she isn't shocked, she is sad. So sad, that knowing how kind and beautiful you are, fun and sparkly – you're now in hospital with horrific injuries.

We had a little cry together again before she left. It felt good to have her there with me, to make me feel like I wasn't going mad or making it about me, which was how it felt at first. Mags made me feel calmer, reassured that this situation is affecting everyone around us, no matter how they knew you – and that's OK. It's a good thing we're all devastated by it, because it shows how loved you are. And then the reality hit me – that this is truly shit. It's shit and sad and devastating. Mags reassured me that it's OK for it to feel hard and heavy right now. It should absolutely feel hard and heavy.

It's now 4 p.m. I still feel nauseous. I'm still in shock.

I've just realised no food has passed my lips since I sat here this morning, scoffing a huge bowl of porridge that was too hot to eat, burning the roof of my mouth as I rushed to take Milo out for a long walk before I left the house for the day. I haven't even had a coffee since then – I'd usually be at least three down by now.

I'm also aware this whole thing has triggered so much for me. Although you and the other girls know about my many years of abuse, I have never really spoken in depth to you about the repeat attacks, the sexual abuse, the injuries from each incident . . . or the final one, a year before I met you, where I was operated on in the same hospital you're in now.

I have so many thoughts on the immediate future, and how it looks for Woody.

Woody.

All the stuff flying around my head about what will happen to him now. What has he been told? Right now, he's staying with Jo and Jamie – we made that choice because he's as obsessed with Jo and Jamie's youngest daughter, Dotty, as she is with him. They're months apart in age, and we felt it's probably best for him to be there, out of all our homes, because he has the distraction of all their kids and a busy house with everything he needs.

I can't imagine how he will feel. He absolutely adores you – and what an affectionate and incredible mum you are to him. It feels like it's just been the two of you forever, even though you only left Craig a few months ago. It reminds me so much of my boys and me – an unbreakable bond where, being their mum, you know everything they're thinking or feeling without them saying a word. Although Woody is still not yet three, there is no one else that matters to him like you. You make his whole world go round – don't forget that when you wake, Martha.

I know from my own experience how easy it is to let the guilt and shame consume you. It's impossible not to blame yourself, to feel like you're a bad mum – but none of this is on you. It's on Craig – every single bit of it. And the love you have for Woody, the love I've had the honour of witnessing over the last two years – it's irreplaceable.

I remember the day I met you, when you popped into the café with Woody after seeing the **'*Staff Needed*'** sign outside. By this point Jo and her mother-in-law, Pat, had taken over the café, but I was living above in the flat and would pop down most days – for my own need to be around them, as they were a huge support to me at that time, as well as to help them transition as smoothly as possible with the takeover.

Woody was in his pram. He had just turned one, and I remember smiling at how similar you both were. Your hair was the exact same colour – all these different shades of blondes including white, a straw yellow and a honey colour. Beautiful locks, you both have, all the colours entwined together – yours falling down your back and Woody's around his ears in ringlet curls – wild and untamed. He was dressed in an oversized Rip Curl T-shirt, black leggings and little black-and-white Vans socks – the bottom of his chunky legs on show, tanned from spending his days with you on the beach. He was sucking on a bright teething necklace, trying to shove as much of it as possible into his drooling mouth. It's funny how you don't ever want to be judgemental but you still make judgements. It's like your brain just does it automatically – it can't be helped or stopped. *Trendy*, I thought, when I set eyes on him. Trendy, because of you.

You were so beautiful. That was my immediate thought when I saw you. Beautiful and tiny, about a size six. You could have easily passed as a teenage girl from behind. You were wearing black cycling shorts with tanned legs like Woody, cute matching black-and-white ankle socks and Vans trainers, topped with a Santa Cruz oversized T. *Trendy*, I thought again, studying you over the top of my peppermint tea. *Trendy skater girl.*

You were super-tanned, glowing, but you triggered me immediately. Something about you made my belly flip. I could feel your anxiety – you were hyper-vigilant, eyes darting everywhere whilst making no eye contact with anyone – as if you were scanning for danger. I convinced myself I was being crazy – I used to do that a lot. Not so much now. Over time I have begun to realise that when it comes to me meeting new women, I get it right with the red flags more than I get it wrong, so I question my gut far less than I used to. The gut, I have come to realise, is one of the most powerful things in our bodies. I raise my boys to know that – to listen to their gut when it talks to them, especially when their head and their heart are uncertain.

Jo gave you the job on the spot. She liked you. I liked you, and I hadn't even spoken to you – you hadn't even seen me, sat in the corner behind my laptop, watching you and your son. You would start the following Monday – three days a week. I heard you say that your partner was a lighting technician, but he had just lost his job, so you were looking for something immediately to help tide you over. The flags were just getting redder and redder, the more you spoke to Jo and Pat, and I felt the butterflies in my belly flutter more quickly.

I wasn't there the first day you started, but I asked Jo how it had gone that evening, in the WhatsApp group we had – the same one you've now been in for the past two years, and which, for the past few hours, you've been noticeably absent from. It's a group the girls originally set up after I left David, and it was a lifeline for me. Megan, Jen and Jo became my soul sisters in the days and weeks after I left him, and I'm not sure I'd be here, writing this to you, without them. I hope when you wake up that same WhatsApp group can provide the same lifeline for you.

Jo replied saying you'd done really well and she liked you. Nothing else. Jen and Megan then said they'd both popped in that day for brunch and met you, and that you seemed lovely and sweet. No red flags raised by any of them, so I simmered down again. I reminded myself it could all be in my head. I prayed at that point that it was all in my head.

I remember the first time I knew my gut was right – that you were being abused. Your neighbours called the police after hearing Craig losing it, and he was arrested. You called Jo a few hours later, when you got home after leaving hospital. Jo rang me and I rushed straight to your house. I already knew it wasn't the first time he'd been violent. You'd never told me, but the signs were there.

Woody was at home when the incident happened – Craig had stopped him going to nursery the month before he attacked you, to save money. It was just after lunchtime when I arrived. Two social workers were leaving as I came in: one young and straight-faced – I couldn't work out if it was because she had no emotion or because she was trying to hold it together – and an older lady who smiled at me sweetly on her way out.

You were in shock. I knew the look as soon as I walked through the door and saw you. I could tell how you were feeling without you even speaking.

I can picture every detail of your injuries right now. You had dried blood at the front of your perfect middle parting. I could see the glue from where the hospital had seen to the wound. Your left eye was swollen – not closed over, but I knew it would soon be black. Your beautiful long fingernails were still intact, but had blood around them, where you'd eaten away the skin with the stress of it all.

Woody was awake, buried into you. You gripped his hand the whole time as you rocked back and forth with his whole body snuggled into your tiny frame, reassuring with words like 'It's OK, bud' or 'We're fine now, baby, we're gonna be just fine'. I felt the love instantly. I felt that mother's protection, pouring from your entire being into him. Even though the purple bruising covered the limited amount of your skin that was on show, I could see you still had that fight within you. Instantly, I felt relieved that I was your friend. Although there was a sadness inside of me for you, there was also a deep-rooted knowledge that came to me of how life could look for you if I could get you the support and help that you needed and deserved. I knew I had to help build you and your baby back up, and let you see what your ever after was going to look like . . .

It doesn't feel like that right now. It feels like somehow, I didn't work hard enough back then. I feel like I took my eye off the ball. I thought you were coping better than you were. I keep feeling all the same feelings I had just over three years ago, when I was lying in that hospital bed, listening to all the machines beeping, the doors around me opening and closing, doctors and nurses rushing in and out. The bright white ceiling I spent days looking up at, wondering where it all went wrong, whilst I lay beneath it, covered in hundreds of injuries and scars – some years old – from a man I had once believed that I loved – like you did yours. A man who was also the father of my children . . .

We know you have no family, from the things you've told us. Your mum died when you were seventeen, something you and Jo have in common – although her adoptive mum had cancer and your mum died from alcohol poisoning. You never knew your dad, and you don't have any family you were raised around, none that you know of – or that's what you've always told us.

Mags has been told that Craig isn't talking in custody – he went 'no comment' throughout his police interview, despite still having the brick in his hand, covered in your blood, when they arrived. And despite two independent witnesses giving statements as to what happened. One was an eleven-year-old girl, on her way to a dental appointment with her mum. He goes to court first thing tomorrow, but they're hopeful he will be remanded in custody. I can't help but think he should have got a harsher sentence than community service after the first attack, and then maybe we wouldn't be here today, who knows?

We are worried that there might be friends and family from your past that we just don't know about, but we can't locate your mobile phone so we can't check your contacts. Jo said your social media doesn't have anyone other than people locally on it, so I genuinely don't have anyone to contact to tell them about your situation. And that feels wrong, and so sad, given how incredible you are – I want the whole world to be up in arms. I want crowds in the street to come together and pray for you to get well. You deserve to feel love everywhere. I don't understand how the only people you have supporting you are four women you've known for just twenty-four months.

I've thought a lot about what I needed when I woke up after David's final attack on me years ago. If a domestic abuse survivor who had been through a similar ordeal as me had written parts of her story for me to read – to show me she could, and did, escape and become free and happy – I feel that would have not only occupied some of the longest, saddest, scariest days of my life, lying in that bed, but it would have also given me strength – to see I could do it too. That I could free myself of him forever, and my boys and I WOULD be OK.

And although we've spoken about my life with David, and some of the things that happened, I've decided to write you some of my story – which is so similar to yours in so many ways – so that when you do wake up, which I know you will, you'll know you're not alone.

You have to wake up, Martha, like I once did. Even if you open your eyes and feel devastated, you're still alive, because the reality is just too much to deal with – the pressure of everyone knowing, the guilt, the shame and the blame – you have to, because you have an innocent little boy that needs you. He has no one else. There is no choice for women like us. Survival is the only way. It's all we know.

I began journalling three years ago, after the attack. Jo encouraged me to. She was my best friend then, as she continues to be today, along with the rest of our girl gang – you included. It's something her therapist encouraged her to do when she was at her worst, and it's been as life changing for me as it was for her.

It was something I'd never even thought to do. I couldn't – wouldn't – because I would never have been able to write the truth whilst married to David, for fear of him finding it – and what was the point of journalling lies about being happy and having great memories? That wasn't my life. It would have been pointless. Infuriating even.

So this letter to you is going to be my story – the story of me – your friend, Louise – much-loved daughter, mother of two incredible boys, domestic abuse survivor.

# TUESDAY

The beach, which you can see from my apartment, is bustling today, which is strange considering it's May and the kids are still in school. It's been this busy since I stepped back into my apartment this morning.

The sun feels angry; it's been almost thirty degrees for the past three days. The heat is overwhelming – burning down from the sky and radiating up from the tarmac on the road. Most days I hate the high ceilings at home because of the cobwebs I can never reach, but today I'm thankful for them, for making me feel less claustrophobic, not as trapped – a little more free from spiders, their homes and all.

Sitting at my lounge window, I watch all the families sprawled across the miles of golden sand. Milo has spent the day skulking around, trying to find fresh pieces of cold wooden floorboards to lie on in shady corners of the flat. I walked him at 6 a.m., before I woke George for school, and I'll take him out again after sunset. It's too hot for him to go out in the daytime. It surprises me how many dogs I still see walking past my home – cockapoos like Milo, but so many other breeds, too – panting like mad and lying on the hot pavement every time their idiot owners stop to browse in another shop window. So many of them stop and drink from the dogs' bowl outside the café like their life depends on it. I know from experience that Pat and Jo will refill that water bowl several times a day for those poor dogs.

Mostly though, today – probably because of you, because of this situation – I focus on the dads. Or maybe the stepdads, or uncles – who knows. But it's men: I focus on all of the men. What I do know is that I'm focusing today the same way I first did all those years ago, when I first started looking out of this window. I know I'm doing it as soon as I start, because my heart races faster and my neck feels flushed. I'm annoyed at myself immediately. I want to stop – I tell myself out loud to stop – but I can't. I know I can't. It's begun again.

I study these grown, adult men building sandcastles with little boys, pulling tiny girls through the sea on their blow-up inflatables. The ones chatting away to their partners, giving them the odd hug or kiss whilst tucking into sandwiches from their cool boxes, sitting on their striped deckchairs that they hire from Greg in the hut beneath me. When I can't see close enough, or I convince myself I spot 'that' happening, I get my binoculars and I zoom in to really 'check'. They're clever though, I know this. They hide it so well.

All anyone else would see out of my window today are happy families, making memories and having fun – and I've realised, for a while now, that that's what I've begun to see again. But not today. Today has made me aware that I *was* almost there, back to seeing what other people see – 'normal people', you know? People who aren't like me. Who aren't like you, Martha. Who haven't lived lives like ours and who don't look at things in the way we do.

But since this morning, and perhaps even since yesterday, after Mags left – after hearing the news about you, after finding out that right now you're only being kept on this earth by machines in intensive care, whilst doctors are making decisions about how to keep you alive – I've quickly realised that I'm straight back at square one.

Today, when I look out of my window, I see what was once my family. I see your family. I see women repeatedly smearing their precious children in sun cream to protect them from the sun's rays, like I used to do, whilst drinking tea from their flasks. Taking the odd glimpse at a novel in between refereeing sibling rows and sighing at how great the weather feels on their skin. I see them loving their husbands and being loved back. I see them smiling and laughing. I see them looking content and happy. But I feel them . . . I feel them dying inside. I feel their pain and confusion, their hurt and their anger. I hear the screams inside their own brains that are so loud they feel like their ears are bleeding and they don't understand why no one else on the beach can hear them. I feel them repeatedly looking around for someone to notice, anyone – and then I see them questioning themselves because they feel like they've gone insane.

I see them realise that no one sees them. No one other than me, who they can't see, and I know I'm helpless, because as much as they're looking around for someone to notice them, they're also hoping at the same time that nobody does. The fear of someone seeing them is often far worse than the fear of staying invisible. I spent so many years trapped in this state of confusion. Desperate to be seen, whilst praying to stay invisible forever.

I remember when we came to this same beach two weeks ago. You, me and our three boys. Harry was home from uni for the weekend, and he and George doted on Woody – it was so nice for me to see that side to them; the side I see whenever we are at Jo's, where they spend their time playing with Dotty. They have all this patience to play games and teach the little ones how to catch a ball and build a sandcastle, and again, it breaks my heart. I shouldn't even notice it. I don't think for a minute that Megan notices it when her eldest stepson does the same with her younger children, nor Jen when her kids play with Dotty or Woody – but for me, I study my boys to see how they interact with people, with any person. I'm constantly trying to figure out what they're thinking, how they're feeling, but most importantly – how they treat others, as the young men they now are. Until my dad came back into their lives a few years ago, the only male role model they had ever known was their biological father, who had zero patience and was arrogant, angry and aggressive. To watch them spend that day on the beach, actually enjoying taking care of your little boy, finding stuff he said funny and wanting to be in his company, made me feel things I never want to stop feeling. I don't think there'll ever be any words to explain my relief that they haven't morphed into David, that they don't copy his behaviours, that they haven't inherited his arrogance, attitude or nastiness. It's as if they give other people everything they never had from him.

I know from speaking to Harry that this is a huge worry for him. He has been having regular therapy for over six months now, from a therapist based close to his uni. Sometimes he calls me after he's seen her and we talk through his session; he asks me questions about certain incidents he remembers, or things that he wants confirmation of or answers to that he's unsure of. It's hard, but I always answer him honestly with every memory I have. He deserves no less than that. Other times, I text him post-session to ask how it went and he just replies, **It was OK** and doesn't elaborate further. Sometimes I get kisses and other times I don't. I respect any response he gives me. It's a journey; we're all healing in different ways. I think we will be forever healing from the years we spent being controlled and abused by the one man whose duty was to love us and keep us safe.

For George, it's different. He got a diagnosis of autism just over two years ago, which has felt more positive than negative. For him, everything's so black and white that he sees that his dad is a bad person, and has almost locked him away in a box out of sight and thrown away the key. He talks about the time we spent with him factually rather than with any emotion, and sometimes that's more upsetting for me – especially because he will recount incidents in front of my parents or friends, where he makes reference to the violence, the screaming and shouting, or my injuries and he just says it how it was. Like, 'Remember the time he said you overcooked the broccoli and he dragged you into the conservatory by your hair, then beat you with the gold lamp base so Harry and I could hear, and then you had to go to hospital and we all had to lie and say that it was an accident?' There is no emotion, it's just a statement – but I wonder what that must have done at the time to an autistic little mind which thrived on routine and safe people – and which had the exact opposite, living with someone who displayed a million different personalities and behaviours.

It's devastating. The effect David has had on all of us is lifelong and heartbreaking, but we have each other – and we are free. We no longer live like we once did. I don't think George even thinks of the future, or makes decisions based around his dad's behaviour, but for Harry, it's the opposite. I know it's a huge fear to him that he might be like his dad, that he could go on to hurt someone he loves. As of yet, no amount of reassurance has convinced him otherwise, and he refuses to even take girls on dates because he doesn't want to risk getting into a relationship and it becoming messy. That part feels life-shattering for me. I wonder if that damage is forever, because when I hear about his friends – and when I see Jo's kids, who are the same ages – it wrecks my heart. I want Harry to be like them – having fun, feeling the stuff teenagers feel for each other. I hate that to him, the risk of all the 'what ifs' is too great for him to even try it.

I often wish that I could share more parts of my story with the women I support at work. That I could say, 'Me too' when they summon the courage to share something with me that they're embarrassed or ashamed of. I want to remove the fear they have of being judged or misunderstood. When they arrive at the centre to go into the refuge, even though they feel cared for by us, the staff, I know that if I were able to share my wisdom from the experience of having once been where they are now, it would help them so much more. So many women go back again and again. I did it myself for almost twenty years. Every time I planned to leave and started prepping my escape, I talked myself out of it. If I had known someone who had been where I was, someone who could have held their hand out for me and my boys to grab onto, it would have been so much easier; we could have fled so much sooner.

But that's the thing with domestic abuse – it keeps you silent, it stops you from talking. Both when you're living with it and once you've left. More so once you've left, because once people know the level of abuse you suffered, once they understand what you've been subjected to, they just think you'd never want to return. They assume you'll want to stay away because you'd be crazy to go back – and you do, you desperately want to stay away, but so often you don't know how. When you've been controlled for so long, you don't know life without your perpetrator. Admitting how you truly feel to yourself is hard enough, so to talk about it out loud, to other people – it's just too much. How do you tell people you miss a man who treated you like that for so long? How do you confide in people that you want to take your child back to someone who caused you both such pain?

I remember when you first confided in the girls and me about the abuse you were enduring – not the full extent, but parts of it. You told us how he hadn't hurt you but he smashed and slammed things round the home. How he called you names and expected you to do everything in the house. You told us what we needed to know to be aware you were a victim of domestic abuse without telling us the whole truth. I know that because I see it every day – because it's what I tried to do to Jo the day she turned up at my house after David assaulted me. You told us enough to test us – to see if you could trust us and hoping we would help save you.

We already knew, or I knew – and they knew, because I told them before you told us. After those first red flags, it became glaringly obvious to me the first time I saw you and him together. I'd spent a lot of time with you at the café by that point, and to see your body language change, and even the way you spoke, how you lowered your tone and looked around to ensure no one else was around or listening in. When he turned up unannounced at the café, it cemented to me what I was already fearful of. You were a shell of yourself when he was around. It was like looking back at my old life. I asked you if you were OK, told you I was there for you – but you brushed it off, as if I were seeing things. So I knew you weren't ready. But I also knew that you knew I would be there when you decided you were ready – and that was all I could do. It's all any of us can do, and I knew the day you began to open up to us was the start of your journey to change your and Woody's life.

I remember when you first came to the centre for support – you were going on the domestic abuse course, but because we were friends I couldn't directly work with you. After you'd had a few sessions, I checked in with Mags to see how you were getting on. I remember her first reply, which was: 'What an incredible mother she is.' And you are, Martha. My god, you are. You always have been. Woody is the centre of your universe, and the adoration you have for him shines so bright, no matter what you're going through or feeling. No matter how relentless Craig was, or how difficult he was making life, both when you were with him and when you weren't. It's as if Woody lit up your world by just being around you.

So many women arrive with us – both for outreach support and for placement at the refuge – and they try to be the most incredible hands-on mums. They pretend they're absolutely fine and happy, for the fear of what we will think of them and the worry they have that they'll have their child or children removed from their care if they're sad, emotional or angry. So many women arrive at the refuge and act like the fact they've had to flee from all kinds of horrid abuse, and stay in an unknown location in a huge, unfamiliar house, where they live with total strangers and are supported by staff they don't know, has absolutely no impact on them and they're absolutely A-OK.

You didn't do that when you came for support. You never did that – you never pretended to be fine – not to the team at work, and not to us as your friends. It's like you were too broken to even try and make out things were OK, so you just allowed yourself to feel – and I was relieved you allowed us that, the insight into both your bad days and your good, your irrational intrusive thoughts, your fear at what the future looked like, the worries about what your son had endured. The panic attacks in the middle of the night, where you'd call one of us girls to just be on the end of the phone with you so you weren't alone. The sleepovers you had at mine and Jo's because you knew you needed company – you didn't ever shy away from that and try and go at it alone.

What I never said to you, and I wish I had, was how beautiful it was for me to watch what an incredible mum you remained even when you were so unbelievably fragile and lost. You asked Jo or me for help when you needed a break, and it quite quickly got to the point between us where you no longer needed to ask us to step in with Woody, we just knew when to, because we both recognised it from our own journeys. Possibly Jo more so, because once upon a time she did have to go it totally alone. She had no one to pick her up with three tiny babies in tow, so she was adamant we would all be there for you, like she had been there for me a few years before, without question.

I remember that day on the beach two weeks ago – it was a bad day. I saw your eyes fill up as you made another sandcastle with Woody. You began wringing your hands and rubbing your thighs with your palms with a force that was uncomfortable to watch, dealing with the thoughts inside your brain that I knew wouldn't go away. Throughout the afternoon, I just showed interest in whatever Woody was doing so he would interact with me, giving you space to just breathe and refocus your thoughts. I knew that you knew what I was doing. I also saw the look on your face that said you were relieved I was there to do it – to give you just a few minutes to get over the trigger. To pace about, wipe away your tears or do some deep breathing. It showed me you were processing it all – and that you were healing.

We didn't speak much about how life had ever actually looked for you before you met Craig. Sure – you told us you had no family but it wasn't something you ever discussed with detail or ease, so I never pushed it. It was skimmed over, factually – but I didn't want to force a conversation you weren't comfortable having – I wanted it to be something you chose to raise, brought up and chatted about naturally, and I knew from my own journey that some things take a long time to talk about. Years, even. I hoped we would get to the point where you would discuss it without me asking, but because it remained unspoken, I couldn't work out for sure whether you did in fact have any family or close friends who you loved that he had taken you away and isolated you from or whether you'd genuinely had no support network before your entered into that relationship. The thought of you having no support seems odd to me, given what a beautiful, kind and incredible human you are – that there would be no one, other than us, desperate to come running to your side right now. I suppose we will know soon enough – once the authorities do their thing and look into where you used to live, and trace anyone who was once close to you.

I remember everyone focusing on my childhood when it happened to me. After the final attack, everyone probed, from the nurses to the police officers. I was even asked about it when I gave evidence during his trial – as if him abusing me could somehow be my fault because of something I may have endured when I was a child, before I met him. But overall, I had a happy childhood – other than what happened with my Aunt Peggy.

# Eleven years old

I went into town with Aunt Peggy earlier. She's met a new boyfriend called Jez. Mum doesn't like him, Dad hasn't said much. Dad says Mum worries too much about Aunt Peggy because she's like her mum. Aunt Peggy lives with us – she has done since I was born because my mum's parents aren't very nice. I've never met them and we don't know them. She kind of feels like my big sister and my mum feels more like her mum to me too. Aunt Peggy's different looking to my mum. My mum is shorter, rounder – she's still pretty, but not as pretty as Aunt Peggy.

Aunt Peggy always dresses in pink and dyes her hair white blonde, and she always wears it in pigtails or plaits. She puts cute hair bows in and wears bright-coloured clothes and big goth-looking chunky boots. She wears her make-up so cool, with lipstick the same colour pink as the Hubba Bubba pack, and her black eyeliner has a huge flick at the corner of her eye that's just perfectly drawn on. She's super tiny and always smells good. Her feet are so tiny that I almost fit into her shoes – she says I can borrow them when they fit me properly. When she goes out with her friends at night I take one of her scarves or cardigans to bed with me because I can smell her perfume on it and it helps me to sleep better. Some Saturday nights, Mum and Dad go out with friends for date nights and dinner parties, so it's just me and Aunt Peggy at home. We walk to the takeaway at the top of the road to get chips and gravy, and she lets me stay up late and we watch cool films like *Beetlejuice* or *The Lost Boys*. She's really cuddly and she lets me stay in her bed and tells me crazy stories about things she did when she was a teenager that make me laugh until I cry.

Last week I asked her about the babies my mum lost before me. My mum told me about them but Aunt Peggy told me more. She told me how sad my mum and dad were. She told me the stuff my mum didn't tell me, about how they didn't know whether two of them were a boy or a girl because they were too tiny to tell, but that the last baby was a boy, my brother, and he lived for a few minutes after he was born. She said he looked just like me – he was smaller because he came too early, but he had the same nose and lips as I have. She told me my mum is too sad to talk about it all properly. My mum never thought she would have a baby after all of that so when I was born, she and my dad were really, really happy.

I wonder how much my mum still misses my brother and the other two babies. I think it's weird they don't talk about it. I wonder if they took any pictures of my brother. Aunt Peggy said she doesn't know. Maybe I'll ask Dad – he doesn't get sad like Mum does.

I told Aunt Peggy that Mum doesn't like her boyfriend; she says he is bad news. Aunt Peggy said Mum says that about everyone she dates and she will do the same to me when I start dating. She said I should ignore her. I think she's right. Aunt Peggy is too clever and pretty to go out with an idiot.

I stayed home alone for the first time on Friday because my mum works that day, baking for the local bakery. Usually I always have to go with her, but now I've just turned eleven I am allowed to stay home by myself for a few hours – I'm just not allowed to answer the door if anyone calls over.

Mum always brings me back some mini Cornish pasties and a lemon slice. She doesn't make the pasties, she only makes the sweet things for the weekend. People queue for ages on a Saturday morning to buy Mum's cakes. She is really good. She's already taught me how to bake loads of things and Dad says my doughnuts and custard tarts are as good as hers now. Mum taught Aunt Peggy to bake – she's as good as Mum but she says she doesn't enjoy it. I know Mum's hoping I will become involved when I grow up so we can make it a family business, but right now I want to be a hairdresser.

# WEDNESDAY

The hospital called today.

We won't know how well you will recover for a while yet.

You may have permanent brain damage.

They said that they are keeping you in a medically induced coma. They want to take things really slow and keep a close eye on you while your brain settles back into a more normal position. You have what looks like an actual bolt in your skull – the doctor said it is monitoring the pressure. You have a breathing tube in your throat, as well as medication tubes and monitoring wires everywhere. Part of me feels terrified about seeing you, but Jo said the doctor was keen to get people visiting as soon as you are out of intensive care. I am keeping everything crossed.

Craig has been charged with attempted murder, and he will be held in prison until he goes to court. I wonder if he will plead guilty or not guilty. I remember David pleading not guilty. I went through that whole trial adamant he would get away with it. He didn't – and actually, him pleading not guilty was the best thing he could have done, because although we all had to give evidence (which I was terrified about), the police submitted a huge amount of evidence, too – they found google searches he had made, so many hospital notes of all of my injuries over the years, and so many notes from professionals with concerns of domestic abuse, plus the witnesses at the last attack – and it all led to him getting the sentence he's still serving today. I feel relieved for you that Craig's being remanded. I know when you wake up it will also be an instant relief when you know he can't get to you.

I took George out after school today. He walked towards the car when I arrived and I wondered how he's as big as he is ... He's just shot up, all of a sudden. I don't understand how Harry is eighteen and George is twelve; time is just going too fast and there is nothing I can do to slow it down. We went for ice cream in town and to look at the boats – you know how obsessed George is with boats! He's learned the names of all the local boats now, and when a new one moors we have to go and investigate it. He loves the trawler day boats and has begun learning facts about them. My dad knows a few of the fishermen, so has been taking him down on weekends to chat to them and ask all about the specifics of what they fish for and how it all works. The joys of George's beautiful brain and the things he loves.

As well as the worry I have for you and Woody, I am also concerned about the effects this could have on my boys. They are so close to you and Woody – more so since you left Craig, because you spend so much time with us. I'm scared they will think men beating women and putting them in hospital is pretty normal now, because it's not only happened to me but also to you. I explained to George most people won't experience this kind of violence in a lifetime, so the fact he's experienced it twice before he's even become a teen is really rubbish – it's unfair and it sucks. As always, he remained black and white. He wanted to know the facts – whether you will get better like I did, and when, and if not, what happens to Woody. His mind works in ways ours don't – I often feel it's so refreshing, his logic, his planning, his way to work through stuff without the levels of emotion clouding his thought processing and decision making. Still, the situation right now with you being where you are, and Woody being where he is, it's clear to us all that it's making George anxious and upset. It's outside of his normal and he knows it's not OK, so that feels hard, because I have to navigate my way through supporting him, with the way his brain works, in the best way I know. It's new to me too.

I also spoke to Harry – he is so mature and grown up, he continues to blow me away with his take on things. He meets everything with such calmness, even when he should be raging like a beast. He asked if he could visit you, which I thought was sweet. He hasn't been into that hospital since I was there after his dad attacked me. The fact he wants to go back there, to see you, makes my heart feel proud and broken all at the same time. I told him he can – I think you would love to see him too, when you wake. Your relationship with Harry has been lush; you're like a really big sister to him, and he finds you funny and cool. The hit of this, for everyone, has been hard, and it's reminded me how loved you are. I hope you feel that love from us when you open your eyes.

It's cooler out today, which means the beach has been less busy, which in turn means my brain has had a rest from studying the women on the beach and how their lives might look. I wonder if this will ever stop? I hope it does; I feel exhausted with it at times. My eyes are physically sore, desperate just to close and rest, but my mind is wild – it's like the two things are in a constant battle with one another.

It's 6 p.m., we've only been home an hour, but George wants to go out again. That's how I know he's anxious, because he walks and walks.

I'm going to take the dog out for a hike with him. We're going to go from home, up over the cliffs and back around – the loop we've walked together so many times. He wants to take his binoculars to see the day fishing boats coming in for the night, and I'll take my book and read up there on a blanket for half an hour. We're going to get a chippy tea on the way home because I cannot be bothered to think about dinner, and it will be nice to have a treat together.

I continue to pray that tomorrow's news brings change, that you start responding, that you open your eyes, that you survive. I pray you survive, Martha.

# Eleven years old

I hate Sundays, mainly because it's when Mum and I clean Dad's offices.

Dad owns a building company. The offices are for his workers who book in the jobs. I hate the office building. It's old and ugly from the outside. It makes my insides feel sad when I look at it. It's a building that always looks sad, even when the sun shines on it in summer. Inside the desks are the darkest brown wood, and shiny. Some workers keep them really tidy and clean, and others are gross and dirty – usually the men's desks.

I polish the bookshelves, too – they match the desks, but the wood is shinier on the shelves, I think because they don't get used as much. There are so many bookshelves. They go across the whole back wall and they're annoying to polish. They have rows and rows of folders on them, all in perfect lines, all in alphabetical order. The same writing on the edges of the folder – neat, calligraphy-style writing in black; they never go out of line. I wonder if everyone keeps them neat and tidy or if it's just one person who does this job.

I like it, though. I like neatness. I think it might be Sandra that does this. We never clean Sandra's desk; she always keeps it super clean and tidy. She even has a vase of dried flowers next to her typewriter and her own pretty notepads with flowers on, and shiny fountain pens rather than the boring plain ones out of the stationery cupboard like everyone else has. I like Sandra's desk. I like Sandra. Sometimes in the holidays I come to work with my dad and she's always pleased to see me. She keeps a stash of pens for me, and pastel-coloured card, so I can draw. I draw my wedding day mostly, and my bridesmaids' dresses. I like drawing the dresses. I'm excited to get married when I grow up and have children. I want a baby girl and I want to call her Katy Jane.

Everyone's nice to me at Dad's work. My favourite man here is called Alan. He works in accounts and he is Scottish. I can't understand what he says a lot of the time, but I'm too embarrassed to tell him, so I just giggle or nod when he talks to me. I'd never heard a Scottish voice before I met him. I wish I was Scottish – or from Liverpool. They are my two favourite accents; I practise them all the time but I can never get them right, they're too hard to learn.

Alan taught me how to make paper aeroplanes. His desk is always a mess. There are always thick brown coffee rings covering the coaster next to his typewriter, and his mug always has coffee drips down it, which makes me feel sick. He also has an ashtray, which is always full of cigarette butts, and the black ash overflows onto the desk and sticks to the coffee.

So many desks are dirty when we clean them. They have crumbs scattered everywhere from the half-eaten packs of biscuits, and there are piles and piles of papers and letters spread and crumpled everywhere – most are in no kind of order. It annoys me. I wish everyone could be like Sandra and put stuff in neat piles with elastic bands, or in labelled folders.

The men's bins under the desks are always overflowing with all kinds of rubbish. Mum walks in front of me with a big black bin liner and I empty all of the little bins into it, as well as the ashtrays, from the desks that have them. The smell when we empty the bins makes me feel sick; it's a mix of the sweet minty smell from the little bits of silver foil off the Wrigley's chewing gum everyone has, with the tangy smell of tobacco from the hundreds of empty cigarette packets that we throw away. There are so many newspapers too. Most are folded in half on the front page, but others are left open at the topless girls on page three. Boobs are so weird. There are so many different shapes and sizes. I'm so embarrassed in front of my mum when we throw away the papers on the boob page. We both pretend we haven't seen it, but I know she has and I know she knows I have. Gross.

Whenever I go into Dad's work with him, all his staff sit the same way, facing forward, so when I walk into the main floor through the double glass doors they all look up at once, smile like they're pleased to see me, then they look straight back down. They remind me of robots. Although I like Sandra and Alan the best because they're so nice to me, they all give me biscuits and cups of lukewarm, sweet Yorkshire tea when I go in.

We polish everyone's phones. I don't mind this job. They all have the same phone; it's the colour of a cooked mushroom – a grey-brown.

Some of the phones have loads of dust in the holes where you put your fingers in to dial the numbers, and some don't. I wonder whether that's because some people don't use their phones much, so they get dusty, or if everyone uses their phone the same amount and some people are just better at keeping them clean, a bit like their desks. Mum takes everything off these desks and puts the items on the chair or the floor, then she gives the desk a good scrub and polishes everything with a duster cloth. Even the typewriters. Then she puts all the things back as neatly as she can.

I organise and stack the messy paperwork into neat piles next to the now-gleaming telephones, and then we both leave the offices. I am warm but not hot, but Mum is always dripping with sweat when she finishes, because her last job is hoovering everyone's crap up. Every time we leave, she flicks the light switches off, locks the door, gives me a smile and says, 'That will make them all happy! Until next week.' I smile back, but I secretly wonder why we have to be the ones to clean up for so many men that just can't be bothered to clean up after themselves, when all the women can.

Mum is in a really bad mood this Sunday because Aunt Peggy's moved in with Jez, into his flat. I haven't been over. Mum says I'm not allowed. She said she's heard the place is a dump. I told Aunt Peggy, but she told me she's decorating it and making it more girly, then she thinks I'll be allowed to go round. I asked Dad what he thinks of Jez and he rolled his eyes and said, 'Let's just give it time to fizzle out like the others.' I don't know what that means. I'm not going to ask Aunt Peggy what it means, because I think he's saying she's had loads of boyfriends, which isn't true, so I don't think he's being kind, which is weird because my dad's always kind, especially to my Aunt Peggy – she always says my dad is like her big brother. I know he loves her very much.

# THURSDAY

There has been no real change since yesterday. You're still being given the same drugs and monitoring – they're hopeful they'll be able to give a more positive update really soon.

We went to my parents' for dinner tonight. It's something we do regularly, as you know. They love having visitors and Mum is an amazing cook. I often just watch them when I'm there; I do this with most couples, in fact.

My mum and dad are happy – they've always been happy, I think. I mean, some stuff now that I'm here today, at this place in life, after what David did, makes me question a few things that have gone on in their marriage, but I imagine I will be like this forever. Where if I peered into most relationships, I'd spot some red flags, somewhere. When you come from where I have been – when I was lying in that hospital bed with those injuries that final time – it makes you over-analyse everything and everyone forever, I think, and I have no doubt your life will look like mine in the future, Martha. It's a secret club neither of us wanted, or knew we were joining, until it was too late and we'd become lifetime members.

My dad has always treated my mum well, treated us both well, taken care of us and loved us, and I suppose him not doing much around the house when I grew up was because 'back then' it was the way society was. That was normal for everyone, not just them. But it's a bit like the 60s, when drink driving wasn't against the law, or the 70s, when women would give birth, then smoke cigarettes on the maternity wards whilst breastfeeding their babies. People did things that were deemed acceptable until they realised it was unacceptable.

Now Dad's retired and they have me barking about everything that's gone wrong in the world, he runs the hoover round most days, cooks in the evenings, solely maintains the garden, and even deep cleans the bathroom regularly, which is good, because it shows he isn't one of 'those men'. It shows he's part of the change. We all learned something from David. My dad realised that things need to change in society, but also inside his home – and that's how it should be, because relationships are about being equal; they're about learning, evolving and understanding how important it is for us to share roles, no matter who is earning money.

David never lifted a finger round the house – any of the houses. Not when I was pregnant or a new mum in London in an apartment, or when we moved to Cornwall and lived in a much bigger house. Even when I took on the café and began working full time, everything at home still fell to me. The secret rage and frustration consumed me during those days. I refused to raise boys who would go on to think this was normal and do it to another woman when they grew up, so from the very start, they did their bit. They both had jobs – whether it was to carry the washing upstairs, stack the wood next to the log fires or empty the dishwasher. As they got bigger, they hoovered and mopped, cleaned bathrooms and cars. Part of me thinks that they did it without complaint because they could see their dad did nothing, but I also think it was just their normal, like turning the shower off when you've finished washing your body, or switching off the TV before you go to bed. It became something they did without question – even before we fled when Harry was a teen, even after we left and moved into the flat. Both my boys have always just cleaned up after themselves and others without question, because I wanted them to be the opposite of everything their father is. I was trying my best to ensure they grew up knowing how important it is to do their bit, to ensure they never go into a relationship and make their partner feel like I did.

# Eleven years old

Mum let me go over to Aunt Peggy's on the basis that Jez was at work. I was allowed to stay for tea, do some crafts and then Aunt Peggy had to bring me home. An hour after I got there, Jez came back. Aunt Peggy wasn't expecting him and she looked worried – probably because she thought Mum would go mad. I don't know why. He was really nice, and funny. He brought me back a can of pop. Mum doesn't let me drink pop so I was well happy, even though I felt bad because I knew it wasn't allowed. Jez told me the odd can is fine and that Mum is being silly.

Aunt Peggy made chicken and chips and the three of us ate together at the little table. The flat is cute. Although it smells a bit funny, like it's damp, and the wallpaper is old and hanging off in parts. The bathroom is really tatty and old, and the furniture isn't very nice, but Aunt Peggy said she's going to change it all and make it nicer over time. She's filled it with pink trinkets, rugs and blankets, and I know soon it will look really pretty, just like she does. We ate dinner and then Jez said, 'OH MY GOD LOUISE!' I said, 'What?' And he said, 'You've peed on the table!' then picked up two peas that had fallen off my plate. We laughed so much. He's really funny, and I think Mum has got it wrong about him.

Aunt Peggy and Jez walked me home. It got a bit awkward, as Aunt Peggy asked Jez to wait at the top of the lane whilst she ran me in, because of Mum, but he was OK and he gave me a high five to say bye. As we walked up to the house Aunt Peggy asked me in a whisper to keep it a secret that I'd met Jez, as Mum might not let me come again if she knew. We pinkie promised with our little fingers, then she gave me a kiss goodbye and I ran in the house.

Mum asked why Aunt Peggy didn't come in and I instantly lied and said she had to rush off to meet Jez. 'Oh,' she replied. 'She's still not come to her senses, I see.' I wanted to tell her she was wrong about Jez, but I didn't. I thought I'd work on Dad instead. He hates saying no to me when I ask for things, and I want to spend more time with Peggy, and Jez – so I just need to get him to convince Mum.

Later, Dad wasn't sure if he'd set the alarm at the office so I drove into the office with him to check. I wasn't sure what time it was, but it felt late at night. I love riding in his car at night. Soon it will be Christmastime, and we drive around every night looking for houses that are dressed up with lights. Ever since I was little, there's been a really good one next to the traffic lights on the way to my school. They have Santas and reindeer, and the whole house is usually lit up, but this year it isn't. I felt sad when I saw it was all just in darkness, and I can't stop wondering why they haven't decorated it. Maybe they moved, or maybe he died. I feel like it's a man that does the lights, or it is in our house anyway. Or maybe he split up with his wife, or she's the one who died, and he's just sat in there all lonely and sad in the dark. I really wish I knew why the house wasn't decorated. I miss it being lit up, and I feel annoyed that it's making me feel sad when it's just a stupid house with lights on.

Anyway, we drove through town and it was busy. People were having fun. There were so many girls dressed in pretty dresses and high heels, laughing and shouting at each other as they crossed the road holding hands or linking arms.

We got to Dad's offices – which still looked as ugly at night under the street lights as they do in the daytime – and he went round checking the windows were closed and everything was turned off, while I played hopscotch on the carpet tiles. They're those large, square carpet tiles in two colours, in a diagonal pattern. One is a leaf-coloured green and the other is a chocolate brown, like the colour of a tree really, the trunk and top part. I hate playing hopscotch, but I couldn't stop myself. I tend to convince myself that if I land on the wrong tile, bad things will happen to me. Some weeks I only let myself walk on the green squares, some weeks just the brown. I did brown last week and said in my brain, 'If I accidentally go over the line onto green, I will have an accident when I next ride my bike.' I went over the line and haven't ridden my bike since.

Tonight, I hopscotched, and I said in my brain that if I went over the line then me and Mum would have a car accident when we're next in the car together, and she will die. I didn't go over the line. I feel so relieved. I really want to stop playing this game, but I can't. I want to ask Dad or Aunt Peggy if it's normal, but I don't think it is. None of my friends have ever said they play anything like it and I think I'll look weird if I mention it. I wish I was normal.

# FRIDAY

You had a temperature last night and your heart rate went up, so now they are keeping an eye out for an infection. The doctor didn't seem worried; they were genuinely reassuring and said it's quite common, after all you've been through. We just need to hope that these antibiotics they've given you work. I'm praying they do, fast.

Today was my day off, which I was relieved about. It feels different at work since this has happened. I know word has gone round like wildfire, and affected so many of our ladies who are all living the same or similar lives to you, with their ex-partners that they're all now even more terrified of. It's very much hit home for them that this could have been any of them. You've done that, at least – made so many other women see how easy it is to end up where you are. You've made them see that this kind of thing doesn't just happen when you watch TV dramas or read the newspaper; it's happened to you – and it could easily happen to them. As devastating as all of this is, I can't help but think that you going through this has saved so many other women. Maybe now they won't have that secret meet up, or think about returning 'home' to perpetrators, because you've made them see that the danger is so very real.

I wrote until the early hours of the morning, then I slept for a few hours, and wrote some more around sunrise. It's amazing, the amount of words you can get in when you need to fill your time and keep your brain busy. I haven't really slept much since I found out you were in hospital. In fact, I haven't really slept much since I met David twenty years ago. He stole my sleep when he took over my life. I used to love sleep before him. Before I moved to London, I would lie in until midday when I could, and I looked forward to going to sleep. But when things became bad with him, sleep kind of just stopped, and then I think I just got used to not sleeping. One day I hope to be able to get into bed, close my eyes and wake up the following morning without a night of intrusive thoughts and night sweats.

I looked after my Dotty and Woody today. I picked them up from Jo at 9 a.m. Pat had gone straight down from her house to open up the café, so I sat and had a cup of tea with Jo whilst the kids coloured in the playroom.

I remember when I realised Jo was my best friend. She was the first proper friend I ever had. Yes, ever.

I had friends when I was younger, and in college, and they were all lovely, but it was more of a huge group friendship – and it was also short lived, because of David. I didn't ever have just one best friend who I could go to, with anything at any time, or who could come to me too. Soul mates in society are always dressed up as someone you have to be romantically involved with – and I really wish that wasn't the case, because I have witnessed first hand how females coming together can change lives, you included. You have helped me in so many ways since we became friends, Martha. But I also got everything I needed from Jo after David left, and I've realised now that I don't need a partner.

Of course, there are times when I think how lovely it would be to have what Jo, Meg and Jen have with their husbands, the nice parts they share . . . And also on the shit days, I wonder how it would feel to have someone to share the load with. Because I've never had that, ever. But I also feel happy by myself now, and the thought of entering into another relationship still terrifies me. I know the girls and my parents would love me to meet someone and be happy, as would Harry – he worries about me growing old alone. But for now, I'm good. I'm better than I have been in almost two decades, in fact, and all I want more than anything is for my boys to have healthy relationships as adults where they're loved and cared for.

Jo, I think, is the leader of our pack – you can let me know if you agree with that statement when you read this! – the matriarch of our girl gang. She's someone I trust without question; she would do anything for me (and for any of us) but she also challenges me, she pulls me up when I need it, and through her I've recognised how important it is to not only communicate with others, but also to hold yourself accountable. At first, it felt so hard to take responsibility when I wasn't being the best version of myself, but I've realised there is no shame in that. We are human: none of us are perfect, no matter how it looks on the outside. By openly holding yourself accountable you become a better person, and in turn, it encourages other people to do the same.

I hold myself accountable now because I saw Jo do it without any shame or embarrassment. I used to sit and watch her pull herself apart, but then she would openly talk about where she went wrong, and why, who she needed to make apologies to, and what she needed to do to reflect and be a better person in the future, and not have the same reactions going forward. It was glorious to watch. Having Jo by my side, I am forever learning. Because of her, I am much kinder to myself about the bad decisions, the wrong choices and the times I could have done things better – because she has a way of making me see we're all human, and even good humans are capable of making terrible choices throughout their lives – which sometimes, in turn, hurt other people.

Jo was sad this morning. She said Woody is crying at bedtime for you. I said I would have him and Dotty for a sleepover tonight. I'm feeling so relieved that, for the past few months, you and Woody have had so many sleepovers with all of us. As much as we did that for you – to keep you safe and give you company – it now means he's comfortable with all of us at our homes, so this situation right now doesn't feel strange to him. George is at my parents' overnight, which is part of his routine now; he stays with them every Tuesday and Friday. It means I can work late on the Tuesday – plus he has clubs until 6.30 p.m., so my dad goes and watches him, which he loves. It made me realise what my boys had missed out on, when Dad started doing this for both of them as soon as David was gone. It was another thing David didn't do. He never showed interest in any of their sports, and even when he wasn't working away, he wouldn't come to any of their games or practices. The boys thrive, now, from having my dad as a male role model – giving them love, support and encouragement, but also having the difficult discussions they need without making them feel awkward. He's a young grandad, and probably feels more like a dad to both of them, especially because they never had a good one.

I am sad my dad never got a son, because I can see he would have been an amazing boy-dad. He's so involved; he speaks to both the boys each day, whether it's by text or phone call, and he runs round after George all the time. Any weekend football games, he watches – he knows all the other dads on the sideline and gets involved in it all, which is not only amazing for George, but also me.

I couldn't face going out in public after I was first out of hospital, but also when the trial began, and then David got his prison sentence. It was on the news on local TV, online and in the papers. To me, it felt like it had been broadcast worldwide. It seemed to be all anyone was talking about. When I saw people, I would either be questioned or avoided; there was no in between. I felt so sick and anxious, I couldn't leave the house. I was so grateful I had a support network – like my dad – to scoop my boys up and give them the love and support at that time that I wasn't able to provide in public. They needed that, and they got it without question.

I took Dotty and Woody to Primrose Farm today – somewhere else we kept promising we'd visit but never got round to. You will love it, when we do come again. It's not really a farm; it's a load of land with some farm animals that you can pet and feed, and a large indoor and outdoor play area. It also has a farm shop which sells local meat, veg and condiments like honeys, jams and cream. They sell gifts, too, and I found the most beautiful card which I am going to send Jo, about getting through tough times. I can feel her overwhelm right now, just by being in her presence.

Primrose Farm also has a large café which serves delicious local food. It's dog friendly, pretty noisy, and the perfect place for two crazy toddlers. The kids love it here, and I'd made over half a day of it by the time they'd played in both the areas, walked round and fed the animals. and had lunch.

I realised today it's the first time I've had them both by myself. Usually I come along on outings with you or Jo, or I just have one of them to help you out with childcare. Watching the way they both interacted with each other today was just the cutest, and honestly, Martha, Woody is doing so well. He's happy and coping with all of this amazingly. They ask each other questions because they are genuinely interested in the answers – I mean, some of those answers started a row, such as when Woody disagreed that Rebecca Rabbit isn't the best character in *Peppa Pig*, or when Dotty got annoyed that Woody's favourite flavour milkshake is chocolate, not strawberry, like her. For most of it though, they chatted like a little old couple. They giggled constantly at each other and had the best day. And so did I.

Despite the reason I am here, caring for your son, I had a day that left me feeling happy and high. Just being around two tiny, innocent souls took me away from the reality of how life looks right now, and reminded me that one day this will be how all our days, including yours, look again, all the time.

I'm going to put the double airbed up in my room for the kids tonight, so they'll be in with me. Remember when we bought that when you and Woody came to stay with me when you first left Craig, and we just ordered the airbed, not realising you needed a pump? And we sat there for an hour, taking it in turns to blow into it, feeling like we were going to die because we were both so out of breath and a bottle of wine down? Then we gave up and ate Chinese, and the three of us stayed in my bed.

That was a good night. I've not thought about that night since, but now I am, I realise how happy it made me. How much we laughed and giggled, how much less alone I felt, because I had you and Woody and the boys in my company. How lush it was to see George play trains with Woody.

I want more nights like that when you wake up. We need a weekly sleepover, where we laugh like we did that night. Best-friend sleepovers are so underrated.

I love you, Martha.

# Eleven years old

Dad worked his magic, and I had my first sleepover at Aunt Peggy's with her and Jez. We went to the cinema and it was fun. We got a hot dog from the fair on the way home with the money Mum gave Aunt Peggy for me. Aunt Peggy said we couldn't go on the rides because they didn't have enough money. I thought that was a bit weird because she's always had money and we've always done things together before, but I think she's saving to make the flat nice and has been spending her money on buying things for it, so that's probably why.

On the Saturday morning Jez went to work early. Aunt Peggy said he's working lots of overtime to save money so they can decorate. She made me pancakes with syrup and we watched TV under the blanket on the sofa until Dad came and picked me up.

When I got home, Mum asked me four million questions about Jez. She kept making me promise he hadn't done anything to upset me or Aunt Peggy, and asking me what he was drinking. In the end, I told her she was being crazy, and she said, 'Believe me, there's a reason for me being crazy which I hope you never have to understand.' She walked into her bedroom and shut her door. I heard her cry. I never hear her cry. I looked at Dad and he just shook his head and said, 'Leave her, pet, it will be OK.' I feel like she's going crazy.

# SATURDAY

I called Jo when the kids woke this morning, to tell her they were OK and to check in on you. She's spoken to the hospital – they said that if your stats and pressure under your skull all stay stable, they may take the bolt out on Monday. Mags went up to see you. She said you look peaceful, but like you're not really there, if that makes sense. I don't know if it made sense to me, really. I'm scared about seeing you – I want to, but I don't. It's all just a lot.

I dropped Dotty back to Jo after lunch today. She was shattered, as we had a late night last night, so I thought she would probably nap this afternoon, which means Jo will get another break. I am keeping Woody overnight again. I think it will be nice for Dotty to have her mum to herself but also Woody settled really well here last night and I can see Jo is absolutely worn out. You know what it's like when they spend too much time together, too – the fights are hell!

I put them down with their comforters around 8 p.m. last night. Dotty was asleep within seconds, but Woody was just looking up at the ceiling, eyes wide, giving intermittent big long blinks, even though I knew he was knackered. I knelt beside him and asked him if he was OK. He said, 'I miss my mummy, Aunty Lou.' I felt like my heart was snapping. Before I could catch it or wipe it away, a tear splashed onto my jeans. 'I miss your mummy too, buddy,' was all I could reply. He began to cry – but it wasn't meltdown or loud hysterical sobs, it was like he was all out of energy, like his heart was just getting used to feeling sad and he just cried silently, with tears falling from his eyes and the edges of his lips turned downwards. I wanted to tell him it would be OK, that we would see you soon and you'd be home, but then I thought – what if that doesn't happen? What if you don't wake up, Martha? What if you don't get better? What does that do to him, if I make a promise I have to break?

I fucking hated Craig at that point. I wanted him to be here, watching his son in this state and say, 'YOU DID THIS, YOU FUCKING BASTARD.' I want him to feel the pain we're all feeling, the knowledge of how life looks for you. I hate him. I hate all abusive men and their angry tempers.

Instead, I told Woody that I love him, that I love having him to sleep over, and it makes me so happy when he's at my house, and it makes his Aunty JoJo happy when he's at her house, because we all love him and we all want to hang out with him. I asked him if he wanted to sleep in bed with me. He said yes – I know after Craig left, you had him in with you, and I know how much Harry loved being in bed with me when we left. Not George – he is a stickler for routine, and his routine has always been his own bed – but even at fourteen, Harry wanted to sleep in with me. I always wondered if it was so he could keep me safe, or so I could keep him safe. Maybe it was a bit of both, but it's something the two of us took great comfort in at the time. So I brought Woody into my bed and he scootched straight over and snuggled into me, holding his muslin square that Jo has sprayed with your perfume. I watched his eyes roll to the back of his head whilst he rubbed the end of his nose with the silky muslin label, and he fell asleep. I didn't want to leave him. I stayed there, and breathed in his scent and yours. I cried. Silent tears ran across my nose that made the pillow under my cheek feel damp and cold. My throat stung where I was holding back from releasing it all. I could feel my heart bending again, trying its hardest not to snap.

Woody looked so peaceful, but every now and then he let out a huge sob from when he had been crying for you when he was awake. The sobs in his sleep were in harmony with mine. Weirdly, I fell asleep – straight to sleep – and I only woke at midnight because he stirred. Four hours of solid, uninterrupted sleep, where I wasn't woken because I'd had a nightmare. It felt good – good for a second – then I was flooded with sadness again because of the reason he was with me in my bed.

Please get better, Martha, we need you. He needs you. We all need you.

# Eleven years old

Mum is no better with Jez. He still isn't allowed at ours, and Aunt Peggy has stopped coming over at all. When I stay with them, Dad drops me off and picks me up. When I ask them what's going on, they're all saying nothing is wrong, but I know everything is wrong. Mum and Aunt Peggy aren't speaking at all, and I feel angry at Mum for it, even though I don't know why they're not speaking.

Mum questions me every Saturday and I tell her everything is fine – and it is, most of the time. Jez does sometimes get angry with Aunt Peggy, though – but over really dumb stuff, like the washing not being dry, or her taking too long to walk back from work. He says things like: 'Useless fucking bitch.' He says it quietly, but I still hear. I'm not sure if he wants me to hear or not; I can't work it out. I pretend I don't hear when he's there, but when he goes to work and I ask Aunt Peggy why he does that, and why he's got so moody, she begs me not to mention it to Mum or Dad. I wouldn't anyway, because I know Mum wouldn't let me come again if I did.

Aunt Peggy says that Jez is stressed because he hates his boss and his job. I don't know why he doesn't just get a new job rather than stay somewhere that makes him so miserable. I don't really want to stay this Friday because it doesn't feel nice when he's there, but I know if I don't go, Mum will start questioning me more about why, and being even crazier, so I'll just go and hope he's in a better mood.

I found a book on Celtic FC in a charity shop and he loves them, so I bought it. He's the second Scottish man I've met, but I don't like him as much as Alan, and he can't make paper aeroplanes. Hopefully the book will make him happier.

# SUNDAY

Woody settled last night without any tears.

George was at home, so Woody slept in his bottom bunk bed and he loved it! He kept saying, 'I am such a big boy.' I put pillows all down the side of the bed and on the floor because I was paranoid he would fall out. He didn't. I gave him his muslin. which still smells of you – I keep catching myself holding it to my face and inhaling it. It's weirdly comforting and devastating all at once. It never stops amazing me, how powerful smells and music and places can be, if the person you have memories of those things with isn't around to share them.

I kissed Woody when I tucked him in, told him how much I loved him. He rubbed my forehead with his tiny hand and said, 'Love you, Aunty Lou-Lou,' and rolled on his side. I stood out of his view, hiding between the door and the wardrobe, to watch him fall asleep. I thought he was going to get upset, turn and look for me, but he didn't. He just soothed himself, rubbing the label on the end of his nose again, and fell straight to sleep. He woke just after 6 a.m. and shouted for me. I took him into the lounge for a cuddle, then we got dressed and took Milo for an early walk. I bumped into one of my old customers, Ruth, who I haven't seen in a long time. She's the loveliest woman. She was walking her collie and we just started strolling along together. We dawdled at Woody's pace all the way along to the second beach – the one you're allowed dogs on. Woody took his shoes off and paddled in the sea. Milo and Ruth's dog, Oscar, ran in and out of the sea, and Woody was squealing – he was almost toppling over because he was laughing so hard.

Ruth was telling me that her youngest daughter has just got her first job as a buyer for a Zara. She is in her mid-twenties and is travelling all over the world. And Ruth's son is getting married to his fiancée next month in the most stunning castle in Devon. She showed me the venue on her phone – it looks incredible. Just as I was wondering why some people are happy and settled, she told me they'd brought the wedding forward a year because Ruth's husband has been diagnosed with Motor Neurone Disease – he's fifty-nine. It's rapid, she told me, the deterioration in him. And she's struggling because her mum is end of life with dementia, so she's trying to split herself in two caring for them both, and her three children all live far away with their own lives and busy careers, so she doesn't want to worry them and plays down how hard it all is. She said she feels like she's drowning, most days. And just like that, I was reminded that no one's life is perfect; we all have our own shit going on, no matter how it looks. Everyone's shit just differs.

As we walked back along the beach, I gave Ruth my number – told her to give me a text and I would pop over for a coffee, or we could arrange more dog walks. What I loved, walking off after we said our goodbyes, was that other than her asking me if I was OK, she asked me nothing else. She didn't seem to know anything about the situation, didn't wonder why I was out at the crack of dawn with a tiny child that wasn't mine – and it felt refreshing. For so many years people have either ignored me out of embarrassment or asked me intrusive questions that leave me embarrassed – there's never really been an in between. It was nice, today, that we didn't speak about me at all, just her – for me to peer into someone else's world rather than them peer into mine, to smile at their highs and offer sympathy at the lows. It felt easy. I pray that one day I'll just be known as 'Lou, the support worker' again, rather than 'Lou with the psycho husband who's in jail for nearly killing her'.

After Ruth left, I grabbed the towel I'd left on the table outside the café and gave Milo rub down to get the sand off him. Woody said, 'This has been a great morning' – matter-of-fact. It made me sad, that you're not here to see him at the minute. I can't wait for you to get better and hear his little sayings that we used to melt over together – because I know that 'morning' would have made you look at him; you would have bitten your bottom lip, cocked your head to the side and said 'God, I love you so much', like you did all the time. I know seeing him laugh like he did on the beach this morning, when he was jumping in the waves, would have made you belly laugh, and me, and then we'd have given each other that look that we have when we see the glimmers in our days – the ones that remind us we *will* be OK, as will our boys.

I called Jo when I got back, to make arrangements for the day. She had no plans, so I said I'd drop Woody back this afternoon. We went home and made pancakes with George. I am amazed at what this boy eats, Martha! He had yoghurt, blueberries, squirty cream – the lot! George likes plain and beige everything, so pancakes for him are always just lemon and sugar. I like fruit, but I just got out a selection of stuff and Woody pointed to it all, so I popped little bits of everything on his plate and he just wolfed it! The lot! What an incredible appetite.

I needed to clean the flat and get on top of the washing, as I have done no housework this week, so Woody watched *Peppa Pig* in the lounge and I brought up some toys from the café. He played with the Duplo for hours, his muslin in his hand or on his lap the whole time. Occasionally he would stop to watch Peppa and stroke his nose with the label. I found myself watching him and just being overwhelmed with sadness.

George is so incredible with him. He got Jenga out and repeatedly built up the tower, then when Woody knocked it down, pretended to be surprised until he was crying with laughter. They did it over and over, and I think George enjoyed it as much as Woody. It was so lush to watch.

After the house was back to normal, all the beds were changed and the uniforms were hanging on the airer in the sun to dry (I hate not having a tumble dryer!) we left to go to Jo's.

Jamie was out with some of the kids when we got there. He'd taken them paddle boarding with Meg, John and their kids. Jo's eldest kids – you remember, Belle and Art – were at the beach together, so it was only Jo and Dotty at home. It felt weirdly quiet because their house is usually really busy – a lovely busy, bustling with love and laughs – whenever I leave, I leave on a high. It gives me hope for the future, as this is Jamie and Jo's second time around, as you know, but they feel like a proper family – no steps or halves or weird dynamics, it all just works as a complete, loving family that works through tough times together, under one roof.

Woody was happy when we arrived, and he and Dotty played together in the garden. We had one of Pat's cream teas and sat in the sun, chatting through Jo contacting her biological mum. It's something she's been discussing for a long time, but she's not read any of her adoption papers, so she has no real idea what she's going to find or walk into, but I can tell she's intrigued. And knowing Jo, and how her mind works, once that feeling is there it never goes away. She's going to speak to Pat about it later, as she's read all the papers, and then make a decision on what to do.

I went to leave and said goodbye to both the little ones, as I always do. Woody immediately became upset that I was leaving. He wasn't just crying – he was inconsolably wailing for me not to go. I felt shit that he wanted to be with me over Jo – I could see Jo also felt shit that he didn't want to stay with her, and I didn't know how to make it any better. I bent down and told him that tonight he would be staying with Aunty Jo, then me again in a few days, but he just wouldn't have it. I was fine to take him with me, but I also didn't want to overstep the mark with Jo, or confuse him. Before I could say anything, Jo said, 'I think he's just knackered'. I agreed. I kissed him as she held him, but he was in between kicking and screaming, then begging and sobbing. It was gut wrenching.

I closed the door and the tears came. I sat in my car outside of the house and I could hear him screaming for what felt like forever. A text pinged through.

**Are you still here?**

**Yes, outside**, I replied immediately.

**Get back in then, because he wants his Aunty Lou.**

I sprinted inside and scooped Woody up. He buried his head into my neck and calmed immediately. A few heavy sobs every thirty seconds as I stroked his hair to soothe him, like the ones he did the first night he fell asleep at mine. 'Shhh. It's OK,' I whispered, with his whole weight against mine on the sofa.

I know none of him wants me, really – all of him wants you – but Jo's house is busy, she has a child pretty much the same age, plus five elder ones, a demanding job, a husband and a dog. She doesn't have the time or the headspace to have Woody too – as much as the idea made sense at first, mainly because we thought being around other kids would help him, in that moment we both came to realise that right now, all he needs is to have someone make him their entire world. So that's what I'm going to do, until you're better and out of hospital.

Jo packed Woody's bag, placing your bottle of perfume on the top – Pivoine Suzhou by Armani. I'd never seen the bottle before, but it reminds me of you, pretty and pink, with the delicate scent of peonies inside. She gave me the instructions – one spray, every few days, after I wash the muslin, which Woody calls his raggie. Jo loaded my boot with toys and she hugged me so tight I almost passed out.

'Thank you,' she said. 'I mean it, I think you both need this.'

I knew at that point she was happy with this decision. I didn't know if it was the right one – I wasn't sure how George would react – but my heart felt happier than it had done all week. Woody held my hand the whole way home as we drove and he fell into the deepest danger nap within seconds. Jo was right, he was knackered!

# Eleven years old

Dad dropped me off at Aunt Peggy's last night.

I was so excited to see her as I had got a new My Little Pony for my birthday that I had brought with me, and she is the best at braiding their tails. I don't tell my friends I still play with My Little Ponies, and my mum hides them away if friends come over so they don't laugh at me. They all have stereos and Walkmans, but it's so boring.

Dad waited until I got to the top of the metal steps and opened the door, then he flashed his lights like he always does and drove off round the corner. I walked in and Aunt Peggy was sat on the sofa, crying. The house looked like it had been burgled. Stuff was everywhere, and there were smashed mugs and glasses on the lounge floor. I couldn't work out why they'd been smashed in the lounge, not the kitchen.

Aunt Peggy saw me as I walked in and said, 'Shit, shit,' over and over. I asked her what was wrong and what had happened to the flat. She got up and started walking round in circles really fast, shaking her head. She said she'd forgotten I was coming and she thought it may be best if I didn't stay the night. I asked what she meant, and she said Jez was in a really bad mood. She started walking forwards and backwards and crying, looking up to the ceiling and whispering, 'No, no, no.'

I felt really worried in my belly. The flat was really bad – it looked like they'd been burgled but nothing was missing, like everything had just been smashed and thrown around. It didn't feel like Aunt Peggy and it didn't look like her – she was dressed in weird men's clothes: a big, blue, baggy T-shirt and jeans that kept falling down and that were too long. Her hair was wet and she had no make-up on. There was an awful damp stench mixed with the smell of a roast chicken that was cooking in the old white oven. I wanted to go home. Aunt Peggy told me to call Mum and ask her to get Dad to drive back and pick me up. I knew it would be ages before I could leave, though, as Dad would have to drive the half hour home before Mum could tell him, and then he would have to drive the half hour back for me. I was stuck there for at least an hour.

'Where is he?' I whispered.

'He's gone, but he will be back and I don't want you to be here when he gets in, Lou.' Aunt Peggy started crying again and I wanted my dad like I'd never wanted anyone before in my life.

'I bought him this,' I said, holding up the Celtic book.

Aunt Peggy started crying really badly then. 'Oh, baby, I don't deserve you. I'm so sorry.'

'Come with me,' I said. 'When Dad comes, come home with us?'

'Just call your mum, honey,' she said. But part of me, all of a sudden, really didn't want to. Part of me hoped Jez would calm down and it would be OK and Mum would never need to know about this, because I knew if I called her that would be it, no matter what – I would never be allowed to this flat again, and if Aunt Peggy didn't leave with me and Dad, I might never see her again.

But I felt really scared and not right and I still just wanted my dad. I wanted to go home.

Mum picked up the house phone after just one ring. It was like she was waiting for my call. I explained Jez wasn't happy and Aunt Peggy thought it would be a good idea for Dad to get me.

'Oh, Jesus fucking Christ,' was all my mum said, which was the strangest thing in the world to hear, as I have never heard my mum swear before. 'I'm calling the police, Louise.'

'How long will they be?' I asked my mum. Aunt Peggy started shouting at me not to let my mum call the police as Jez had done nothing wrong, and Mum started screaming to Aunt Peggy so she could hear, 'I fucking warned you about him! This is my baby! I am hanging up now and I am calling the fucking police, Peggy!'

The phone went dead. We heard footsteps coming up the metal stairs. Aunt Peggy quickly ripped the wire out of the wall. I knew at that point Mum wouldn't be able to call back and I felt even more scared. Why would Aunt Peggy do that to me?

Jez opened the door and said, 'What's all the shouting about?'

Aunt Peggy looked at me and said, 'Show him.'

I thought I was going to be sick. 'Show him what?' I said.

'His present,' she laughed.

'Oh,' I said. I picked up the Celtic book off the table and said, 'I bought you this.'

'We weren't shouting, I was singing some of the Celtic songs to Lou that you subject me to every time they play in the pub!' Aunt Peggy said.

I couldn't believe how easily she lied to him, so quickly without even having time to think about it, and he just believed her.

'Oh,' he said. 'Thanks, Lou, at least I have one girl in my life who thinks of me.' He threw the book on the table without looking at it and got a beer out of the fridge. 'When's dinner ready?' he asked Aunt Peggy, as if she didn't look like she had gone completely mad and his flat hadn't been smashed to smithereens.

'It's ready now,' she smiled, jumping towards the kitchen. 'I was keeping it warm for when you got back,' she carried on. 'You wanna help me plate up, Lou?'

I put my three My Little Ponies I'd brought to play with on the small dining table and went into the kitchen to help Aunt Peggy dish up. I love her roast chicken so much, but I felt sick, like I'd just got off the roundabout at the park after being on it for too long. The smells were making me gag.

Usually Jez would chat to us when we plated up, or get the table ready, but last night he just stood, drinking his beer and staring at Aunt Peggy the whole time without saying anything. Glaring at her without blinking. She was really nervous, I could tell. Jumpy and twitchy. Everywhere she went, his eyes just followed her. I'd never ever seen her like it before. I carried over my plate and the gravy jug to the table and Aunt Peggy followed with his plate and hers. The three of us sat down and Jez said, 'Where's the fucking salt and pepper?'

'Sorry,' she replied immediately.

'I'll get them,' I said, and as I stood up, Jez reached forward and held my arm really tight, forcing me back to my seat.

'No you won't. You'll sit back down. She'll get them. Because she's the one that fucking forgot.'

Aunt Peggy stood up to fetch the salt and pepper. She looked at me and I could see she was going to cry. I could hear my heart pounding in my ears; I didn't think it had ever beat as fast before. Aunt Peggy placed the salt and pepper on the table and Jez started pouring tons on his dinner. He was whispering under his breath the whole time. I could tell he was angry, but I couldn't understand what he was saying. He was scary. He bit into the chicken and spat it straight back out, then stood up.

'Fuck's this?' he shouted.

'What?' Aunt Peggy replied quietly, like a little mouse. 'What's the matter?'

'What do you fucking mean, what's the matter? Are you trying to poison me with this shite?'

Before Aunt Peggy could answer him he just started going crazier, screaming at her that she was trying to kill him with her cooking. Aunt Peggy was as scared as me, I could tell. Maybe more scared, actually. She kept saying she was sorry. I wasn't sure if she was talking to him or me as she was looking down at her plate, saying the same two words over and over like she wasn't a real human. She started trying to speak, but she wasn't making sense because she couldn't get her words out. Eventually she managed, 'Please, Jez. Think of Louise.'

'Fuck Louise!' he screamed back. 'And fuck her mum and her dad, and fuck you!'

He held his right hand out in front of him, pointing in her face as he screamed at her. I'd never realised until then how big his hands were. He grabbed the whole of the back of her head in his hands and smashed it down into her dinner. She screamed. The dinner was still so hot. When he let go, she lifted her face and there was food all over it. I screamed, too, before clamping both my hands over my mouth to force myself to be quiet.

Jez turned around, picked up his plate of dinner and smashed the whole thing into the side of her face. Aunt Peggy fell off her chair with the force of it, right onto her pretty pink rug. I wet myself on the dining chair. Aunt Peggy was screaming in pain and crying about the gravy being hot and Jez just got angrier. As he bent down and picked the roast chicken and carrots off the floor, she managed to stand up, but then he straightened back up, walked towards her and smacked his big red forehead into her tiny little pretty one and started walking so fast she was running backwards into the kitchen whilst he was crushing food against her head, smearing it all over her face, ramming it into her mouth with three of his big fat fingers until she was almost sick. He just kept screaming, 'You fucking it eat it! You fucking eat this shite!' Aunt Peggy was choking and begging, saying, 'Please, Jez, please no,' over and over and over.

I wondered if he had forgotten I was there, because he didn't look at me. Not once. I was too frightened to move in case he saw I'd had an accident on the chair; I was scared he would get angrier. But I wanted to run to help Aunt Peggy so she wouldn't get more hurt, then I wanted to run out of the lounge so I couldn't see what was happening. I sat and shut my eyes so tightly that instead of it being pitch black like it normally is when you close your eyes, it was bright white, like the light that shines in your eyes when you go to the dentist. Like the light I always thought you'd see when you walk into heaven.

I began humming to drown out Jez's shouts and Aunty Peggy's screams. The next thing I knew, there were loud smashing sounds that my hums wouldn't cover and I thought I was going to pee again. My tummy felt like I was on a fast fairground ride. My legs were bouncing up and down and no matter how hard I tried I couldn't stop them, even with the weight of my hands pushing them down. I heard lots of shouts from voices I didn't know and I opened one eye and three policemen were running into the lounge. Two were on top of Jez, wrestling him to stay on the ground, and one was leaning over Aunty Peggy, who was lying on the kitchen floor. One was shouting down his radio about getting back-up and an ambulance, and he was saying, 'It's Jez Brown. I repeat, the offender is Jez Brown,' as if he were famous. Aunt Peggy looked like she was sleeping. The carrots were still mushed into her cheek. Jez must have walked back to the table when I had my eyes closed and picked up the gravy jug, as he had poured the rest of the gravy over her head and the jug now lay smashed into a thousand tiny pieces beside her. There was blood all over Aunt Peggy's hair and on the front of her flowery apron. One of the My Little Ponies lay next to her, its pastel-coloured tail and mane now covered with her blood.

All I can remember is being at home later, waiting while Dad ran me a big bubble bath. As it was filling up, he wrapped me in a warm bath towel he'd pulled off the radiator and rocked me on his lap. I felt too big and really tiny all at once, and I cried and cried.

# SUNDAY

George was happy when he saw Woody tootle through the door in front of me. Mum and Dad were at mine, Dad holding the bottom of the ladder whilst Mum was trying to attack the cobwebs with the end of the broom. It made me laugh – the two of them are forever doing the jobs that annoy me but I can't be bothered to tackle.

I set Woody up in George's room with the Duplo and asked to speak to them all. We sat in the lounge and I explained that Jo was struggling to juggle Woody with the other kids and the café and I thought it would be a good idea if he stayed with us until you were out of hospital. To my surprise everyone agreed, and I could tell George was happy with the idea. 'He can have the bottom bunk,' he said. 'And there's just over a metre in the room where you can fit a second set of drawers for his clothes. There's no room for his toys, though, because I don't want the room cluttered, so they'll have to stay in the lounge,' he added, matter-of-factly. We all smiled and I agreed.

I'm happy George is happy, and I'm happy my parents are supportive because I will need their help to navigate this, as always. I know they love me to need them – it's all they've ever wanted and they had too many years of feeling as though they weren't needed, even though they desperately were. I hope when you wake up, Martha, you think we made the right decision. We're all just winging it right now, trying to do what's best, but none of us really have a clue.

I'm going to call the social worker in the morning to check it's all OK and that they're happy Woody's with me, but I spoke to Mags tonight and she said it will be fine. She's coming over to chat to me tomorrow and to make a plan with work.

I think this happening to you has made me analyse all my friendships. But my friendship with you in this situation has also made me reflect on how incredible Jo was with me after David attacked me for the final time.

Jo had just moved to the area when we met.

I remember the first day I saw her. It was a few days after David had fractured my wrist. She was at the café – she had already met Jen, so she introduced us. She had the most perfect shiny straight black bob, sharply curled under her chin, with the most beautifully arched eyebrows to match. They say eyebrows should be sisters, not twins – which I always remind myself of whenever I try to pluck mine and it goes wrong – but Jo had some incredible identical eyebrows on the go. They were pretty mesmerising to look at.

She was dressed in all black – leggings and a top, I think – all clinging to her incredible figure with an oversized oatmeal chunky cardigan. She leant forward to greet me, and the waft of her perfume smelt divine. It's funny, I remember when we later spoke about that first encounter, after becoming best friends, she sent me a picture from her journal from the day she met me, all about how beautiful I was – mentioning my wild red hair, freckles and clothes. And there I was thinking the same about her, for the way she looked, and at that time we both felt shit about ourselves. Crazy, isn't it – the way we don't see the beauty in ourselves that we easily see in others?

I'm not sure if you know, but Jo originally moved here from near London with her husband Jamie and their children. She began working at my café shortly after relocating here, and months later, after I'd left David and with the trial pending, I decided I needed a change. I just couldn't continue in the café when the boys needed so much time and support. I also had so much to process and heal from myself, and due to the local papers, our family were the talk of our small town. I felt like I needed a fresh start, which was why I leased the café to Jo and her mother-in-law Pat, who had moved to the area too. They now run it as a family business – the same idea my parents had, when they first opened it all those years ago.

Jo and all her family gave me the most incredible support throughout my separation, the court hearings – all of it. Jo gave evidence in court and was just amazing. Spending my days hanging out with her, especially spending so much time with Dotty as her godmother, helped to heal my heart in so many ways. I was never allowed to enjoy my boys when they were tiny. I always knew I was being watched, even when David wasn't around. Everything I did, I had to overthink. I had to consider the consequences and outcomes of how I interacted with the boys, what I fed them, where I took them, how much I loved them. The pressure was so high all the time that I could never just be their mum with the freedom I should have had.

I often wonder what that's done to them – the damage of them feeding off who I was as a person back then. My nerves and anxiety; my absence, even when we were together, because I was battling so much in my brain every single day. Even when I was present, I was never truly present; I know that now I can just hang with Dotty, I can play with her, be silly – any decision I make won't be questioned or frowned upon. In fact, decisions I make for her aren't even looked at, because no one's watching me – and she isn't even my child. It just makes me feel so unbelievably sad that I was never able to parent my boys with this freedom and ease. To begin with, they got two different mums: the mum I was when David was away on business and the one I was when he was home. Although I learned quickly I had to be the same mum at all times, as he would interrogate them once they could talk. It also felt unfair to them to be more fun and free when he was away – I was terrified they would then blame him, hate him, and it would make things worse for us. It was such a constant head fuck, knowing the level of control that was over me at all times, even when the person doing the controlling was absent, even in another country for weeks at a time.

I know it was the same for you too, with Woody, and I really hope that when things are better for you, you start feeling how it is to live a life with him like I never got the chance to do with my boys. He's young enough for you to make those changes and be present. He won't ever remember you being the mum I was throughout the first nine and twelve years of my boys' lives.

But I have to focus on the positives. I am now finally present as their mum and I am lucky enough financially, with the settlement, to be able to parent them both with every part of my being. And I can be present as a godmother to another tiny precious being, which I feel so fortunate about, because it is one of the most glorious feelings in the world.

Harry called this evening after I'd put Woody down (he went straight to sleep again without any issues, in the bottom bunk!). He asked to come home from uni for a few nights, as he has an assignment he has to work on which he can do from home. Remember how torn he was, when he was choosing between sports science at Bath and sports psychology at Liverpool? He's settled well in Bath, though; it was the right choice for him.

I told him that Woody was staying with us for a while so it would be a squeeze, but I assured him we would make it work. He said he would crash at my parents' house – to be honest, their house is pretty similar to how our old one was; both boys have their own rooms there – it's pretty spectacular, compared to our tiny flat. My parents also treat both boys like kings, and cook them their favourite foods – they love being with them. They're pretty young grandparents and still considered quite cool by both my boys; the boys aren't embarrassed by them in any way.

Anyhow, then I began to overthink that I'd upset Harry with Woody being here, so I started rambling about how wanted and loved he is . . . He shut me up in one sentence. 'Mum, you're doing for him what no one ever did for us, or for you. I want to stay at Granny and Grampy's, and I'll come and hang out with you loads. Don't stress. I'm happy.'

He told me he's going to a gig tomorrow night with his sister, Molly. They're super close now, which is nice – given they only found out they were half siblings a few years ago. Since I became best friends with her mum, Jaclyn, Molly has become like a daughter to me. I worried it would be weird, as they were already friends, but they've both embraced it. I think that having each other to get through the past few years has helped them hugely. They speak and message constantly and Molly goes to Bath to stay as much as Harry comes back here.

Did I ever tell you how I found out about Molly and Jaclyn? It was after David's final attack on me. Years earlier, I'd seen this stunning, heavily pregnant woman at David's London office – Jaclyn. Well, after the attack, I found out that the baby in her belly at that time had been Molly . . . and her father was David.

It turns out that David had been dating Jaclyn for three years when he first met me in Cornwall when I was seventeen. He was actually there staying with Jaclyn, at her aunty's place. Jaclyn and David had come to Cornwall for a holiday; she returned to London after a week, as originally planned, but by then, David had met me . . . so he stayed for the summer to love bomb me.

He told me the house was his parents' and I wasn't allowed to visit because they were 'odd'. His parents have never even been to Cornwall!

Anyway, he and Jaclyn were already living together in London at that point, Jaclyn was pregnant, and they were engaged to be married. David managed to keep me hidden from her for a while at first – until he didn't. I imagine she must have cared more than me, to do her investigation work. He was always pretty shit at hiding his infidelity, but I never cared enough to trace who the other women were. Later, Jaclyn told me that David was a bit of a dick when they were first together – arrogant, big headed, chauvinistic – but never violent – until she found out about me, straight after she gave birth. She confronted him, and he lost it. When she threatened to tell me, he choked her until she almost became unconscious. She fled back to her aunty's empty house in Cornwall with a broken heart and a newborn baby and began working in a local solicitor's firm. Jaclyn didn't have any other family. Her dad had left her mum for another woman when she was tiny, and never stayed in touch. Her maternal family were extremely wealthy – her mum and aunt inherited this huge house – but her mum passed away when Jaclyn was just fifteen, so she lived with her aunt until she left to study in London. When her aunt died too, the house was left to Jaclyn – who thankfully hadn't married David at that point as she'd found out about me before the wedding went ahead, so she managed to keep herself financially secure. Like me, Jaclyn knew nothing of David's parents, other than that they lived in Somerset, and as far as she knew, he had no siblings.

David moved us all to Cornwall – to follow her, unbeknownst to me – after my parents moved away. I thought it was to punish me when he made the choice to come back to where I grew up once my parents had emigrated, and to a degree, I suppose it was – he needed to ensure I had no support network around before we relocated – but mainly it was to stalk Jaclyn. He put Harry in the same school as Molly, so Jaclyn pulled her out. She stopped Molly being in private school, just to keep her away from him. David tried to get a job at her firm but she threatened to tell her partners, and me. He got a job at a firm close by instead, and she told me he loved the thrill of going up against her in court, representing clients he knew would mean their paths would cross. All of it was this weird, sick game. Jaclyn told me there were times, so many times, that she would come to the café and psych herself up to tell me, but then she would sit outside in her car and watch me work and she just couldn't do it. She later sold her aunt's house and bought a new home that was gated and secure, to try and keep away from him. She thought about moving away again, but knew he would probably follow. He was – and probably still is, by the sounds of it – obsessed with her. Or obsessed with the fact he can't have her.

The reality was that Jaclyn could live without him – and David always wants what he can't have. I often wonder if that's why his levels of violence and control were as bad as they were with me, because he wouldn't have been able to bear two women seeing through him and disappearing, so he had to keep me under full control. I also feel that he blamed me for him losing Jaclyn; I often feel like she was the 'one', and somehow, in his warped mind, he was angry at me that it went wrong for them – as if he had absolutely nothing to do with it and it was all my fault, even though I had no idea she and Molly existed.

Jaclyn told Molly the truth when she was fourteen, after David dropped her home from school. Molly knew 'of' him because of her mum's work, as we live in a small town. She had hopped in his car to grab a lift when he'd 'just happened' to be driving by and pulled up next to her outside her school and offered. When Jaclyn decided to tell Molly, she told her everything. She told her how David had assaulted her, that they had fled, that he had followed, that Molly had half siblings that lived in the same town. She told her the real reason she had pulled her out of the private school she loved – all of it. Molly was devastated that Jaclyn had lied to her for so long, and their relationship really struggled for a while. But it sounds like it was never great, because David broke Jaclyn's heart so badly after she gave birth that she just focused on work from the minute Molly was born. She was an incredible solicitor and it was the only thing she felt good at. She had no role models or support network to teach her how to be a mum, and she felt so lonely when she landed in Cornwall. She'd got pregnant because it was what David wanted; they were going to share the care of Molly with the help of a nanny. He had a dream of a family, and that's what Molly was planned to be born into – Jaclyn planned to continue with her career after she gave birth, but go part time for a while, with the love and support of her fiancé – and then that plan changed overnight. Jaclyn found out that I was around – a pregnant teenage girl – and she wondered whether David really did want a family, or whether he just wanted to trap Jaclyn for her inheritance.

I suppose it became easy for Jaclyn just to keep going out to work once she started. Molly loved her nanny – she was settled and happy. The nanny did everything with ease that Jaclyn felt she was drowning with, and so the bond between Molly and her mum just wasn't there. Their bond now, though – well, it's the stuff dreams are made of. There's had to be a lot of forgiveness on Molly's side, and a lot of accountability, communication and explanation from Jaclyn's – a lot of which Jo and I have supported her with, because it's been beyond tough for her some days. It's felt at times like we were teaching a baby to take their first steps – you give them all the encouragement – you know they can do it, but instead of putting that foot forward to take their first step, they sit back down, because it's too overwhelming to try something new when they know they're safe sitting down. That's what it was like at the start, when Jaclyn was trying to explain things to Molly. To tell their story to her, she had to dig deep; she had to remember stuff she'd blocked out in order to survive, and not only did she have to go through the pain of feeling it all again, she had to explain it all to her own child – who needed and deserved answers – and who now, as a teenage girl with a huge range of emotions, had so many questions.

Today, Molly has two extra mother figures in Jo and myself. She is beyond loved, welcomed, cared for and listened to in all of our homes; she showers her mum with love and affection, and Jaclyn now reciprocates it all back. It's a joy to watch. It's been a glimmer for me during some very dark days. It's the bits David didn't spoil or take away . . . and it shows that actually, we won, and reminds me he is powerless.

I asked Jaclyn whether she hated me when I first found out, before we became friends. I asked her if she got angry on the days she came to the café and watched me through the window. She told me she didn't. She closed herself off to feeling anything, I think. She just wanted to make David stop, to leave her alone

– but realised in the end that telling me would most likely cause him to worsen, make her life even more difficult, destroy mine, so she continued to manage him as best she could – boundaried as fuck in private, and polite in public, when they were at work. Knowing what a lunatic he was, she always lived with the fear, though, of the 'one day', what he might do, and what life would then look like for Molly.

He is due out of prison in two years – he got a ten-year sentence, incredible for this country – but he will only serve half if he behaves. Which he will. He has an incredible little lump sum put away, and although I am told he won't be able to relocate here, he could move close enough for us all to worry about still having to see him. I don't know what that will look like for us all, how it will feel. None of us know if he will seek revenge. He was a power-hungry, successful lawyer before he went to prison, at the top of his game. His life will look very different when he comes out, and I don't know what that will do to him – and in turn, what he will do to us because of that. What I do know is that we have an amazing community here. All the years I feared not being believed, people doubting me, questioning me – but that didn't happen. Turns out David was known for being an arrogant narcissist by his own colleagues and other organisations. He'd lost many clients because of his own behaviour.

At first I used to think it was harder, having Jaclyn in my life. The truth she gave me left me with so many questions – so much guilt and shame, anger and rage. But then I'd remind myself we were both involved with the same monster, our children are siblings, and I feel fortunate she gets it, she gets me, my children – and our situation. It means I have someone to speak to, to share the thoughts and feelings I truly think only she can understand, and vice versa. I also love that I have Molly.

She has been a rock for me at times, and I'd like to think she feels the same about the boys and me. It's an odd dynamic, but one that I now feel relieved about. Jaclyn and Molly have got the boys and me through some really dark days, and I will be forever grateful to them.

I've realised, since processing stuff after leaving David, that some people are just good for your soul. You can feel it in your gut. It's something I never felt when I was with him; I didn't ever get close enough to anyone to have those amazing feelings. Yet now, I gravitate towards those people. The ones who, no matter how you feel when you see them, leave you feeling happier, calmer and brighter – even when things feel super shit.

When Jaclyn first came over and met Woody, it was really intriguing watching them interact. It surprised me. Knowing how she raised Molly, because of the torment of what she went through with David, has always left me wondering if she just switched her heart off to children – but it was clear she genuinely enjoyed playing with Woody, to the point that she took him to the landing outside George's room to where the other toy box is, and played with the Duplo Lego with him for ages. I could hear her chatting away to him and it made me wonder if she was ever like this with Molly while she was growing up. Before I knew about anything with David and Molly, I really disliked what I'd heard about Jaclyn from Jo. I thought she was a terrible mother, and I felt so sorry for Molly. I still do, in many ways, but I also now feel sorry for Jaclyn too, because I understand the situation. I really hope both of them have some glimmers of the first fifteen years they spent together, whilst David had so much control over their lives – that they remember some good times. I know that their relationship now looks totally different; they enjoy each other's company, Jaclyn is affectionate towards Molly, and that's well received, which is incredible, given it isn't something she's ever had.

I can't imagine how it must have felt for Jaclyn. She was literally about to give birth when she found out David had got an eighteen-year-old pregnant and had set up home with her – and then he led two lives that he dipped in and out of, and controlled and abused both of us. Jaclyn knew he had me and the boys, yet I knew nothing of her and Molly. I feel like I got the better deal, looking back. Ultimately, I believe it happened for a reason: we have each other, my boys have a sister, Molly has gained two brothers and we are all so close. I feel very fortunate. I think we all do.

Well, that turned into a long story! It's only twenty past nine, but I'm whacked, so I'm going to sleep. Goodnight, Martha. I love you.

# Eleven years old

Aunty Peggy has stayed with us for the last few weeks, since she came home after the attack. Mum didn't let me visit her in hospital, which I was upset about, because I wanted to tell her I was sorry for not helping her. Dad told me I didn't need to be sorry – he says the only person that should be sorry is Jez, for what he did to both of us, but I feel so guilty and sad all of the time that I should have done more to stop him.

Mum decorated Aunt Peggy's bedroom and bought her new clothes, make-up and a hairbrush. She painted the walls a pastel pink and got her a new floral bedspread and lampshade which matched – it looked soooo pretty.

Aunt Peggy looked different when she arrived. Thinner, which made me sad, because she was already so thin. She'd stopped dyeing her hair so her black roots were long, and it had a yellow tinge to it, like the colour of hay. I didn't like it. She also stopped washing it, it seemed, so it was greasy all the time too. She reminded me of my friend's grandma who has a stick and walks slowly – she looks like she's going to fall over any second. The shape of her face looks different. Her jaw has been wired, Dad told me, because Jez broke it so badly. For a while she could only have drinks to eat, like soup and mashed food, and she had to drink through a straw in a glass. She didn't talk when she came home and she was sad all the time. I heard Mum whisper to Dad in the lounge that it feels like he's killed her but she's still alive. She's right. It's like she's walking round, but it's not her any more.

Her arm is in plaster – Jez broke it from kicking her, Dad told me. I asked Dad how Jez could kick that high up and he told me that he couldn't. He kicked her when she was lying on the floor, asleep.

She has a scar on her stomach from a wound that needed stitching. That happened before I got there, I found out, which is weird as she still managed to plate up dinner and walk around. He was chucking mugs and glasses at her from the kitchen when she was in the lounge. She managed to dodge them all, and they smashed on the floor or against the wall, but that made him so mad that he attacked her and when she was on the floor one of the bits of glass cut her badly. She said she fell onto it, but the police think he did it to her – I overheard Mum telling Dad. I wondered if that was why she was dressed in his clothes when I arrived. She was definitely dressed in men's clothes, anyway. I want to ask her, but I don't feel like I can any more. Before Jez, I could have asked her any question in the world and she would have answered without any awkwardness or lies, but I don't feel like she would any more.

After a week or so, Aunt Peggy said she was well enough to go back to her job at the local chemist. Mum wasn't happy and told her it was a bad idea, but Aunt Peggy said she was going crazy doing nothing and she just wanted to get back to normal. Mum dropped her each morning and Dad picked her up on his way home from work, to make sure she was safe and didn't need to walk home alone. Her boss called my mum to say Jez was hanging round the chemist but Aunt Peggy wouldn't let him call the police. Mum went mad when she put the phone down. She kept shouting, 'Do you want to get killed, Peggy? Is that what you want?' Aunt Peggy just cried lots and didn't argue back, and Dad tried so hard to be nice to both of them.

Everything feels different. The house feels different, Mum is different, Aunt Peggy isn't even herself any more – I wonder if she ever will be again. It is like she has just given up. Died inside, but her body is still walking around.

Jez was in our local paper for the attack – only a small piece written about him, halfway through the paper. There wasn't even a picture of him. He got a fine and some stupid punishment. Mum and Dad are angry that he hasn't gone to prison. One morning when it was early and I sneaked out of my bedroom, I sat on the stairs and listened to them in the kitchen – Aunt Peggy was still in bed. Dad was saying, 'The bastard's kept his job, Pete and Sue are still serving him beer in the Crown, and he's still buying cigs off Bill in the newsagent's. We should be making a stand. Instead we're all treating him like he's done nowt wrong when he's destroyed our Peg's life.'

I've heard Aunt Peggy crying alone in her room at night. It was a quiet cry, but our rooms are next door to each other so I could hear her sobs. I wonder why she is still sad when she has got away from him. I wanted to go in and hug her. I wanted to tell her it would all be OK, but I felt like I couldn't any more. I feel like I don't know her any more, not like I used to. It's like she went to hospital and someone else came out inside her body.

She and Mum had a huge fight last night. It was late at night and it woke me up. It's the first time I've ever heard Aunt Peggy raise her voice to Mum like that, or at all. Mum was screaming at her to get rid of it or it would destroy her life. Dad was trying to calm them both down, asking them to 'shhh' so they didn't wake me. He kept telling them both that it would all be OK, whatever

Aunt Peggy decided. The shouting got worse: both of them were screaming at each other, Mum sounded angrier whilst Aunt Peggy was yelling back, but really crying. She was crying so much I couldn't understand what she was shouting.

I felt so sick in my stomach because I'd never heard them argue like this. I had never heard Mum sound this angry in my whole life. I wanted to go out and ask them to stop, but I was too frightened. I wet the bed. I was scared to go out and tell Dad, so I made a bed on my floor out of my cushions, blankets and dressing gown.

I must have somehow fallen back to sleep, because the next thing I knew, I was being woken up by Mum for school this morning. When I walked past Aunt Peggy's room to go to the bathroom, it was empty, and her bed was stripped. Mum was perched on the end of it, clutching all her bedding in her arms, and I asked her where Aunt Peggy had gone. She wiped away a tear and said, 'To hell, darling. She's gone back to hell.'

I carried on walking to the bathroom. I knew Mum meant she had gone back to Jez. My tummy did a little flip because I was worried he would be nasty and hurt her again, but I didn't ask Mum any more questions as I didn't want to make her sadder, even though I still have a million running round my brain. I wondered how Mum let her return. I would have done more to stop her. I wouldn't have let her leave.

Dad came in to the bathroom and asked me if I was OK. 'I wet the bed,' I said. He hugged me and told me not to worry, then he walked in to Mum in Aunt Peggy's room and whispered, 'This stops now, it's not our battle. We need to do better for Louise. She's wet the bed again.'

# MONDAY

Mags came over first thing. She told me the social worker would be visiting me this morning and she wanted to check in on me. Woody had woken at 6 a.m. and we'd left early to take George to breakfast club at school – he goes to breakfast club a few days a week as he likes the way they toast the bread. No matter how much I try, I can't get it the same. The three of us had taken Milo on the beach for a run before I dropped George off, so Woody was exhausted and went straight off in the bottom bunk when I put him down at 10 a.m.

Mags and I made a decision while Woody was napping. Well, Mags did, and I agreed because we both know there isn't really another option here. I knew it would be pointless arguing with her, but also, everything she said makes complete sense.

I can't do my job right now. Not like I did prior to last week – I'm not sleeping and my head's fried.

Mags thinks I need to just concentrate on taking care of Woody and being able to visit you as soon as you need me, so we've agreed I'm going to take some leave until things look different.

The job requires me to be switched on at all times to work with the women we support and right now, if I'm honest with myself, I know I just can't give that to them. Everything has changed overnight. My focus right now needs to be on Woody, and myself, and you. It's temporary, but it's the right choice for us all currently, and that's all that matters.

The social worker came over. She was super sweet – she'd only just qualified, but I saw that as a good thing, because she was keen and passionate. I am so happy Woody has her in his corner.

They are fine for him to stay with me. I don't think much will happen other than them checking in until you're better. With Craig being in prison, the risk to Woody is minimal, and no family members from either side have come forward to ask about him, which hurts my heart – but I'm also glad, because I know he had no relationship with any family members, and I would hate for him to be placed with a stranger just because they're a blood relative.

The hospital told Mags you've had another temperature in the last ten hours, but the infection markers in your blood have stabilised. It feels like a relief – I don't know why, because part of me thinks I shouldn't feel relief. I don't know what the right thing is to feel; I don't think anyone does. They said they are back to planning to remove the external ventricular drain bolt and wake you up. Mags has asked if they've done another brain scan to look for what the damage may be. Her brother died after a motorbike accident, but went into a coma first, and I worry this is super triggering for her – but my god, I'm glad you have her to ask questions on your behalf. She is advocating for you in every way possible, like nothing I've ever seen before. The doctor said at the moment he wants to wait. What are we waiting for? Not knowing how much of you we will get back feels like torture.

# Twelve years old

We've been living in Cornwall for almost six months now. We arrived at the beginning of the summer holidays. No sad, dragged-out emotional goodbyes. I just quietly disappeared, in between school changes. I don't think anyone really noticed.

I don't miss my old school. I had friends, but I hated the politics of friendships, the fights and fall outs, the taking sides. I preferred to help the teachers at break and lunchtimes, or volunteer to help the younger kids in other classes with their reading and spelling. I do miss the dinner lady, who always gave me a bigger portion of roast dinner on a Wednesday because she knew I loved it so much. She had grey curly hair and smelt like butter. Her apron was always covered in food, but she was smiley and kind to everyone. I wish there were dinner ladies like her at my new school, but high school isn't really like that.

I think Dad misses his old job – he had worked hard on building his business, but when the big company came along and made him an offer to buy it, he couldn't refuse. But he also loves our new life in Cornwall, and getting to spend more time with Mum doing something totally different.

We all love our little café on the front, overlooking the beach. Mum does all the baking and the food prep and Dad is front of house and makes the drinks. The change in him was instant. He loves talking to everyone and anyone that comes into the café, telling holidaymakers the best coastal paths and beaches to explore whilst serving up Mum's famous carrot cake and pots of tea, then wiping down tables and mopping the floors. He takes such pride in making sure the front of the building is freshly painted each season, and decorated with the biggest, brightest hanging baskets full of purple trailing lobelia and hydrangeas, and he made cute bench seats by hand, which he's painted in fresh nautical colours.

I head to the café every day after school with my friends. We get ice-cream milkshakes and sunbathe on the beach. Mum always keeps fresh towels and a load of clean swimsuits in the back room so all my friends can just hang out there too until the café closes at teatime.

I don't miss Yorkshire, apart from the dinner lady. I do miss Aunt Peggy, though, and I know Mum does too.

I write to her a lot. I love writing letters: I decorate the envelope with gems and stickers, and colour in the writing paper, make borders with little hearts and crosses and spray the paper with my 'So . . .?' body spray.

She always writes back. Mum and I read the letters together, and when I reply she always says, 'Tell her to come and visit' and 'Tell her how beautiful it is here'. She gives me photos she's had printed to put in the envelope. Photos of the beaches and house, me eating her Victoria sponge – which is Aunt Peggy's favourite cake. I think she's trying to get Aunt Peggy to leave Jez and move to Cornwall to be near us.

Aunt Peggy always says she is happy, that Jez has changed, that he is sorry for his past behaviour. They are having a baby and she's due really soon. If it's a girl, they're going to call it

## A Letter to Keep You Safe

Katherine Louise (after me!), and if it's a boy he will be John James. She's promised to send photos when the baby comes and says she will visit as soon as she can. I can't wait to meet my baby cousin!

# MONDAY

Harry arrived just after 11 a.m. He looks bigger, older, more tanned and more handsome – which I didn't think was possible.

Every time I see him, he feels bigger and looks different. I want to feel like his safe place, but today when he walked in the door and hugged me, he felt like mine. His huge arms wrapped round me and his smell felt so familiar. I felt a mix of every emotion and I tried so hard to hold it together, then he rested his chin on the top of my head and said, 'It's gonna be OK, Mum,' and that was it, I was gone. I wonder if I'll ever run out of tears. He didn't ask why I was crying and I didn't explain, and for the first time ever I didn't apologise for crying – because I'm not sorry.

One of my best friends is lying in a hospital bed because of the father of her child, just like I lay in a hospital bed too many times over too many years because of the father of my children. It just feels a lot so much of the time right now, and that's OK. It's OK to show my emotion to my son, who's also been through this. It's OK to grieve for the lives we didn't get, that our children didn't get, that we all deserved and should have had – so that's what I did. I sobbed in the weight of my son's arms while he just held me, and it didn't feel awkward or horrid; I didn't get an overwhelming feeling of shame wash over me like I usually do when

I get upset in front of him. I just felt relieved he was there to care for me, and as he reminded me of all the good things, all the positive parts of this journey and the life we have now, I felt like he felt the same.

I took Woody to the monkey sanctuary with the boys and Mum and Dad; my parents met us there, as we couldn't all fit in one car.

Oh god, Martha – Woody absolutely loved it; I cannot tell you how excited the monkeys made him. There were some enclosures that you could walk through where the monkeys ran in front of you and he was literally squealing and jumping. When you're better, we *have* to take him again. Meg and Jen came with their kids too – they met us there. After we'd walked round for a while, we pulled out our blankets and got our picnics out. Mum had also packed one of her famous spreads: homemade pork pies and lemon drizzle cake, and Meg had stopped off at the café and brought along some of Pat's incredible brownies – it was a midday feast and it was so nice just to sit in the sun together, eating amazing food and chatting. I can't wait for you to be a part of it again.

Dad then took the kids off to the park, which was just in front of us, so us girls had a bit of time just to enjoy the feeling of the sun on our skin whilst we had a bit of peace from the chaos all the little ones bring.

I watched my dad with all the kids. The bigger ones were taking turns putting the little kids on the zip wire and guiding them down, whilst Woody stood next to it screaming with excitement every time one of them launched past him at speed. He was so happy just being a part of it all. Jen asked me how you were – I told her there wasn't much change. We chatted through how we are all going to support you when you come out of hospital. Mum suggested having a rota in place where we can all care for you, so it's always covered, and we can spend time with you so you're not alone. I don't want people to feel obliged to help, especially when I know they have young families themselves, but actually it's clear that everyone thinks the world of you, and Woody – and they want to support and love you. I watched both boys today playing with Meg and Jen's kids, and I realised I now had true friends that I can just sit and chat to about life. I realised that I'm part of a real community here – as are you. For the first time ever, I have a whole bunch of really cool, kind and normal people around me – I have my family – we all have each other, and my, oh my, it feels so good.

We drove to the seaside afterwards and ate fish and chips on the beach – they definitely taste better out of the wrapper rather than on a plate – and then we drove home. This was the first beach I ever ate fish and chips on, after we moved here suddenly when I was eleven and a half. It was a huge change, Cornwall from Yorkshire. Even though we had Scarborough beach up there, it was a drive, and we didn't go often. When we moved here, we were surrounded by all these beaches that were within walking distance from us. Mum and Dad wanted to move to Looe to start with, but then they found the café up for sale, which they loved, and they looked at houses there instead.

# Twelve years old

It can't be true.

It was late last night when the police called. Mum had the phone tucked under her chin because she was carrying a vase of roses to the table. I couldn't hear what was being said, I just saw Mum drop the vase of roses and it crash to the floor.

She started screaming, 'He's done it, he's done it!' over and over again. Dad didn't even speak to the person on the other end of the phone, he just picked the handset up off the floor and hung it up on the cradle.

Mum started to wail. It sounded like the noises our cat, Tabby, makes at night outside my window when she's in season. It was so loud, and it went on and on and on.

Dad knelt beside Mum. He scooped her up onto his lap on the armchair next to the big sash bay window, and rocked her like a baby, I just stood in the doorway thinking how he looked so big compared to her. He stroked her cheek with the palm of his hand, wiping away the tears that just kept coming, and repeatedly saying 'shhhh' over the never-ending sounds of her shattered heart, the two of them surrounded by pretty cream roses and thousands of pieces of broken glass.

I can't get my head around the fact that my beautiful aunty, my aunty who cooked the tastiest roast chicken in her cute little floral apron, who sang songs in the shower with the most unique voice, has been beaten to death on her bedroom floor, nine days before she was due to give birth to her baby girl, my little cousin – who also died in such a cruel, brutal way – inside her protector's belly.

# MONDAY

Woody slept the whole journey back this afternoon, so I know tonight will be a late one, most probably, as he had a full danger nap – but I'm just chilling writing this, and he's snuggled on Harry with his raggie, watching cartoons on the TV. Harry is doing nothing, he's just enjoying soaking in Woody's cuddles. I can't work out if that's strange, for an eighteen-year-old boy to just lie with a toddler watching *Peppa Pig* without the distraction of a mobile phone, but it's nice. It feels special. He's giving Woody the love he clearly needs right now, and I feel like subconsciously Harry needs it too.

He's going with Molly to a gig shortly, then they're staying at Jaclyn's tonight.

You haven't spent as much time with Jaclyn as with the other girls – partly because Jaclyn and I were friends for years before meeting you and mainly because she's a workaholic, but she's messaged me every day to check in on you and keeps asking if there's anything she can do. She asked Molly what things Woody likes and she's going to drop in a load of Peppa toys, more Duplo, and she's also bought him some more summer clothes and sandals, which I thought was super kind of her.

Right then, I'd better go – Harry is almost ready for the gig, your baby boy needs his dinner and a bath, and I need to get George organised too.

Goodnight, Martha, sleep well xx

# TUESDAY

The tiredness won yesterday, I think; although I managed to sleep for periods last night, I don't feel like I did. It was the weirdest night's sleep. Random dreams that made no sense, then I was going from being in and out of deep sleep to being suddenly wide awake, so now I'm knackered, I have a headache I can't shift and I feel groggy.

I've never slept well since meeting David – although I've definitely begun sleeping better in the past year. In fact, I've done most things better in life in the past year – without questioning and overthinking every decision I make. I remember my therapist explaining to me how hard it is for me to make even basic decisions because I've been controlled almost the whole of my adult life by one person. When I thought about that, it made me so mad that he's had that – all that power over me for all of those years, where I second guessed everything I did, all day, every day, because I never knew what the rules were at that time – he changed them frequently to match his mood. For years, I didn't know if I was coming or going, so it feels pretty triggering right now to go back to having these awful nights – I forgot how long and lonely they feel and it's reminded me of how often I used to pray for it to just get light so I knew a new day was coming.

Separating from David left me being single for the first time as an adult. I'd met him when I was seventeen, and it felt so weird to think *I am not in a relationship*, knowing I was answerable to no one for the first time ever.

I had one proper relationship before David. I mean, I was a child and it lasted less than a year, but I lost my virginity to Jason, and I genuinely believed I was in love with him. And then there was Tom, and although theoretically we weren't in a relationship and we didn't sleep together, I felt a connection to him like I'd never done with anyone. But one day he just disappeared and ghosted me. I wonder about him at times, you know. I always have over the years, but more so lately. I wonder if he went on to marry and have children, or stayed single. I wonder where he is – if he's even alive.

I remember feeling, when Jason broke my heart at the age of almost sixteen, that I would never get over it. I still remember those feelings to this day, even though I'm not far off forty and have my heart broken far worse since. But I don't think we prepare our teens enough for how it will feel when it happens to them. I certainly wasn't aware, and when I got treated like shit by a boy I really liked and trusted, I thought there was something wrong with me for how terrible things felt. I remember it feeling so rough, so unknown. It was the first time in my life I had ever felt any abandonment or rejection, and I realised humans can really let you down, even the ones you really love being around, ones you thought loved you. I suppose it's quite an achievement that I'd never had those awful feelings before, given at that point I was almost sixteen, but right then and there I felt like the most unloved, inadequate, dirtiest girl in the world. For a few long months afterwards, I went to bed and woke up with a sick, anxious feeling I'd only experienced with Aunt Peggy, and I hated it.

Woody was at nursery all day today, so I napped on the sofa this afternoon while Harry went to the gym and George went fishing with Dad. My parents have asked me to go over for dinner tomorrow. Usually I'd stay overnight – they asked if I wanted to, but I just think it will be too much for Woody. He's been all over the place, and I just want to settle him into a proper routine.

The hospital called Mags.

There is no change; you're critical but stable. Not the news I wanted, but they are running scans. Mags is going up to see you this afternoon. I asked her to tell you that I love you, that Woody loves you, and that we miss you. She promised she would. I am praying with everything you wake up soon so I can bring him to see you. Right now, he would just become so upset and worried if he saw you like you are, so we have no option but to wait.

# Fifteen years old

Rachel and Sally keep giving me dirty looks when I walk past them at school. They're the year above me, so they're in sixth form. I don't know why they hate me so much. I know Rachel dated Jason before me, but he didn't cheat on her with me; they were split up for ages before we got together. It makes me feel sick whenever I see them because they just start straight away with the dirty looks, the OTT giggling, and comments loud enough for me to hear they're talking about me but quiet enough for me not to make out what they're saying.

I've been with Jason for nine months now and we've decided we're going to have sex. I want to, I feel like I'm ready and I love him.

We've decided we are going to do it straight after school, next Thursday afternoon at my house, as I know Mum and Dad won't be back until just after 5 p.m. and we've been trusted a million times to be home alone together before.

I am worried. It's my first time and his third. I'm worried that he will be really experienced and because I'm not he will hate it or go off me. I don't know what I'm doing. I just want it to be like the stuff I watched in films with Aunt Peggy, where they start kissing and then it happens naturally without it being awkward or weird.

I'm scared it will hurt, and I don't know what to do if it does, or if it hurts so much I can't do it. I wish I had someone to ask. I can't ask Mum, she wouldn't know what to say and she would probably be angry. I wish Aunt Peggy was still here. She would answer all my questions and I know if I could speak to her, I wouldn't be worried at all right now.

# THURSDAY

Sorry I didn't write yesterday – George fell when he was fishing with my dad and took a chunk out of his leg on the rocks. He had to have it stitched at hospital and it was pretty traumatic. I was also worried about going to the hospital as the last time we were here was when he was visiting me after the attack. On top of that, he doesn't cope well in busy places, or with the unknown, so having stitches in a heaving hospital with bright lights, strangers and new smells took up most of the day and night. When George first got his autism diagnosis, I felt so overwhelmed, out of my depth – like everything now made sense, but at the same time, made me feel petrified – I was panicking so much about how I was going to raise my son properly . . . I remember my dad reminding me that I'd already been raising him. It's not easy when George dysregulates, but it is good that he can be himself – however that looks – and he knows that we all love him through all of it without question or judgement.

Harry stayed over and took care of Woody with Mum whilst Dad and I were at the hospital. I genuinely don't know how I'd cope without my parents now, and what I love the most is that I know that's exactly how they want it. Harry and Molly took Woody to the beach together, and then for dinner. They sent me so many pictures I have kept to show you; Woody had the best day and I think Harry genuinely enjoyed it – I can tell he has a huge soft spot for Woody. He asked me if I want him to come home for a bit – away from university – to help me with the boys whilst you're in hospital. I told him no, absolutely not. He spent his whole childhood having to be hyper-vigilant, listening out as to whether I was safe. It's now his time to live, to be free, to put himself first. I am reassuring him I'm fine, that we're all fine – but I know he is a natural worrier.

Good news, though! Mags came over this morning. They have removed the shunt from your skull, hurrah!

The nurses are super lush, Mags said. They told her that they are weaning the medication that has been keeping you still first. I hate that we can't visit you yet, but I love hearing how you are doing and you have been having some movements in your left arm and leg, but no movements at all from your right side yet. When Mags asked about this, the doctor brushed it off, reassured her it was again normal. I can tell that Mags is desperate for a peek into their minds, to have one ounce of a clue what this all might mean for you now and in the future.

# Fifteen years old

It was awful. I feel so sick.

We got back from school just after 3.15. Usually we eat some food, chill on the sofa or in the garden, then watch TV together, but as soon as we walked in the house Jason said, 'Let's do it straight away, so your mum and dad don't come back.'

We went into my room and he pulled the covers back on the bed. I really wanted to shower first and brush my teeth, but I felt it would be stupid to say that, so I didn't bother. Jason told me he was going to take his clothes off and left my room to go to the bathroom.

I quickly stripped off under the covers in case he came back, so that he didn't see my body, and I lay under the covers naked. My heart was pounding out of my chest at all the 'What if?' questions that began flying around my brain. He returned in his boxers, then perched on the edge of my single bed, pulled his underwear to his knees and began trying to get a condom on his penis. It's the first time I've ever seen a penis and they're so ugly. He had so much hair around it, too, that it made me feel a little bit queasy. Should it? I didn't know if that makes me the weird one. Maybe other girls like hairy boys and the look of dicks.

He really struggled to get the condom on and was getting angry, whilst I was totally silent. The cat meowed at my door the whole time to be let back in, and the whole thing felt so awkward and gross.

I had the idea to start kissing and cuddling, then try the condom again. We got under the covers, but we started sweating from the heat. Jason grabbed the condom – that he'd stolen from his older brother's top drawer – off the edge of my bed, but by then it wasn't in a great state from the amount of times he'd tried to get it on. I knew from rolling one on a banana in sex education last year that you have to make totally sure there is no air in the tip, but I was sure there was still air in the tip, and we needed to make sure it didn't have any so I didn't get pregnant. Jason kept getting annoyed, and shouted, 'It's gone soft again now!'

When it first went in, the clock on my bedside table said it was 3.49 p.m. and I worried that if we were going for too long, my parents would come home and catch us.

It hurt. It felt like we were trying to fit something into somewhere it wasn't supposed to be. I kept waiting to feel my cherry pop, like so many girls at school said they had. That didn't happen, it was just this weird feeling with pain and a dry, friction kind of sensation. Then I waited to have an orgasm like every girl at my school who had lost their virginity told me they'd had . . . but again, nothing. All I had was the continued dry, burning sensation where it went up and down. Everything felt tight and sore down there, and I wondered if we were even doing it right because no part of it was nice.

I needn't have worried about getting caught by my parents because before I knew it Jason made a weird groan in my ear, clambered off me and handed me a condom with a top knot with the contents of what looked a tablespoon of warm watery milk in the bottom, and said, 'I'd better go.'

## A Letter to Keep You Safe

He walked to the bathroom, got dressed and left without saying goodbye.

It was 3.55 p.m.

I want to be sick.

# FRIDAY

Overnight, you had a seizure, and they decided to rescan you again. There are some areas that are whiter than they should be, on a few small parts of your brain, which they have said is worrying – but they've said most of it looks OK, and your brain is back in the middle of your skull, which is absolutely incredible. The doctors have started you on some epilepsy medication to prevent more seizures, and are now finally happy to start waking you up! Good news is, it's one step closer to me being able to visit – which I now can't wait for!

I called into Jo's tonight with George, Woody and Milo after I collected George from school. I thought how lovely it is that George gets on well with Jo's kids – even though their house is always total chaos, isn't it? Always full of the kids and their friends. Pat and her dog are often there too, and I love how George never gets overwhelmed or worried. The dogs love playing together in the garden, so it's a bonus that Milo gets worn out. I wish my house looked like Jo's – it's always welcoming, full of people, chaos and laughter.

It's mesmerising to watch Jo and Jamie in action, having six children between them, all living with them full-time.

I remember Jo explaining the family dynamic when I met her originally. At that point, Jamie's two kids, Will and Ruby, were just about to start living with them full time, and Jo had her three, and I thought she was Superwoman. I never came round when I was with David, but after I left, her home became my safe haven. I always felt welcomed and wanted, and any time now that I look at her huge comfy sofa, I silently thank it for all the days it held me up, allowed me to snuggle my broken body into it and heal. Jo would wrap me in soft blankets that smelt of her incredible fabric conditioner, and her kids would entertain my boys in their rooms or their garden, giving them a safe space and an abundance of love which they'd never had before. The three of us would spend days here in our comfies, not knowing how the future looked, but knowing for the first time ever, we had a family. Even though we weren't related, they just embraced us and loved us and helped us so much – they are the entire reason I am now sat here, writing to you.

Ruby and Will are off to see their mum this weekend. They haven't seen her since she moved away with her partner and their new baby a few months ago, so Jo said Jamie is feeling nervous about how it will go. I love spending time at their house, where you see that DNA and surnames are irrelevant. It's refreshing to be in that house, for me. Watching the way Jamie parents forever reminds me not to settle until I find what Jo and he have. It's not perfect – but even when it isn't, it still feels like it is, because they love each other and their kids. They are united, and prioritise each other over everything. It's a beautiful blended family that feels right even when it has its issues.

Ultimately, I think Jo and her family are all happy, they support one another and love very hard, and I think they're quite proud of their family dynamic and how well it works – and so they should be. Blended families can be so difficult to manage and navigate, so when you see one getting it right, even when the world is often against them, it's pretty heartwarming to see.

I just love that it's a house you can always drop into – there always seems to be someone home, and even if it isn't bustling with the usual chaos, it still feels like home. It's a real skill, I think, to be able to have a house that feels safe to so many people. It's a dream that one day I hope to have a home like this myself. It still feels so far away for me yet – but I really would love this for my boys, and whoever they bring into our lives.

After a while, when all the kids were playing tonight, and we were sat in the garden, Jo asked me how I'd feel about reading her adoption papers with her. She and her two siblings were adopted from their birth parents when they were tiny. Jo didn't feel ready then to look when she first got them, but wondered if now it would be something I could do with her. She pulled out many files and folders, all containing hundreds of notes, reports and paperwork. I scanned through – the notes had been written on a typewriter, some by hand – the most incredible, scrolled calligraphy writing I'd ever seen.

I didn't even question it.

I felt honoured that Jo had asked for my help to dissect it all. We made a date for next week, to spend the day at her house trawling through it all while Dotty and Woody are in nursery. Pat will be there too; she is going to get everything into date order for us, as she's already been privy to it all so she could be another support to Jo. I have a feeling it's going to be really heavy and overwhelming, but Jo has been there for me, so I want to be there for her.

# Fifteen years old

Since Jason and I had sex, it has been the worst three days of my life.

I felt sick all night because I didn't understand why he went straight after it happened. He usually stays until about 5.30 p.m. – some days, he will eat dinner with us, then leave about 6.30 p.m.

We always meet on the corner of my road at 8.30 to walk to school, but the next morning he wasn't waiting to go in together, like he had been every other day of our relationship.

I walked into my form group on the Friday morning and all the girls started chanting, 'She did it, she did it!' and I wanted the ground to swallow me up. I asked how they knew and one of my friends, Lucy, said, 'Everyone knows.' I wanted to die. I just wanted an earthquake to happen so I would just die immediately, right there and then. I was so confused and angry.

I felt like I needed to see Jason immediately, to ask why he had told people, but I couldn't because I had to get to my first class.

Two hours later, which felt like forever, it was break time. I went to the science block, where we always meet at break, but he wasn't there. The realisation of what was happening was hitting me, and I felt sick with panic.

I still feel sick with panic.

I started walking down to the green where my friends would be, and as I passed two of Jason's mates, one shouted, 'Make sure you get all the air out the tip!' and I stopped myself from crying again. I walked straight to the medical room and told the school nurse I had been sick. She took my temperature and said it was OK, but I did look flushed and my pulse was high so she called my mum and said she thought I was coming down with something. Mum came and got me straight away and took me home.

She totally believed I had a bug and tucked me into bed with a bowl, a towel and a glass of water, and told me to call the café if I got worse. If not, they'd be back around 5 p.m., as usual.

I waited until 3.30 p.m. and I called Jason's landline. His mum answered and said he wasn't back yet. She was really nice and seemed a bit taken aback that we weren't together as usual after school. She said she would get him to call as soon as he got home. I felt relieved she didn't know anything, and thought this may all be an accident and we were going to be fine.

He didn't call.

I rang him again yesterday morning, which was a Saturday, at 9.30 a.m., knowing he would be up as he leaves for football at 10 a.m. His mum answered again. She told me he was in the shower as he had woken late. I feel like she was lying, from the way she was stuttering. She said she would get him to call me back after football.

He didn't call.

I called again this morning, and she sounded so upset when she said, 'He's asked me to tell you not to call again. To be honest, darling, I just don't think he's ready for a girlfriend at the minute.' I started to cry, because I am so angry and sad that he used me. It makes sense to me now, why Rachel and her friends hate me – I bet he did this to her too. I still can't stop crying, though, because I really love him and thought he loved me. I don't get how he can go from spending every day with me for nine months and then just stop talking to me.

# SATURDAY

You're awake!!!

I honestly thought this day would never come.

I still haven't seen you – no one is allowed at the minute, which has been hard – but Mags went up to the hospital and was allowed to visit you as she's your support worker.

She said your eyes are pink; they look dry and sore. They've taken away the big oxygen mask and now you just have oxygen from a tube that rests over your top lip. She did say the bruising is now fully visible. One side of your head is a mix of green, blue and purple. That made my heart hurt, knowing how that feels. Hopefully by the time you look in a mirror, it will be gone.

Mags said when she asked you if you were OK, the corners of your mouth turned upwards and you squeezed her hand. I am so buzzing and emotional right now.

It's been such a good day today. Harry's been offered a new job in a bar in Bath city centre. It's a cocktail bar – he has to go on a course, to learn how to make the cocktails properly. The money is good and they have said tips are also great because it's a bar that you have to book to go to – quite posh, I think. He seems excited, so that's good. Other than studying and playing sport with the lads he's met at uni, he doesn't really do anything or go anywhere other than occasionally with Molly. He assures me he's happy just doing this, but I wish he would live a little more, like most eighteen-year-old lads do. Like the stories Jo and Meg feed me about their kids and stepkids.

I think Harry's feeling a lot of things, especially since starting his therapy – and he isn't sure what that's doing to him, but in order to process the difference in the life he lived for the first fourteen years and the one he's been living for the past three years, he absolutely needs professional help. I hope, in time, the therapy helps him do more of the things I know he wants to, but can't. Hopefully, this job will help too. I am beyond proud of him. Obviously I'm petrified every day that he's actually not OK, that I might one day lose him. I know he already has more demons to battle than most of his friends ever will. But we speak and message every day, and I truly believe he feels more light than darkness overall, or that's what he shows me.

And the next bit of good news today – Jo has found her mum. She traced her pretty easily, it seems. Social services got back to her within days with all the details, so I am assuming her mum was looking to be found.

Typical Jo, finds her birth mum before she's even read the adoption papers and figured out if she wants to meet her or not.

She also found out her dad died seven years ago – she isn't sure how. Her mum still lives in the same area as where Jo was born, but a different property – Jo has the address. Her mum wants to make contact with her and her siblings. Both Jo's brother Joe and her sister Kitty don't – they don't feel the need right now, and Jo gets that, I get that, but Jo's life looks different to theirs. Kitty still lives abroad – she met the man of her dreams two years ago and is planning her wedding before they move back to the UK and start trying for a baby as she's about to turn forty and worrying she might struggle to get pregnant. I don't think she needs the stress of meeting her biological mum right now. And Joe is in the forces and also away a lot – he's really high up, and Jo thinks he just doesn't want the hassle – he stays away from anything that could cause him issues where he may not be able to do his job to the best of his ability. He's also in the midst of a divorce, as his wife became super lonely and sad after not having him home for so many years and was tired of living like a single mum – they're trying to remain amicable now the divorce has been definitely decided, but I think they've both got so much of their own stuff going on that he just doesn't need the added heartache this could bring. They're both OK with Jo reaching out, which is good, and maybe (situation depending) it could bring them all together somehow, who knows?

I feel Jo is in a different place to her siblings altogether. She and Jamie are so in love and settled, their kids are smashing life, Jo has the best support in her mother-in-law, should meeting her bio mum go wrong, and I think the main thing she's taken from what Pat has told her about her case notes is that her mum was a victim of domestic abuse. She was extremely high risk and that, in the end, was the main reason that Jo and her siblings were removed. Now she's recognised she's been a victim of domestic abuse too.

I'm starting to realise, whilst writing this letter to you, that life is too short. Sometimes we have to just get on and do whatever it is we're thinking of doing whilst we're feeling brave enough to do it.

# Seventeen years old

I'm so happy at sixth form.

Thank god I didn't let Jason breaking my heart stop me from passing my GCSEs. I'm really proud of myself for passing every single exam. I know I didn't put in as much effort as I should have done, so I'm so grateful I managed to get through them somehow. Someone must be looking after me somewhere!

I can't believe I almost didn't go to sixth form because of Rachel and Sally being in the year above, but given it was a toss-up between college with Jason and his mates or sixth form with those two, I suppose I didn't have much choice! It's funny to think back on how we girls felt about each other, when now we all get on really well. To think we hated each other, when actually, Jason dumped Rachel pretty much as soon as she did it with him too. And he only took five minutes with her as well. The guy really was a total cock.

My friendship group is actually pretty incredible – boys and girls across two year groups, mine and the one above. A lot of them drive already, as they are seventeen and eighteen, which means we can go out of town to different beaches in the summer, and drive to theme parks and big cinemas further up country – we're able to do things which just aren't available in Cornwall. The boys in the group are really grown up and decent compared to Jason and his friends, who were what I was used to before I met them. They take care of us girls, but like big brothers rather than in a weird or sleazy way. I mean, occasionally we all get so hammered that one of us girls *might* do something sexually with one of the lads, but it's never discussed – no one ever takes the piss or makes you feel wrong or dirty. I think we all feel like we're just teenagers, we're experimenting and having fun without any judgement and jealousy, because we're all such good friends and it works. I feel included, like I've met my tribe for the first time ever. It's nice.

We all hang at each other's houses, and they come to the café most days to see me when I finish work. A few of them got part-time jobs working for us in the holidays when the café's busy. Mum and Dad always make them welcome, and it feels good.

I've got my practical driving test booked next month so I'm doing extra lessons – I really want to pass so that I can go to more places, see more, like so many of my friends do. Dad's been taking me out for extra lessons too, so I am praying I can do it.

This summer we've got really into the rave scene. There have been loads of raves on within a few hours of where we live – Plymouth Warehouse has them every Friday night and we have literally all just worked and saved to make sure we could go to them all. Us girls dress up in neon Lycra, put our hair in French plaits and finish our look with a face full of glitter and sequins. The boys have actually got really into it and rock neon paint across their torsos, wear cool shades and bucket hats, and we climb on their shoulders and wade into the crowds and just sing and dance to the music. Another lesson I've learned this year: the power of music. How different beats, lyrics and words can make me feel a million different things. This is my second summer with the same group of friends where we are all just together, dancing all night. That freedom, mixed with the fun of just letting yourself go in an arena full of strangers – all of them happy and buzzing from just being there too.

When we're not at raves, we create our own events.

One of the boys, Dan – his dad owns loads of land where we live. They have a huge farm where we set up tents around a big campfire and play music into the early hours, doing all of the same stuff, and when we stop dancing we all just all sit and talk about everything and nothing, enjoying each other's company even when it falls silent. We go really deep at times, talking about our childhoods, our experiences; we plan our futures, and although we all have such a huge contrast of plans, hopes and dreams, even though so many of us want such different things out of life, and others (myself included) have no idea what we want, we've all promised each other that 'this' would never change, that the sleepovers, the campfires, the nights out, the get togethers will never change. We've made a promise that we will always come home, together, and that we will always, always remain friends, no matter what.

# SUNDAY

Jo went up to the hospital this morning and said you were awake and smiling, with a nurse sat beside you, chatting away.

My heart feels so full and the anxiety has lessened so much! I want to tell Woody you're awake, but I know he will want to come and see you and then it will upset him more. I am so excited for bringing him to see you when you are up to it. I am going to come and visit tomorrow, now that we are all allowed, as soon as I drop him to nursery.

Jo said you were holding her hand, and when she went to leave you got tearful, which made my heart hurt. I'm wondering if you can understand everything yet. Jo said it was busy with visitors while she was there, but the nurse assured her there is a team in place that will be working with you daily to give you the best support possible. I'm praying – I don't know who to and I don't know what I believe – but I am praying, so hard and so often, that you come out of this OK.

# Seventeen years old

I'm meant to be going to a birthday party of a friend of a friend tonight. I don't know whether to go because I have my practical driving test tomorrow morning and I don't want to be hungover, but also I haven't been out since Tom left and I'm sick of crying.

I don't know the girl whose party it is. I mean, I've met her a few times, but we've never said more than hello to each other.

We all kind of do this. I suppose living in a small town means there aren't many events to go to, so we all have this kind of unwritten rule that we just turn up to each other's without being invited, and it's mostly cool and accepted. It is something that's always gone on, but I've only really felt confident enough to do it in that last year – since Jason has been fully out of my life and my new friends have given me the confidence to remember I'm not all the things he'd made me feel like I was. There really isn't any drama in Cornwall, not within our friendship group – and not that I know of anywhere else.

Tom left for Cambridge last week and I haven't heard from him since. I really didn't want to like another boy again after Jason, and I went eighteen months without liking anyone else – but then I met Tom this summer. He is so good looking. He has dark olive skin and the biggest chocolate brown eyes. He doesn't live here, his family are from London, but they have a holiday home around the corner from our house. It's absolutely amazing and has a massive swimming pool that we've all been hanging out at. His dad is quite a bit older than his mum and Tom has two older sisters that are in their late twenties from his dad's first marriage. His dad's first wife died suddenly when the girls were a few years old, so Tom's mum has brought them up since they were pretty small. They are all so trendy and nice, they all have proper London accents and they get on so well. It makes me wish I had a big family. I hate that it's always just me at home, with no one to chat to or mess about with. The whole family were really nice to me and I spent so much time there through the holidays, while Tom hung out with my group loads. He's the year above me and he's just left to study medicine at Cambridge. His dad is a surgeon at St Thomas' in London, so it's in the family.

We had a thing for eight whole weeks, which seems like no time at all really, but I really like him – he is the first person I've properly fallen for since Jason. But we both knew he was leaving and it wasn't going to work. Tom also wants to concentrate on his studies as he has worked super hard on getting his placement at uni. We agreed from the very start it would be nothing more than friends with benefits, and although we haven't had sex, we have literally slept together when we've all camped or all stayed over at Dan's house, and then we kissed and did stuff. Tom stroked my hair and arms until I fell asleep on him and he cuddled me all night. He would ask me all kinds of questions about my life, from how my childhood looked to what my goals and dreams are in the future. He gave me butterflies like I've never had before. I still think of him when I wake each morning and before I fall asleep each night. God, I think of him every minute of every day, and it makes my heartbreak over Jason seem inconsequential right now. In all the weeks I spent with Tom, he was nothing but kind and nice and respectful, and I feel so gutted he's left. I tried so hard to not get feelings for him so I didn't feel like this when he left, but I did and I do.

It feels harder in a way that he was such a good guy and not a wanker, just after sex like most other boys our age. The connection we had was so good, like nothing I've ever felt before, nothing like what I felt about Jason. The goodbye was more painful than I'd expected and although I managed to hold it together when he gave me hundreds of kisses all over my face and hair, and bear-hugged me into him against the bonnet of his car, we both welled up with tears and he said, 'I'm gonna go before it gets worse.'

I wanted to say 'What about long-distance?' I wanted to tell him I'd travel to him, I'd make it work . . . but if he wanted to do that, he would have suggested it, so I didn't. He said he would stay in touch, that he'd call me when he got there just to let me know he'd arrived safely.

When he drove off, I had never felt anything like it. It's been all I've thought about since he left last week – I felt like I was going to have a panic attack, my chest went so tight and my throat fizzed with pain. I can still physically feel my heart throb and I have this desperate feeling deep inside me, which I hate myself for feeling because I've sworn to myself I'll never go here again, yet here I am. I can't even tell any of my friends or my mum how it feels because we agreed to just be friends and I knew that this day was coming . . . So I've played it cool to everyone, and no one knows how bad I'm feeling or how sad I am. He hasn't called like he promised. I keep checking the answer machine, but I haven't even left the house since he went, so I know I'd have heard the phone ring. I wonder if he knew he wasn't going to call me – like, do all boys and men just fucking lie? I keep looking at my dad, wondering if he is as good as he seems to my mum, or whether he's the same and she's just stupid and I don't see it. Maybe they just get better at lying and hiding things with age, or maybe there are some genuinely decent guys out there, I'm just incapable of finding them . . .

# MONDAY

I saw you today for the first time.

I was so happy to see you, and we were both so emotional. I can tell your body is just surviving right now, though, and you aren't 'you'.

Your speech is really slow and quiet – a whisper. You look so fragile and unwell. Although Mags prepared us, I don't think we could ever be prepared enough. Even for me, with my past, this was a shock.

Although you don't sound like you – you're slow and slurred – you are saying words and listening to us talk, which is more than we were hoping for so soon.

One side of your face doesn't match the other when you speak, but the doctors say you're in the early stages of recovery and all of this stuff takes time. Whenever we ask the doctors what we can expect from your recovery, they say it's up to you, that you will need to work really hard, but it's all doable.

Tomorrow you will be 'going downstairs'. This means to a neurology ward, where they can help you even more to get better. Most importantly, this means we will all be allowed to visit, and I think this will support you most because you need people around you who love you to spur you on and help with your recovery. I've decided that, although you're awake and although I can talk to you, I am going to keep writing here. Not just because the doctors have said you may forget things to start with, but also because I wish I'd had something to read back on from my days that looked like yours to remind myself of how far I've come.

Your face lit up when I told you about how well Woody is doing, how much he misses you and that he will be coming to see you now. I hope you are pleased he's living with the boys and me; I hope we are all doing you proud whilst you get better. You kept squeezing my hand and smiling when I told you anything he did that was funny or amazing, and that made me so happy.

# Seventeen years old

God, what is my life?

I went to the party last night. I met a new guy there and I passed my driving test today.

How the fuck has all that happened in the last twenty-four hours?

I have never been to a party like it in my life.

It was crazy.

A huge event: waitresses walking around with trays of canapés and glasses of fizzy champagne bubbling away. There were two DJs playing, one inside the house and one out in the garden, in front of the huge water fountain.

The birthday cake was as tall as me and sat on a table in the middle of the entrance hall, with a gated rope the entire way round it to protect it, like it was a waxwork.

It had been thrown for a girl called Sammi. It was her eighteenth.

Her family, quite clearly, are extremely rich. She is quite well known in our town, and she is actually quite nice considering their wealth. She got a white convertible BMW and a gold bracelet with the sparkliest diamonds I've ever seen for her birthday, which were presented to her with a drum roll from the outside DJ, and the cheesiest slow 'Happy Birthday' song I've ever heard.

She didn't seem that bothered about her bracelet – or her new car. I mean, she thanked her parents, but she didn't even open the BMW doors to peer inside it. I wondered if maybe she was embarrassed about them giving her the presents in front of hundreds of people, some of whom (like me) she hardly knew. It was all really grand, and personally, I would have hated it – I kind of felt sorry for her.

Still, my parents bought me a battered old canary yellow Vauxhall Nova for my seventeenth birthday (the one I've been learning to drive in) and when I walked out onto the drive and saw it, it literally made my life complete. Dad kept reassuring me it was better to have a first car I could smash up, but I didn't even care what it looked like, I just felt the excitement of learning to drive – knowing soon I would be able to get in my car and drive anywhere, at any time. That made me feel so happy – I am still so grateful to them.

But Sam nodded over to her dad, mouthed, 'Thanks' to her mum, adjusted her new diamond-encrusted bangle and returned to the dance floor without paying any more attention to either present. Words rang inside my head that my dad had told me a million times: 'Money doesn't buy you happiness, pet.' I'm beginning to think he's right.

Then I saw him.

I felt him looking over at me a lot. It was like he was staring into my soul. None of my friends know who he is. I hadn't ever seen him before, but I got butterflies in my tummy every time I saw him looking at me. Then I felt guilty, because I still feel heartbroken over Tom, and I knew if he'd walked into that party at any moment, the feelings for this new guy would disappear in seconds. But Tom wasn't going to walk in, he hasn't even called – so thinking about him is pointless. And the girls keep telling me I've 'gotta get under someone to get over someone'. Why does that saying make me feel sick?

When I came out of the toilet, the guy was waiting to go in.

I brushed past him as it was so busy, and he stopped me and introduced himself as David. He asked if I'd like a drink. His hand gripped my wrist – not too tight, but tight enough to show me he probably gets what he wants. I giggled and said yes. I was already tipsy, and if I'm honest, by that point I was angry at Tom for leaving, for not getting in touch, and I just thought: *fuck it*. The guy didn't go to the toilet, instead he slid his hand from my wrist down to my fingers, and led me past the girls I was with – who all gave me the open-mouthed, smiley 'Look at you' look. They were probably wondering how I've gone from being celibate for eighteen months and saying I hate all boys, to having two hot guys around me in the space of four weeks.

I don't even know what's happening.

He took me to the outside bar which was manned with waiters in crisp white shirts and bow ties. I asked for half a cider. He smirked and said, 'A cider drinker? Hardcore.' He got a vodka and coke. Which I think is a bit of a strange drink for a man, or for anyone in fact. I haven't ever really drunk spirits, neither have any of my friends – we have only ever been cider or beer drinkers. Maybe that's a Cornish thing?

We walked to the bottom of the huge garden, away from the loud music, and perched next to each other on a wooden sun lounger beside the swimming pool, which glowed with pretty lights under the huge white moon.

I studied him with a side eye as he sipped his vodka. He's got sandy blond hair that's floppy and he is really tanned – a different tan to Tom, more golden than olive, but a nice tan all the same. He was wearing a navy Hugo Boss polo shirt tucked into jeans with Oliver Sweeney brogues. The lads that are my best-friends dress nothing like this guy. They live in stuff like Rockport boots, Stone Island jackets and Berghaus clobber. He dresses differently to them, and differently to Tom, but I don't mind it. He looked good, and it's obvious he likes to take care of himself. I also knew he was definitely way older than me – which felt exciting, and weird.

He kept looking at me and smiling. I asked why and he told me he's never met anyone before with curly red hair like mine. He asked if it was natural, as if I would want to perm my hair and dye it ginger when it's the one thing I've been bullied for my whole life.

He asked about me. I didn't go too deep, I kind of thought it would be pointless. I told him I was doing my A levels and that the following year I'd be taking a gap year to travel to Australia and Bali with my friends. I've saved £1,600 working at the café so far, and I'm lucky enough that my parents have said they'll match whatever I save. The plan is that we're going to backpack, and when we run out of money we will work on farms fruit picking until our visas expire and it's time to come home.

He smiled through all my life plans and repeatedly said things like, 'You have it all planned out, don't you, Miss Miller?'

I mean, I don't have anything planned out, and all I was doing when we were talking was thinking about another guy who looked the opposite to him in every way, that I'd have rather have been with there and then (and still now as I type this) – but still, here we were and life was there for living, I decided.

The conversation turned to him.

He was twenty-four. I knew it. I'm not sure whether him being seven years older than me is a good thing or a bad thing.

He studied law at uni and has just finished his training contract with a global magic circle law firm (whatever that is!) based in central London. I had no clue what any of what he said meant, so I just nodded and agreed and said things like, 'Wow,' a lot.

He told me his parents had a holiday home close by in the next town; they were wealthy, from what he explained of them. He told me they were odd. They weren't close. He has two older sisters – like Tom, I immediately thought, although then he said they weren't close either – so nothing like Tom, I immediately thought again. He didn't say why none of them were close, or why they were odd, and I could tell it wasn't something he was up for discussing, so I just said 'Hmmm' and 'Ahhh' to the minimal detail he freed up to me, and left it at that.

He said he was here for the weekend visiting, and because he'd made friends with Sam's dad after meeting him at a private members' club, he had actually been invited to her party, unlike me.

I knew immediately we were worlds apart. He has an amazing career in London and I bake cakes in my parents' café in Cornwall – and in a year I'll be backpacking round the other side of the world, with no life plan after that.

We shared a taxi home around midnight. I told him I couldn't stay later as I had my driving test this morning and I needed to sleep, and he left the party with me without hesitation, which I thought was sweet, and weird – what twenty-four-year-old good-looking city guy leaves an amazing party full of hot girls to share a taxi home with little old me?

He dropped me off at the bottom of my drive and told the taxi to wait whilst he walked me up to my front door. I told him he didn't need to, but he insisted. No one's ever offered to see me home safely before – that made me hate Tom a little as he never did that. I'm finding it's easier when I hate him; I cry less.

When we got to the door, he asked for my number, which he saved in his phone. We all have the same Nokia phone down here, but his is different – smaller, nicer. I asked him what his top score on Snake is. He looked confused and asked me what Snake is. I am in shock. I don't understand where he's been. Who doesn't know what Snake is?

He asked if I wanted his number, but I didn't have my phone. I don't really take my phone out much; it annoys me. My friends always have theirs, so I can get hold of people and be 'got hold of' by my mum, as she has all my friends' numbers. At first I told him just to text me, mainly to play it cool – but I then had a surge of panic that, because I hadn't taken his number, if he didn't text me I wouldn't ever see him again. And I really didn't want that to happen because he's taking my mind off Tom. I took his number.

He leant forward and kissed me. Then he asked me if I was seeing anyone. I thought it was a bit of a weird thing to ask after he'd kissed me, but I did an awkward laugh and reassured him I am very much single. I didn't feel it was appropriate to add on that every part of me would actually get married to Tom right now and I can't stop thinking about him, even though I am forever trying my hardest to hate him.

Mum was still up when I got in, icing the carrot cake for the café the next day. 'Who's your new friend?' she smiled. I told her he was called David. David Metcalfe.

'Well, David Metcalfe is very handsome, and I can't wait to meet him,' she replied.

There is still a sadness as I'm writing this, because I'm missing Tom and I wish he would call me. But also, I've got a good feeling for the first time this week, now that I've met David.

I kissed Mum on the cheek, swiped some of the icing off the cake with my finger and licked it, and she gave me a tap on the back and said, 'Lou, I've told you a million times . . . DON'T DO THAT.'

I came into my room, plugged my phone in to charge, and as soon as I'd got changed into my PJs it flashed up with a new message . . . It wasn't from Tom, as I'd hoped, but instead it read:

**Really enjoyed tonight. Fancy lunch tomorrow? And I can't stop playing Snake, it's so annoyingly good!! D xxx**

I replied straight away, agreeing to go to lunch with David Metcalfe – and laughing that I know I've already turned him into a Snake addict!

# TUESDAY

I came up to see you this morning with Jo. I wanted to bring Woody, but he is full of cold and the hospital won't let anyone be around you who's unwell at all. They've moved you to Level 3 from Level 5. Apparently the floor you're on indicates how critical you are – something I didn't even know was a thing until today – which I suppose feels like tangible progress. Above your bed there is a new whiteboard that says your name, age, what you can eat (soft puree only) and what your goals are for the day. Today it said that the goal was to get you out, sitting in a chair for at least two hours. I spoke to the team tonight and they said you managed it this afternoon. I am so proud!

You are in a bay with three other ladies, all of whom are at least twenty years older than you, and all more able – and motherly, from the way they shout across at you from their beds, offering words of advice and funny one liners that make you smile. I'm pleased about that. You need that kind of love right now, and I know, you being you, that you will appreciate it.

You told me you feel safe here, the team are warm and caring and there is a constant supply of *OK!* magazines that you'll be reading in no time, so I reckon you're going to be just fine.

I went back to Jo's after we left the hospital late morning – the team were coming to work with you so we weren't allowed to stay long. Jo and I cracked on with the adoption stuff. Pat had all the documents laid out in front of her when we got there; she had divvied them up into piles. As we settled down around Jo's huge kitchen table, Pat warned us how we might feel after reading certain things within the files and folders. She had gone out of her way to highlight certain pieces she had found particularly hard to stomach and digest with bright pink Post-it notes. She even asked Jo if she was sure this is something she absolutely wanted to do – using the phrase 'opening Pandora's box' numerous times. Jo was adamant she wanted to read it, to know how life had been for her and her siblings when she'd entered the world, and so the three of us began at the very start.

It was clear social services had deemed Jo's parents unfit to care for her, her sister Kitty and her brother Joseph, and they had been removed because of poverty and neglect, but the more I read the more I could see this looked like domestic abuse.

*The mother has no awareness of the damage caused to the children from Mr Addison's violent outbursts.*

*Joseph is being ignored by the mother for long periods when Mr Addison is present – she told us this is to keep them safe, as it lessens his violence towards her in front of the children. However, she is lacking understanding of the harm caused to the children by doing this.*

It went on, and on and on.

It was clear to me that Jo, her big sister and elder brother were neglected and ignored by their mum because the level of violence worsened tenfold when she gave them any attention – that's what I read. And that's often what had happened in my home, for fifteen years. I saw it so much more, reading these case notes. The bottle feeding I did because he banned me from breastfeeding, the 'leaving them to cry' so they didn't become 'spoilt'. Putting them into nursery from being tiny, even though I didn't work, so they didn't become attached to me . . . So many rules to destroy the mother and baby bond, that I always knew could have been so much stronger if things had been different, if I'd chosen a non-abusive partner.

The levels of neglect were horrific for Jo and her siblings. The three of us sat together and cried for those three tiny babies, and their mum.

Social workers had reported them living in poverty. They lived in a council flat in Devon, two bedrooms, one with bunks and a cot and the other one was the parents' room. There were reports of the social workers attending regularly – both announced visits and unannounced. It read like a lot of the social workers were scared of the father; it certainly appeared that way, as they wrote about how he was aggressive and argumentative, but none of them reported challenging him on his behaviours. Instead, it was just catalogued in their paperwork, and he continued with this behaviour. The children, it stated, were being left in soiled nappies, which caused severe nappy rash and infections. The two eldest were reported to be infested with head lice, the house always dirty, no food or drinks in the house for the children, bottles around the house with the remnants of sour milk, and there were fleas – the children were covered in bite marks and scratches which were blamed on the animals living in the family home.

Despite all this, it was clear that Jo's birth mum loved her children. When Jo's dad went to prison several times over the years, she stepped up. She kept the house clean; the children were fed, bathed, taken out and shown love; she accepted responsibility for what she deemed her failings and she worked well and happily with services. But as soon as he got out, things returned to shit within weeks – and from the reports, she spent a lot of time in bed because of her mental health and was often tearful and quiet upon visits, refusing to engage with social workers – never aggressive, rude, defensive or argumentative like her husband, but she wouldn't speak when they tried to engage with her. He was also violent towards the kids. He was witnessed beating Jo's brother, Joseph, in a car park supermarket by a stranger, who reported it to the police. And at home he was reported to be smacking him by a social worker.

I imagine Jo's mum stepping up is why they weren't removed immediately – I suppose because when he wasn't around, there were glimmers of how life could have looked for them. But he was so domineering. And she was clearly so broken and controlled. All of the prison sentences he got were for fighting in pubs or petty theft, so the periods of imprisonment were not long enough for her to get strong or move away and hide. There was alcohol misuse on his side, never hers, and there was no mention of substance misuse for either of them. I couldn't help feel Jo's mum had been failed. The notes from most social workers blamed her, as the mother, for not protecting the children – rather than blame the father, the perpetrator who was raining down violence and control on a vulnerable woman and her three babies.

On the day of removal, Jo's mum was distraught. The social workers and police catalogued she became hysterical, refusing to hand the kids over. They were physically removed from her arms, dragged off her on the green outside the flats on a freezing December morning with a crowd of neighbours watching. They were placed into a police car, the two eldest children also distressed, screaming and crying for their mum. The father came out last minute and dragged Jo's mum back inside the house by her arm, shouting insults at her as they went.

The feelings I got reading it all – and still now, and it's currently 1 a.m.; the emotions – sadness, anger, shock; the nausea, the sick feeling in the pit of my stomach for what this woman and these babies endured; the questions – why didn't she leave? Why didn't they get her into a safe house, in hiding with the children? Why did they allow him to drag her back into the house after they removed the kids? Why are there no follow-up notes after the children were removed? Did anyone ever check on her again? How did her life look afterwards? Did they have any more children?

My brain is still buzzing with so many questions, so I have no idea how Jo must feel; I can't even begin to imagine what she's going through right now. I want to message her to tell her I'm awake, that she can call me, but I worry maybe she will have fallen asleep and then I'll wake her again and cause her a whole more heap of pain if she can't get back to sleep.

She kept questioning whether her brother is lying about not remembering anything. He would have just turned four when they were taken by social services. He would have been three and a half when he was beaten in that supermarket car park.

It was a planned removal, so I wonder if Jo's mum knew it was coming. I wonder if it would have been better if they'd just removed the children during a violent incident. She probably would have been calmer, thinking they'd come back – or would she? Depends how violent he was, I suppose. There are hospital reports of her injuries – broken nose, cheekbone, collarbone and wrist – all at different times, spanning over those four years. Black eyes and bruises were often present on her and all three children when social workers visited. Part of me wonders how they remained in the house for so long when they knew how dangerous he was, when *she* knew how dangerous he was – but at the same time, I'm sat here reminding myself that my boys remain with me, and the only difference in our situation is poverty and wealth. That is the only thing that stopped our lives looking so different.

# Seventeen years old

I've been with David for eight weeks now.

After the first lunch, I agreed to another lunch, then dinner, then walks. I agreed to go shopping, to the movies and swimming in the sea.

David has been staying here with me in Cornwall every week from Thursday to Sunday evening since. He still has to work on a Friday, which is my day off from college, but he's only catching up with his paperwork, so he comes to mine. My parents are at the café on Fridays, so I just chill with him while he works. Mum was annoyed at first because it's my day to work at the café and I'm meant to be saving up to travel, but I've managed to convince her I'm revising for my upcoming mocks as I'm in my second year, so she's cool about it now.

I still think of Tom most days. I drive past his house every time I go out, even when I don't need to. His dad puts up a flag when they're here – it's a standing family joke. But the flag hasn't been up since they left at the end of August. I feel like if I drove past and the flag was up, I'd probably be sick. It's so weird how, as I approach, I'm desperate for the flag to be up whilst also praying it's down. But then when it is down I feel this surge of relief, and also overwhelming sadness. I'm trying so hard to forget Tom and just think of David. I keep reminding myself he's gone, and hasn't been in touch at all – it's history – and I know I need to look at the here and now and what is on offer. And I know that David is a good thing to have on offer.

My parents won't let him stay over. Mum told me she likes him but doesn't want me to rush things. She keeps repeatedly reminding me about my age, how young I am and the amount of time I am spending with him, that I have a friendship group that I need to remember are important to me. It annoys David that they won't let him stay over, but I've told him that he's my first proper boyfriend and I'm still seventeen, so it will just be a matter of time.

The problem is that he was due to go back to London after that first weekend I met him and stay there until Christmas, but now he comes down every weekend to spend time with me. So I feel bad seeing my friends when he's come all this way, and I don't want to tell him that I want to go out with my friends, as it will probably upset him. When he came down two weeks ago, I had plans to go surfing with the whole group on the Saturday afternoon, as the waves were amazing, but he got really annoyed that he'd come all the way and I was going out without him. I invited him along – I've invited him to loads of things my friends have planned – but he says he doesn't feel comfortable. He says they're not his kind of people. It makes me sad because they're *my* kind of people, but I don't want to force him to come and I don't want us to argue.

He keeps saying he won't be able to visit as much in a few months' time as he has some huge cases coming up at work, so I've figured I can see my friends loads more then. And they all know it's normal when you first meet a guy that you spend all your time with them; I'm sure they do. David has no friends here either, so that's difficult. He always asks me who would want to live in this town their whole lives, like it's a terrible thing. I kind of smirk when he says it, I don't answer, but it's my plan after I come back from travelling to return home and stay here. My parents are here, some of my very best friends are planning to stay here, many of them are in apprenticeships and aren't even going to uni – it's a beautiful place to live, but David obviously doesn't think so and maybe he's right. He's seen so much of the world, whereas I've never really left Cornwall.

# WEDNESDAY

I came up this morning, but you were sleeping so I didn't get to speak to you. I waited for an hour, but they said you'd had a restless night, so I thought it was best I left you to sleep. Pat is coming up to sit with you in a few hours, and I didn't want to tire you out. You looked so peaceful, despite having your feeding tube back in – they put it back in your nose yesterday because you aren't managing to eat and drink enough.

You need to eat to be strong enough for all of the exercises the physiotherapists want you to do, but everything is just such an effort. You're struggling with the right side of your body; your face is still different on that side and the weakness is noticeable. The doctors have told us it means you need to work even harder to recover. It all feels so soon to me. You still look so poorly and I can't help think that you should just be resting, but I have to remember they're the professionals; I don't have a clue.

They have started talking about you moving to a residential neurorehabilitation centre, as your recovery is going to take longer and be more complicated than they first thought. It doesn't feel so great today. It's going to be a much longer process than any of us thought . . . but that's OK. It's all going to be OK, Martha.

As I watched you sleep, I wondered if all women who've been in our situation remember the first bad incident, however it may have looked. The one that cemented the fact you're being abused. I wonder if you remember yours, Martha? I think you do. I think we all remember that time, when we have that lightbulb moment and we confirm to ourselves in secret, in silence, in our head, that this relationship is really what we've been telling ourselves it isn't – abusive. And we know deep down we're in massive fucking danger, and we feel trapped, like a caged animal undergoing tests and experiments, waiting for the next bout of pain to come, but not knowing when, and just surviving the days in between these times.

It's weird how the whole thing flips when you go from questioning whether your relationship is abusive to knowing it is. I think I'd have rather questioned it forever than know I was being abused. Because that's the part that's terrifying, when it means it's on you to make the change. Before that lightbulb moment, you convince yourself that they're just a bit moody or snappy, that they've had a stressful day, or maybe you've been hormonal, so you tell yourself you're as bad as each other. But once that line is crossed and you know for sure that they are an abuser, that's when everything changes. Before that, you convince yourself you'd never put up with certain things, you've set your bar high – and you wouldn't accept things like being pushed – but then you do, or being cheated on – but then you do, or being spat at – but then you do, or hit – but then you do, or raped – but then you do, or financially controlled – but then you do, or beaten black and blue – but then you do. And not only do you put up with all of these things, they become your normal. And then you start feeling happy when those behaviours don't happen for a while – so if you go a month without being assaulted or financially controlled, it feels like a good thing. Then you get a shove, but you remind yourself it could have been a smack, and so you feel lucky. And you went four weeks instead of two with an incident, so that's a positive. And then six weeks later you get a smack – but it could have been a beating or a rape – and you went even longer than before, at six whole weeks with no violent incidents, so you think that's a good thing . . . And before you know it, your whole world has turned upside down and you're trapped with a monster, wondering how it ever got to this and why no one knows.

A secret club you never wanted an invite to, but one that only you're in. Alone, desperate, broken. Desperate to stay invisible and screaming to be seen, feeling fully to blame that your life looks the way it does . . .

# Seventeen years old

Things aren't great at home.

David told me to tell my parents they were being out of order about not letting him stay over now that we've been together for a few months, but they still wouldn't budge, and so he told me we would need to start meeting halfway at weekends and pay half each for a hotel because I couldn't stay at his parents' place either. This means I've only been seeing him Saturdays and Sundays. I am back working in the café on a Friday to earn money to go, but it's not enough for petrol and half the hotel for two nights as well as food and drink whilst we're there, so I've been dipping into my travel savings. Some weekends we go out and explore, and others we just stay in at the hotel and have sex a lot. That one time with Jason is nothing like the sex I have with David. I often thought when the girls spoke about having orgasms they were lying, because I'd never had one – until I met David. It was something he was desperate for me to have, to the point it almost became a challenge for him to give me my first orgasm. I mean, I'm glad he did – because I've now realised there's a point to sex for women too, and I do really enjoy having sex now. And it is something we wouldn't be able to do like this if my parents let us stay at my house, well, unless they were out.

I'm still so angry at Mum and Dad because they are just making everything impossible and we're fighting all the time. Why do they have to make things so difficult?

I'm on my way to London now to celebrate my eighteenth with David. I was planning to have a party at home for it, but when I told him about it a few months after we got together, he told me he had already planned to take me away somewhere special – just the two of us.

I told my mum to cancel the party, which felt shit. She looked so hurt and upset because she had planned it for so long. But I knew I had to let one of them down, and I knew Mum would take it better than David. He is so excited about spoiling me in London this weekend, so I knew it was something I just had to do, but I still feel crap. Mum cancelled the room she had hired in the local pub. I know she's lost deposits on the DJ, cake and balloons she had ordered, as I heard her telling my friend Ollie's mum on the phone. Not in a way that's slagging me off; she just sounds sad.

Mum and Dad dropped me at the train station this afternoon. I wish they hadn't.

My mum looked heartbroken, but even worse, she tried to hide it – she told me to have the best time and made me promise to call when I arrived and ordered me to stay safe. She reminded me no matter what time, if anything happens, my dad will drive day or night to London to collect me.

I've hated them for the past few weeks, but now I'm sat on this train feeling so guilty that I feel sick. When I hugged Dad goodbye I saw his eyes well up with sadness too. We've never spent a birthday apart. I did ask David if I could meet him in London tomorrow, so I could at least wake up with my parents on the morning of my birthday, but he sounded hurt at that idea even being in my head. And I am almost an adult. Maybe it is weird I feel like that – like, I probably do need to grow up. David has planned so much and wants to be there with me when I wake tomorrow – on the actual day of me becoming an adult. But then, my heart is aching for both my parents right now – I can feel their devastation, and that's hard because I am happy with David, not sad, and I just wish they could be happy for us.

# THURSDAY

I sat with you all afternoon today, until I needed to leave and pick Woody up from nursery.

You were quiet. You didn't put on your usual brave face or pretend things weren't as bad as they seemed, like you usually do. Instead, you just accepted and admitted things are shit, that life right now for you feels impossible, and rather than try and convince you otherwise I just honoured your feelings and told you how loved you are. It was a hard day.

I know you're desperately missing Woody, but I understand why you've decided it is too soon to see him. It would be too confusing and upsetting for him because you're still unwell, your speech is slurry and you're so frail. You're doing the right thing, but that doesn't mean it doesn't feel unfair – and brutal and heartbreaking.

The team on the Daisy Ward, where you are, have suggested starting you on some anti-depressants, but you don't want them. I knew you wouldn't. Anti-depressants were something you told me ages ago that Mags had discussed with you when you first got support with us, and you didn't want them then either. You have never been on them, terrified of taking any meds. I get it, and I also think we should just wait a while whilst you're recovering, as you're in the trenches right now, and things can only start getting better.

Maybe that will be enough to lift your spirits without prescribed medication, but if not, then we will navigate that together too . . .

As hard as today was, I could see the positives you couldn't.

Your feeding tube is out again, and you're walking (well, shuffling!) to the toilet. The catheters and bedpans are a thing of the past. We're getting there, my darling, I promise.

I picked Woody up, then drove to collect George from school – he doesn't finish until around 5 p.m. most days as he has after school clubs, so the pick-ups work quite well for both boys. We went to Jo's. I felt really sad after seeing you, but I also knew Jo would still probably be sad after reading the adoption papers so I wanted to just have a hug and a cuppa with her.

We arrived and it was a mad house. Molly and Harry were there with Belle, which was lush – I love how my son is chilling in the garden at my best friend's house with his half-sister and I wasn't even expecting to see them. Molly was super affectionate with me, has been ever since we were introduced. It's been a process for everyone to work through – but we have learned through family therapy that we have to talk to get there – we have to communicate and be honest with our feelings. And we have been. Now, years later, I feel like we've all finally found our feet. Jaclyn works in the Cornwall office now; she rarely leaves here any more, and I know from the word around she is the best family lawyer in our area. David's title has well and truly been taken, by a female he also spent two decades bullying. I'm so proud of what she's overcome and how strong she's been in her work arena, as it's been pretty cutthroat at times, what with the politics of law firms and what people have said and done since the trial ended. I feel we have all finally found our place. Harry and Molly are so close; they have the same sense of humour, and cry with laughter at the weirdest stuff.

I didn't get a chance to speak to Jo about anything at hers because we were both surrounded by kids and she was flat out, but she wasn't crying in a heap on the sofa like I half expected her to be, which can only be a good thing. I'm seeing her tomorrow for coffee, so we can chat then, but tonight we all made pizzas. I sliced and prepped all the toppings and divvied them into small bowls on the table, while Jo made the pizza bases from scratch. Jamie got to work with the pizza oven and the kids loved choosing their own things, slathering the base in passata and watching their creations come to life. Stuff like this for Harry and George is so much fun. We would have never have been allowed to do this with David – he would have hated the idea. Dinner times with David were regimented, and we either ate in silence or he fired questions at one or all of us, to start a row. Tonight I just stood, watching all the big kids help the little ones, music playing, Jo and Jamie embracing the chaos, everyone eating pizza all over the garden – but more than that, I just inhaled the laughing – the smiles and the giggles and the fun. This, right here, this is happiness, and I can't wait for you to be a part of it again.

Mags called when I got home tonight. I'd just put Woody down. She was just calling to check in and see how I was feeling having time off. I really did worry about how I'd feel not working, because I love my job so much, but I'm starting to realise how much I needed the break. Not just because of Woody – because of me. I think even when you are out of hospital, when you are well and Woody comes back to you, I would honestly advise you taking some time off, just to have the headspace to process things and breathe a little. I've realised for the first time that I don't need to be busy all the time to cope. I can sit with my own thoughts, and when I've caught up with housework and jobs and I think, *What now?* I can actually do stuff I've never done before. Like take the dog for a walk because I want to, not because I have to. Like take my mum to the garden centre and walk round at a slow pace, because there's no rush. I've realised that when I'm working, I am trying to squeeze everything in everywhere, and the reality is that I have no time. I have no time to do anything without a time limit, without rushing, without panicking that the dirty washing pile is growing too quickly or I have to write a report for one of my ladies' upcoming court hearings. As much as I adore my work, as much as I miss the families I work with, I realise that I need to put myself first for the first time in my life, and it feels so good that I'm doing that – I think for the first time ever. I feel proud of me.

# Eighteen years old

Well, that whole weekend has left me feeling like my brain's going to explode.

I woke on the morning of my eighteenth in a hotel just outside Covent Garden to David popping a bottle of Moët. We clinked our champagne flutes together to celebrate me reaching adulthood. The thought of knocking back alcohol before 9 a.m. made me want to puke, but I didn't want to spoil the day, so I sipped it down and thanked him for the sweet gesture. I'd never tried champagne before, not even at Sam's party, although drinking it always looked so cool in the movies. I wish I hadn't bothered; it was vile.

After I managed to drink my first glass of champagne, I felt a bit pissed. Then David handed me a collection of presents, wrapped in thick, expensive-feeling black-and-white polka dot gift wrap with silver bows and ribbons. I'm sure he must have paid someone to wrap them. He gave me them in the correct order he wanted them to be opened. I am DREADING my parents asking to see what he bought me.

First I opened a gold dress. It consists of (a very small amount) of shiny beads stuck together to form the tiniest mini-dress I've ever seen. It has an open back with just a string to tie it, and a loose front, so my whole cleavage is on show. It is also sooooo mini that it just about covers my lady bits. I hate the idea of having pretty much my whole body on show. It's not my style at all, and I tried my best to hide both my disappointment and shock. I have never worn mini-dresses before. I am more a jeans and T-shirt kinda girl – and at the very most, a floral dress and trainers – and I feel like David knows this too. As I was studying it he took my hand, stood me up in front of the full-length mirror and walked behind me. He then reached over my shoulders, holding the dress against me, then as he eyed my reflection and reaction at the same time, he said, 'That's for tonight.'

I smiled, like I was happy, but I knew that I had purposely let a little of my anxiety and disappointment slip loose for him to feel whilst I was thinking, *Brilliant. I'm going out into the centre of London in fancy dress as a disco ball with my fanny on show.* I had hoped he would let me wear my new jeans and gold T-shirt I just bought, but I could tell he wanted me in the dress he had chosen.

Next was a pair of heels, but not any old heels – these were black velvet platform heels with huge gold taffeta bows on the front, that I knew I wasn't going to be able to walk in. When I said that out loud, David chirped in with, 'Nonsense. All the girls wear them.'

My brain began screaming, *My girls don't! Me and my girls wear flip-flops and Converse and comfy shoes that we don't die in when we walk, unlike these fucking monstrosities!*

But I didn't want to upset him, so I put them on with my silk short pyjamas. Then I tottered up and down the hotel suite like a baby horse that had just taken its first steps after it had fallen out of its mum's vagina, whilst David perched on the edge of the bed nodding approvingly, still sipping his champagne in his white waffle hotel robe, repeatedly saying, 'Nice.'

Next, I opened a vibrator. An actual vibrator.

I felt my cheeks burn with embarrassment and had no idea what I was supposed to do with it. As soon as I opened it, he told me it was for us to use together. He told me I wasn't allowed to use it without him. I mean, thank fucking god for that, because the thought of taking it home to my parents' house and writhing round in my single bed trying to have an orgasm whilst my mum's downstairs whipping up cakes really doesn't do much for me, buddy . . .

The second to last present was another sex gift – a three in one. Again I felt my face turn scarlet, and my heart started pumping so hard I could hear it in my own ears. I am now the proud owner of a leather spanking paddle, a blindfold and some fluffy red handcuffs. I wasn't sure what was happening.

'This weekend we're going to have proper sex,' David said, as soon as it was all laid out on the bed.

I genuinely had no clue what he meant, and if I'm honest, I felt a little pang of panic in my belly because I've really enjoyed our sex – and I thought he had too. I was also anxious about how 'proper sex' was going to look.

The final present was a small, square box.

I had pointed out some pearl earrings I loved in a little local jeweller's when he last came down and when I saw that box, I was so buzzing that he had listened to what I liked. I smiled as I unwrapped the box and lifted the lid . . . but was met with a ring. A square solitaire on a platinum band. My tummy flipped. At that point, David was on one knee. He looked up at me and said, 'Louise Miller, will you marry me?'

I mean, marriage.

Married.

I'm eighteen, I've literally just turned eighteen, and I'm due to start travelling the world soon . . .

But maybe I can still do all of those things. Just because people are married, it doesn't stop them living out their dreams, doing what they want. I'm sure we won't settle and have kids immediately – marriage is just a commitment of your love, and all I've ever wanted is to be loved. I know I'm not going to get better than David, so I said, 'Yes.' I said yes lots of times. He scooped me up and twirled me round, and I could tell I'd made him so happy with my answer.

Is it weird that the thought of telling people makes me feel a bit sick? Maybe we can keep it a secret for a little while . . .

We spent the weekend seeing the sights of London – and he paid for everything, which I was massively relieved about, considering I am now down to my last £700 of savings. Well, I think that's what I'm at – in all honesty I stopped checking my bank balance a while ago because it fills me with anxiety and panic.

Overall, we had an amazing weekend.

We had dinner at the most incredible restaurant, sipped cocktails in cool bars and visited some of the sights. I mean, I was freezing cold in the itsy-bitsy dress I was wearing, and I couldn't walk in the platform stilettos, but David didn't want me to take my coat as he said it would ruin the outfit. He told me it's not something girls do in cities, and I would stand out – which seems odd, thinking about it, considering the majority of women I passed that evening in London were all wearing coats and I felt like the odd one out. Again, something I haven't mentioned as I don't want the row. And he did treat me to a lovely weekend.

And we actually had the 'proper sex' he'd promised. We used all the toys and gadgets he'd bought. He instructed me throughout most of it, and I'm pretty sure we did every position possible. I felt so inexperienced. And sore. And now I'm overthinking how crap he must think our sex has been for the last six months, because it's been nothing like this weekend . . .

I wonder how many girls he's had sex with. I'm now convinced they must all be amazing compared to me. They were probably older than me, but I reckon the sex he had with them would have been much better than we've been having. He was literally telling me where to place my body parts, how to move properly when I was on top, how loud I should moan to turn him on . . . I've been getting it all wrong for so long.

# FRIDAY

It was moving day for you today, Martha!

Mags supported you with the team moving you to the neurorehabilitation centre which you will call home for the next few months. It's around half an hour away from us, which isn't too bad. If they'd had no spaces at that one, the next closest one was a two-hour drive away, which we were really worried about.

Visitors of any age are free to visit you every day, without the restrictions we've had in hospital. Mags and I think it will be great for you, just what you really need to boost your recovery, and I'm hoping we can get Woody to come and see you here soon, when you're settled. I know you're super worried about what he will think, seeing you looking and sounding so different, and him not being able to stay with you, but it's something we can all navigate together. Mags said you have your own room with a little bathroom attached, and you can put pictures up on a pin board. The food apparently smells insane, too, and there's no more night-time blood pressure checks or temperature checks, they're just once a day now, which means you can rest more, without so much interruption, which will be loads better for you.

I gave Jo a call earlier – she seemed upbeat, which I was surprised about. I keep expecting her to be sad, or tearful, because the adoption stuff feels huge, but she never is – she's just taking it all in her stride. She said she has written to her biological mum. She did it late last night, posted it this morning – before, she said, she had time to change her mind or discuss it with any of us, in case our opinions made her question her decision.

She took a photo of the letter before she put it in the envelope and she's just sent it to me. It's a beautiful letter – handwritten.

Jo spoke, in the letter, about how lovely her childhood was with her adoptive parents, how loved she and her siblings were. She said she knew how difficult and heartbreaking the situation must have been for her mum, losing her children. She told her she had left an abusive marriage herself years ago – she spoke about her children, her step-children. She wrote about Kitty and Joe, how well they've all done; she spoke about the café and Jamie, their home and Stanley, their dog, and she said she hoped her mum would write back.

I hope her mum writes back.

# Eighteen years old

I've just left Dan's and I am sat in my car, and I don't know what to do or where to go.

I returned home last night. I got a taxi from the train station. My feet are covered in purple bruises and blisters from attempting to walk through the streets of London in those god-awful stilts. My whole body aches from the sex we had all weekend. I have the start of a full-blown cold – I imagine from the no-coat idea and from venturing out in the cold, at night, wearing nothing more than seventeen gold sequins and a thong. Urgh.

Mum was pleased to see me when I walked in at first. She held her arms out to give me one of her huge hugs, and as I did the same, she caught hold of my left hand, spotting the sparkling diamond engagement ring, and said, 'Oh Lou, no.'

I knew she would be disappointed. I knew she would be sad – but I'd expected her to at least try and hide it, to pretend to be happy for me. She had been doing so well at hiding her dislike for David since she learned his age and the fact he doesn't ever want to live here. She's dressed it up as caring for me and disappointment in my decisions for such a long time now, that this new reaction left me shocked. Dad stood behind her and shook his head at me too, with an identical disapproving look on his face.

'Sweetheart, your mother's right,' he said, totally backing her. 'You're too young for all this nonsense, pet.'

I felt gutted. Really hurt and upset, but also angry at them, because I want them to be happy for me. I need them to be happy for me, for this to work with David.

Immediately, I got on the defence, but they wouldn't back down. It was like they'd saved it all up for my return.

They treat me like I'm a child.

Mum started shouting about all the changes in me since I met David. She said she's spoken to my friends who 'see it too', which immediately tipped me over the edge, thinking that everyone's talking about me behind my back and slagging me off. The paranoia and anger at the idea of people talking about my life sent me crazy. Dad was trying to calm the situation as always, playing referee and mediator, but I could tell he was still on Mum's side. He's always on Mum's side.

'We've all noticed such a change in you,' he was saying. 'You're just not you any more, sweetheart, everyone's seeing it – not just us.'

Mum began to cry. She was angry-crying, whilst screaming the same question over and over: 'What are you doing with your life?'

Seven months of it spilled out – everything she'd been holding onto for my entire relationship hit me like a tsunami – about how I'd let my friends down because it was apparently clear I no longer wanted to travel, then how I'd let my parents down by not working in the café as much any more, how I'd gone from having my life in some kind of order to it being a total mess, controlled by a manipulator.

She hadn't shouted like this since that night, the night back in Yorkshire, when I was listening in . . . and just as that thought was in my head, she turned to my dad and said, 'I told you. I told you, it's happening again. I'm gonna lose her, Tony. I'm going to lose her, like I lost our Peggy.' She fell to the floor and let out the same wail I'd heard all those years earlier after she'd got that phone call. After Aunt Peggy and my baby cousin were beaten to death.

I couldn't breathe. I felt like my chest was tightening and the air wasn't getting into my throat. I felt the same as I'd felt all those years ago. It was too much. I ran into my room and locked the door. On my bed were all my presents from my parents. Perfectly wrapped, like they had been for the previous seventeen years of birthdays, in pink paper and matching bows and ribbon. There were matching coloured balloons dotted about my bedroom, that Mum would have spent an eternity blowing up whilst I was on the train. A huge envelope, with my mum's perfect handwriting, sat on my pillow. It read *'To our girl'*. I felt torn in two.

I just panicked, and filled a second hold-all with my belongings, as much as I could fit, picked up the bag of dirty clothes I had just walked in with from London – which also held my new sex kit, weird mini-dress and god-awful heels that David ordered me to take home – and I stormed out of the house, lobbed the lot into the boot of my car and drove off as fast as I could.

I was halfway down the next hill when my phone began ringing non-stop. 'Home' flashed up. But I couldn't answer.

I started crying. Like I'm crying again now.

I haven't cried like this since we lost Aunt Peggy, since Jason dumped me, since Tom left me. It's the crying where the sobs choke you and you can't wipe your tears away fast enough because more and more just pour from your eyes – the crying where you finally catch your breath and calm down, only to find another wave of sadness creeps in and you start all over again.

My head feels fucked. I'm crying because I feel like I hate my parents and my friends. It's like they're trying to ruin mine and David's relationship. I'm so angry with them all, talking about me behind my back. No one's even asked how I feel, or what I want, or why my plans have changed.

I am happy with David. I'm an adult, and this is my life. People are allowed to change, I am not always going to be the same Lou. My goals and plans and even my fucking personality will change as I get older, and I don't understand why every fucker in this town has an opinion on that – and my choice of boyfriend, sorry, fiancé – like it has anything to do with them. I wish they'd all just leave me alone.

I called David as soon as I left. His phone went straight to answerphone.

This has been happening so much over the past few months. He says the signal is bad where he lives at times. He's moved in with a new group of solicitors that he's flat sharing with and there is no phone signal in certain parts of the house. It's so frustrating. I messaged him and asked him to call me immediately.

I didn't know where to go or what to do. I thought about calling my friends, but then I thought back to what Mum had said, and how none of them had even messaged me to wish me a happy birthday, and convinced myself they all hate me.

I just sat in my car and began to cry again.

It all just felt too much, and still does now – all these overwhelming feelings and thoughts. My negative emotions were flowing out of me like nothing I'd ever felt before.

I sat at the bottom of the lane where Dan lives. It's a huge farmhouse – his bedroom light was on, as well as other lights in his house, which gave me hope that him or his mum, Ange, might be in. Ange is pretty much like my mum but without all the complications that came with being my mum right then.

As I got up the driveway, I saw Dan's car parked outside, and felt a rush of relief. Before I knocked on the door, I checked my face in my car mirror. Thank god I did – my mascara was smeared everywhere. I tried to wipe it away with some saliva, but my mouth was dry as fuck and that made me cry again. I just thought *fuck it*, and went and knocked on their door.

Dan answered the door within a minute of me knocking. His instant reaction was surprise that it was me, but I could tell that he was pleased to see me, which was the nicest feeling. He told me he was home alone as his parents were at some friends' for dinner, and his sister was at her boyfriend's.

I tried to hold it together, but I started crying again. The tears wouldn't stop coming – thick and fast, pouring from my eyes whilst I tried to explain why I was feeling like this – but it was so hard to explain because I didn't even know myself. Dan pulled a spliff from behind his ear, tilted his head to the side, smiled at me and said, 'Fuck it, Lou, let's go and get high.' And we did.

We sat in his back garden on one of the huge tractor tyres I'd sat on so many times before. We shared the spliff and put the world to rights next to the fire pit Dan lit, just as we had done hundreds of times over the previous couple of years. But then again, we had never done it like this – just the two of us. It had always been all of us, or at least a few of our friendship group – and I'd always felt happy. Last night, it was just the two of us and for the first time ever, it felt dark; I felt sad. Dan talked to me, honestly – about how my world had changed, how my goals and hopes and dreams had disappeared. He confirmed to me what we both knew deep down – that I'm not me any more.

I don't why I've changed, but I know that I have. Everyone knows I have, and it was pointless trying to deny or defend it to Dan. He repeated everything my mum had said to me half an hour earlier about how all of my friends felt, him included – but it didn't come from a place of hate or anger or jealousy – they just missed me, they were worried for me. He told me our group wasn't the same without me in it any more. I knew what he was saying wasn't coming from a bad place, but it was coming at me all the same, and I felt so shit.

I agreed with him that I'd changed. I promised I'd start seeing him and all my friends again. He told me they have so many festivals and events planned this summer and I do really want to be a part of that – I want to go with them and have fun like I used to. He said they're booking the flights next week for travelling. I know this is something I am no longer going to be able to do because I've spent the majority of my savings now, and it makes me feel really shit, as if I've let everyone down.

If I'm being honest I feel like I've rushed into a relationship with David to heal from Tom. And I feel like I can't be honest about that to my friends or family as we were never officially 'a thing', we didn't have sex or label what we had but the connection I felt to him this summer is like nothing I've ever known, and the pain of him going and not contacting me has been brutal to manage. I don't feel close with David to what I felt for Tom so I am trying to almost throw myself into this relationship so I never think of Tom again but even now, when I do, it's like a dagger to my insides.

We talked, laughed, smoked another joint, drank cider into the night, and I crashed in one of his spare rooms. By the time I woke at 9 a.m. this morning, I'd had seventeen missed calls from David and three from home. I left Dan's house quietly, without seeing anyone. I felt instantly worried about David being annoyed about not knowing where I was, that he hadn't been able to get hold of me – I was also terrified that my parents may have called him to see if he had heard from me.

I didn't know who to call back first – which party was safest. I drove the car to the bottom of the road and decided to call David back first. He asked why I hadn't answered, and I told him I'd slept in.

It was the truth, kind of. I had slept in, just not at my house – and actually, there is nothing wrong with where I've been, I haven't done anything wrong. And he didn't ask where I'd been – he only asked why I hadn't answered – and I told the truth, I was sleeping.

I felt immediately guilty, though. I still feel guilty. I feel like I've lied. Like I've done something wrong, even though I haven't. Is staying at a friend's house wrong just because he's the opposite sex? Is it wrong, now I'm engaged to be married? As soon as I thought that, I felt sick, because my rational brain knows there is no reason to not tell him, but it felt like by not telling him, I would be breaking some kind of unwritten, unspoken rule ... Or is the fact that everyone's talking about our relationship and how I've changed making me more paranoid that David's going to be angry about something he might not even be angry about?

I was waiting to be caught out, holding my breath for the 'Your mum called me ...' line, but it didn't come. He just said, 'Oh baby, you were tired?'

I acted cool, fought back the tears that were desperate to spill down my face, and tried to swallow the lump in my throat that felt like the size of a tennis ball. David said he had to dash – he was on his way to work and he was assuming, I imagine, that I was on my way to college. I should be at college now. But he hung up, and I've been sat here crying ever since. I have cried so hard, for so long. I've felt so many emotions. Anger towards him, my mum and friends again. Rage at myself, to the point that I've repeatedly punched the steering wheel and sun visor until my knuckles on my right hand throbbed, and now they're still glowing red. Who the fuck am I? What have I turned into? Why can't I just be the Louise I was before David, but still be in a relationship with him?

Last night when I left, I'd planned to tell David about how my parents had been, and I'd assumed he would transfer me the money to drive to him, stay with him, to start a life in London together. But the reality is that he didn't even have any phone signal to take my calls, and when he called me back this morning he gave me less than five minutes of his time and made me feel like I was annoying. A hindrance to the incredible life he's built for himself, where he lives so far away from stupid, pathetic, needy me.

I didn't go to college this morning after I spoke to David, and I didn't go home either. I drove to the top of the hill and parked at the green we all used to hang out at together last summer, and I'm still here now. I opened my car door when I first got here and let my legs dangle into the grass. The sun feels so warm on my legs, but my whole being feels so lonely and sad.

I've kept my car door open to feel the breeze. I reclined my seat when I arrived and fell back to sleep pretty much immediately. But as soon as I closed my eyes, I was woken to the text notification ping and a message from Dan:

**Where did you go this morning – you missed Mum's pancakes? Good to see you Lou, it was fun – remember our promise and don't be a stranger x**

There was no mention of the festivals we'd discussed last night, or the parties. I felt the sting of rejection, but I'm also telling myself now that he didn't actually have to text me at all in the first place. Maybe I'm looking for rejection to justify being estranged from them all. Every part of me wants to drive back to Dan's house now, to tell his mum what's been happening and ask her advice – which I know she would take the time to give me because she's so kind and nice – over her incredible pancakes. I desperately want to get some help from her on how to fix things – but I know David will call soon, as he knows it will be my first break at college. Then he will call again at lunchtime, and so I don't have a big enough gap to spend time with anyone without being called by him.

I was just attempting to ignore the little voice in my head reminding me I *could* ignore his calls, I *could* be busy, I *could* tell him I'd call him back . . . but then, like clockwork, his name began flashing up on my phone. I answered and he asked how college was.

I told him it was fine.

# SATURDAY

Less than twenty-four hours here and you already look much more like the you that we remember from before all of this. You are eating proper food now – nothing too chewy, as you get so tired and are more likely to cough and splutter. They are giving you targets here too. This week your target is to walk with your sticks wherever you need to go in the building – no more wheelchair! We are so proud of you. Seeing you walking this morning has made my week. You told me this morning that you feel lucky to still be here, alive. It's the first time you've felt this positive.

I broached the subject of Woody coming to visit again. It wasn't a no, but it wasn't a yes. You're desperate to see him, but you're also such an incredible mum that you don't want to worry or upset him. I get it. By next week you may be up on your feet again with some crutches, so we will think again about him coming in then. I've been able to tell him you're getting better, though, and he's super excited to see you soon. I'm trying to explain to him that you look and sound different, but I'm not sure he gets it – I'm worried about his reaction when he sees you, and also how that will affect you . . . but he's too tiny to explain anything to, so we're just going to have to roll with it. Hope for the best, and deal with the worst if that happens.

I think he's doing OK, but I know from when I was in hospital that my boys only survived it as well as they did because my friends picked up the pieces. Then my parents returned, and we were fortunate enough to be able to have their constant support until I was better, both physically and mentally. One day, though, you will have to move again, because you won't be safe here once he comes out of prison, and that feels hard and wrong. But for now, we just need to take baby steps, both whilst you're in hospital and when you come out, to navigate our way through what life looks like now and how things are. It will feel overwhelming some days, impossible others – but we will get you there. And you're doing it with a small and mighty team behind you – you are not alone.

I called into Jo's tonight on my way through from work, to see if she'd heard back from her mum. She hasn't – but the letter was signed for, the day after she sent it, by a B Mitchington. That was her mum's maiden name – I remembered it from the adoption papers. She hadn't kept her married name. Jo seemed OK, busy – she had a houseful as usual. Harry and I stayed for pizza with all of her kids, including Belle and her boyfriend. Can you believe how many years they've been together now? Jo was saying she's going to speak to his parents about them moving into the summer house together, as he's there most of the time. And if they were out there it would free up an extra room in the house – which they could do with, as there's so many of them, and Jamie often works from home now.

Molly was there too. As I looked at her, I thought it's weird how you can go through part of your life not knowing something happened or that someone existed, but then as soon you find out, everything starts coming together. You make sense of stuff that once upon a time felt weird, but you never really questioned.

## A Letter to Keep You Safe

Things that you pushed to the back of your mind and convinced yourself you were imagining – but then when you know the whole truth, you wonder how you never spotted it when it was always so obvious.

# Eighteen years old

I've been living in London for just over eight weeks now.

David found my accommodation for me. It's on the other side of London to where he lives, but it's closer to his work, which he said would be better as he can see me more. He has six months left on his tenancy, then he said we can get somewhere together. I mean, I do see him often, but not for long. He never stays over as he says he likes to be organised for work from his flat with his suits and shirts. He doesn't want stuff at two houses, and I'm not allowed to stay at his as part of the house rules from the landlord. The hotel visits have totally stopped. He's too busy to stay over at mine, let alone go to hotels – we still pay half whenever we eat out as I am now working full-time, but even that isn't a regular thing right now, due to his schedule. It just feels like everything nice we used to do has stopped since I arrived here.

He managed to get me a room in a house share just outside central London, and I got a full-time job as a waitress at an incredible French restaurant in the city. I share with three other girls: one had left uni after studying Media and is now a budding photographer, one is in her second year of studying Art at uni, and one is on an apprenticeship with an interior design company that works inside beautiful homes of the rich and famous. Then there's me, working full time with no clue as to what I want to do, and feeling really shit about that when everyone I'm around seems to have their lives together and a future plan in place. I'd planned to study baking and patisserie at uni, after I came back from travelling, but when I spoke to David about it, it was another thing he laughed at, like I was telling an actual joke. So I just parked it and started work full time.

I feel lost. Lost in the capital of the UK, where I am surrounded by so many people every single day – and I am so busy, busy working in a bustling city, wondering why that fact never numbs or stops the pain of feeling lost. I don't have one person to tell. Mum hasn't called much. I went and packed up all of my stuff when she and Dad were at work, and when I was halfway up the motorway Dad called and left me a voicemail to say she was so sad and couldn't stop crying.

I feel so shit, and angry. Angry at everyone, and I don't know why. But mostly angry at myself for how my life looks and the feeling that I can't change it.

# MONDAY

So, Martha, turns out the target was a bit ambitious for week one at the neurorehab centre.

You have demanded your wheelchair back so you can get around in between your physiotherapist sessions, as you are aching so badly and it's too much to walk – but now you're on the move, you don't want to lie in bed or sit in a stationary chair. The team agreed, of course they have, so you have your self-propelling wheelchair which you are now a total whizz at to get you around the building when you have no visitors to push you!

You told me today you'd like to see Woody. We've agreed for Wednesday, as it gives me today and tomorrow to prep him. None of us are sure how he will respond, but I know you seeing him will only be a good thing to encourage you to fight to get well and home. We spoke about him at length when I saw you today. You asked me whether I'd look after him permanently if anything went wrong again. I told you Craig was in prison, reminded you that you were now safe. You took my hand and said, 'Shhh. Just promise me, should anything happen to me . . . you promise he will be safe and loved, Lou?'

I promised. I get it. I've thought the same thought a million times. I still think it, when I picture David coming out of prison in a few years. We have to carry these scars for a lifetime, don't we? I'm lucky that I have my parents, and Jo and Jamie. You don't have that. We agreed that I will contact a solicitor this week to look at formalising this 'just in case'. It's peace of mind, that's all – it's not something that will need to happen because you will get better and we will keep you safe from Craig, and you and Woody will go on to have the most beautiful life – together.

Jo called after I left you. Her mum has written back. She must have responded as soon as she received Jo's letter. Jo was really crying when I answered and I couldn't work out if the tears were happy or sad, so I drove straight over. The letter was written on actual writing paper, the type you'd get as a kid when you had a penpal, where the design of insects or flowers on the sheets of paper matches the envelope and you get so excited about posting it off. Jo's mum's writing wasn't neat – it was scrawny and looked like she'd been shaking as she'd written it – like proper elderly writing. We worked out she would now be sixty-two. The handwriting looked like it belonged to someone much older than this – or someone who was unwell or anxious, perhaps.

She didn't go into much detail, said she wasn't great at writing, she wasn't sure what to say. What she did say, though, was that she's sorry – within the first sentence, that made my heart hurt – and she's desperate to meet Jo.

Jo is panicking. It is all happening so fast. I think when she wrote that first letter, she'd convinced herself something may have happened, which meant she may never hear back, but she did, and she's heard back within a week. What a turnaround!

Jo's asked if I will go with her. Again, it wasn't something I needed to think over. It will be an honour – and actually, it will take my mind off what's happening with you, because I'll be honest, Martha – it feels really consuming right now. I would never tell you that, and by the time I give you this letter to read, we will be in a totally different place – but right now, I'm scared for how things look for you a lot of the time.

I ended up having a really weird but brilliant afternoon. I feel overwhelmed, with loads of different emotions. I drove out to the farm shop – I'm not sure you've ever been, but it's on the back lane out of town. It started off two years ago as a hut full of home-grown veg with an honesty box to pay for what you take, and it's now a full-blown shop where you can buy meat as well as fruit and veg, all grown on the farm – plus they have other local people who sell stuff there – home-grown flowers, butters, cheeses and creams, bread and pastries. They also have a coffee shop where they make the best flat white I've ever tasted.

I went to get some veg for my mum and fresh fruit for the boys; it tastes so much better than the stuff you get at the supermarket. I was planning to do some journalling with a coffee, but just after I sat down, I got a tap on my shoulder. It was Dan, one of my best friends from college and someone I haven't seen for over twenty years. The last time I saw Dan was when I sat in his back garden and we smoked a spliff – just before I moved to London to be with David. His mum was like my second mum, and was one of my mum's best friends. She died after a really short battle with cancer when I was pregnant with Harry. I didn't go to the funeral. There was so much stuff I didn't do when I was with David. My relationship with my parents was so controlled by David that Mum didn't even tell me about Ange, because she knew I wouldn't have travelled back, and it would have just made me feel even more of a terrible human than I already did.

Dan and I chatted for almost two hours, about everything and nothing – the past and the present, but mainly how fucking weird life is and how quickly it goes. Him and his sister sold the farm after his dad passed away a couple of years after his mum. They were both too young and brokenhearted to run it. Once they got the money from the sale and inheritance, Dan went off and travelled the world. He met a girl in Sydney, and settled there when they had a daughter. The relationship didn't last, but he stayed for his daughter, so that's been his base for the past two decades. He showed me all these pictures of his teenage daughter, who's already talking about travelling around Europe – so he's come back to England for the summer before deciding what he wants from life. His sister moved to Canterbury and has four kids with her husband who, by the sounds of things, is a really good guy. It's so weird, isn't it? Like, I always felt envious of their family unit – they had the most incredible farm where Dan's mum would smother both her kids with love, and make pancakes for us all on the weekend. His dad built us a whole space to hang out at with a fire pit, seating and a BBQ area, and they had this amazing farm – yet before he was out of his teens, they were both dead, Dan had sold the farm and was an orphan . . .

The trauma people are dealt with in life, that so many people don't even know about. Whole worlds ripped apart and changed forever in a second, and you're left to cope without a support system that's been vital your entire life. I just feel like I'm in awe of Dan, that he is still such a good guy. His daughter FaceTimed as we were sipping our coffee. She's in Sydney with her mum and stepdad, and I felt so sad when I heard them chatting. Their relationship felt so pure and special – I could feel the love they have for each other through the phone – and I felt this huge wave of sadness that my boys will never have a father who loves them like that. They've had to grow up with one parent – and I know now I was emotionally absent so much of the time, because of the situation.

We spoke about my situation – I told him the whole story – or whatever came into my head. He cried, actual tears. When he wiped them away, the shock in his face reminded me how terrible life has been for my boys and me. I didn't apologise, like I have so often before when I've spoken to the few people I've trusted to tell about what happened to us. I didn't panic I was oversharing, or worry I'd be judged. I felt safe enough in Dan's presence to be able to just be me, and to tell my truth – and I feel so much better for it. Even if I feel an abundance of sadness for how life looked for us back then, I am reminding myself I will be forever healing and this is my journey.

Dan and I swapped numbers and agreed to meet again. I really hope we do, because I feel like a little bit of me came back today that I didn't realise was still in me. The few years I had before David that I had forgotten about sparked back up this afternoon when we were reminiscing, and for the first time ever, I feel excited about the future, rather than just knowing I have to survive it . . .

I rushed from the coffee shop and picked Woody up from nursery. I took him to the arcades and park, just the two of us, as George wanted to stay at homework club, and my dad was collecting him after to go for dinner at their house. It felt nice just to spend time alone with Woody. He spoke about you as soon as I put him in the car. He speaks about you every day, Martha. He told me you were poorly and in hospital – he stated it as a fact, which sounded odd but cute in his beautiful baby voice. He is always black and white, come to think of it now. It *is* a fact – you are poorly, you are in hospital, and that to him (I think) means you are just getting better. I wonder if his reaction is normal, whether he should be crying more – but I don't think there is ever a 'normal' reaction to this kind of thing, especially when you're not even three years old, and he doesn't know why you're in hospital. It's clear from the way he says it that he thinks you're sick. The same as when he gets sick, and needs to rest and take medicine to get better again.

# Eighteen years old

Things are really shit.

I feel like I say that all the time, but each time I say it, things have just got worse. Way worse . . .

I'm pregnant.

David was livid when I told him. I was gutted – at his reaction, but also that I'm pregnant. It wasn't the plan. I mean, there was no plan – for life, for myself – but this wasn't part of anything I've ever imagined or thought about, so it feels shit. Really shit.

It's all been a whirlwind, and as much as we're engaged to be married, there's been no discussion of marriage since David proposed.

I've been promoted to assistant manager at the restaurant and the hours are full on. The restaurant is so busy all the time. I love it, the team and atmosphere are amazing – the food is renowned through London and the customers are mainly nice, and big tippers – but I don't know how I will be able to continue there if I keep the baby.

David's reaction when I told him made me feel like I've somehow done this to myself without any involvement from him. He ranted on about how this could properly fuck him up, how he has only just started out in his career.

We've spoken about me having a termination. David said he thinks it is the best thing for us, that he couldn't see how us keeping it was doable. I agreed.

Then he told me he needs time to think, and he left. He walked out and left me sat on the bed in tears. I tried to call him that evening and the following morning, but was met with his answerphone, repeatedly reminding me I am still very much a lost girl in a busy city. But now I am a pregnant lost girl.

We still aren't living together. If I don't have the termination, and I choose the other option, I wonder how I'll manage a baby, financially, if he decides he doesn't want a part in it.

He still hadn't contacted me and it had been over a week. I was still getting his voicemail when I called, so I decided to get the tube to his office because I felt like I was going insane and I just needed to sort things one way or another.

I've never been to his place of work, but I know he gets a lunch break every day because he calls me when he is in the office on lunch. I got there at 12.55 p.m., five minutes before he would have usually rung me. I waited until 1 p.m. – he didn't call. I called him; I got his voicemail again.

I felt sick, still. Sick about the future of our relationship, about the baby inside me that is growing every day, and about going to his workplace uninvited . . . but I was also angry that he's ignored me since he found out. I arrived at his work and felt this massive feeling of 'Fuck you' because of the situation I am in. I walked through the huge glass doors into the biggest building I've ever been in during my life.

The first woman I noticed when I entered the building looked like a heavily pregnant Swedish supermodel. She had shoulder-length white-blonde hair and the perfect tanned skin. Her jawline was razor sharp and she had the most perfectly manicured nails

I'd ever seen. She leant over the desk in front of me, and the receptionist passed her a brown file. Clearly, she worked in the building as she had the same lanyard David wears around her neck, her badge resting on her perfectly neat baby bump with the name *'Jaclyn Bunting'*. I couldn't see her job title – she walked away too quickly. She was wearing a white fitted round-necked dress. Pretty brave, I thought, given she looked like she was about to give birth any second. The dress met her dainty knees and clung to her bump, and her silhouette was beautiful. She'd teamed the look with nude heels, which were the same height as the ones David had bought me that I've found it impossible to walk in – yet here she was, pregnant and bossing them as if she was strolling in Reebok Classics. I wondered if I'll look as good as her if I do keep the baby. She looks so incredible . . . But then, as I watched her walk up the circular staircase, she turned to face me again. I caught her expression and she looked sad, as if she was lost. It wasn't the face I'd expect from a powerhouse pregnant businesswoman, you know? I felt a slight bit of relief when I looked at her, because it almost okayed how shit I am feeling. Like, if this glamorous woman with her life together – drop dead gorgeous and with this incredible career – looks like her world is about to end, surely it's fine that I feel this crap?

The building is across three floors: glass everywhere, men in trouser suits and polished black shoes, women in skirt suits and heels, all dragging hand luggage suitcases or carrying huge reams of files and paperwork that they look like they're about to drop any second – arms as long as Inspector Gadget and as strong as Popeye to manage it all. It was organised chaos like I'd never seen before. Like when you watch ants at work – all rushing around, busy as fuck, carrying way too much pointless stuff – but in their colonies it all makes sense to them? Yeah, exactly that.

I went to the reception desk, where a beautiful Japanese lady sat on a cream leather computer chair, which she kind of disappeared into. I couldn't work out if it was because she was so tiny or the chair was too big. She had the most perfect slicked-back bun, flawless skin and a smear of red lipstick across her perfectly pouted lips. On one side of her was a huge vase of lilies, and on the other, a glass bowl of white mints, individually wrapped in see-through cellophane. I immediately wondered what type of person picked up one of those mints and ate it.

'How can I help?' she asked me, with a genuinely nice smile.

'I'm here to see David Metcalfe, please,' I replied, feeling like I was going to throw up on her desk. She started clicking her computer mouse button, moving it around until she held her oversized black-rimmed Chanel glasses with her right hand and pulled them down her nose slightly so she could peer over the top to get a better look at me. 'Annnnd, what time is your appointment please?' she asked, still looking at me, not at the screen.

I said I didn't have an appointment, that I was his girlfriend. She couldn't hide her look of shock – still looking towards me, not her screen. I felt like I'd been punched in the stomach, and she looked as if *she* had – I'm still questioning why. Was she shocked because of how I look – maybe she thought I didn't look good enough for David? Or was she shocked David has a girlfriend? Is there a reason he shouldn't have one?

She managed to pick her jaw up off the desk within a few seconds with what then looked like a sympathetic, sweet smile and said, 'Sorry, what was your name?' I told her. She picked up the phone and dialled his extension number without needing to look it up from anywhere. In the same voice, she said, 'I have Louise here – your girlfriend.' She paused before hanging up and before she had chance to say anything else to me, David was sprinting down the escalator, taking two steps at a time, even though it was already moving at a pace electronically. I couldn't work out if he was angry or embarrassed. When he got to me he held my bicep with his hand and began marching me out the door. He didn't greet me – he didn't say anything at all, actually. As I was being escorted out, the receptionist called after him, 'Oh, David? Change of plan. The hospital called – they changed the scan date to tomorrow. I've emailed you both, but just in case you wanted to know sooner . . .'

'Right,' he replied, without turning around, whilst still forcing me out the building. I immediately asked what she was talking about and he said that his boss may have cancer and wanted him to accompany him for his scan at hospital. He never talks to me about anything he has going on in his life. Why wouldn't you tell your fiancée your boss has cancer and you're taking him for a scan?

He was seething. I pulled my arm away from his grasp, but before I could tell him he had hurt me, he put his face into mine and through gritted teeth he whisper-shouted: 'Do not ever turn up at my fucking work again.'

I felt instantly sicker. It was as if I hadn't even felt sick when I arrived. The bile rose in my throat and a flash of heat whizzed down my back, leaving a trickle of sweat.

I didn't speak. I couldn't speak. I kept thinking back to my Aunt Peggy. David saw my reaction and was instantly sorry, immediately apologising for his behaviour. He explained he is stressed at work, and that his management don't approve of people's partners in the building.

I don't know whether David is telling the truth or not. Either way, I'm quickly realising I'm getting used to pretending David doing weird shit is normal now.

I told him I need to make a decision about the pregnancy, and he asked what I meant. He was pacing up and down in front of me, he kept looking up to his office building and rubbing his forehead with his thumb and his index finger, applying maximum pressure on his brow, which had sweat beaded all over it.

I told him I meant that I didn't know whether I am looking at having a termination alone or raising a baby together. He scoffed. His favourite fucking thing to do to me. The same scoff he did when I first mentioned travelling, the same scoff when I spoke about going to uni, the one he made when I told him about the eighteenth birthday party my mum had planned for me. Scoff, scoff fucking scoff.

I was expecting him to tell me I was being ridiculous and that I needed to book an abortion. Instead, he answered with, 'Of course we're keeping it.'

I immediately realised I don't even get a choice with this guy. This is down to nothing I wanted – it's all his decision. I've also now realised I don't have the courage to say this out loud. I feel like he doesn't want to keep it, either, but I don't even have the energy to challenge him on that.

I looked up to the sky, and saw the beautiful heavily pregnant bad-ass career woman in the huge staircase window of the offices. She was stood, briefcase in one hand, holding the edge of the window sill with the other, just staring down on us. Again, looking sad, so overwhelmingly sad. I looked around me to see if there was anyone else she could be looking at, and when I looked back up she was gone, as if she was never there. Maybe she wasn't.

David said he will be in a position to get his own place before the baby arrives, so I can move in with him. He then said he needed to get back inside as he had a big client due in for a meeting. He told me he would be entertaining until late, so he would call me when he finished, and then he walked back inside.

No kiss, no hug, no further reassurance or apology.

He's just left me riddled with anxiety and worry. I stood there, outside his offices, questioning once again what the fuck I am doing, like I'm sat here questioning it now.

All I want to do right now is book a termination, return to Cornwall, apologise to my parents for my temporary insanity and resume my life with my friends like it was before David entered it. But weirdly, I just can't. It feels like it isn't even an option for me, because I also want him to want me. I want the life he promised me when he proposed, and I want us to be happy, together. I also haven't even spoken to any of my friends since I arrived in London and my mum rarely calls any more, and when she does, she just starts crying and it gets weird. I feel like I'm in so deep, I can only plough forwards.

I got the tube home, climbed under my covers and cried myself into a deep sleep. A sleep which I've just woken up from – and now I feel even worse because it's 4 a.m., and as I guessed, there's been no missed call like he promised . . .

# TUESDAY

I didn't visit you today, as I'm not feeling great and we aren't allowed to come if we're unwell. I have started coughing and feel really blocked up, so I think it's going to turn into a cold. I'm praying it doesn't, as I am planning to bring Woody up tomorrow, and I mentioned it to him last night – he is so excited. He chanted 'Mummy' over and over, and then he was chatting to imaginary you in everything he did for the rest of the evening, talking about so much stuff you do together – so sad and cute all at the same time.

Mags came up this morning. She said there is no clinical change, but you seem happier and more positive. You were sat out in the garden, the nurse said you're working really hard with the new rehabilitation programme and you're getting stronger each day. Mags said you spoke about Woody visiting and you are excited for this. I send you so many videos and pictures of him every day to make you smile and to keep you strong and focused when you're having your tough times, which I know from experience often feel far more than the times you feel positive.

Molly and Jaclyn came over for a takeaway tonight. Harry was supposed to come too, but ended up meeting up with some of his old friends from school and going for dinner.

We got Chinese and watched a film after Woody and George went to bed. They've just left now and it's 10 p.m., which is perfect as I need to sleep. I feel like I'm sleeping for longer periods – I still wake, but I can fall back to sleep more easily, which feels good. I cannot stand it when insomnia kicks in when the rest of the world is asleep – it's one of the loneliest feelings in the world.

And Dan has just messaged to see if I fancy a coffee tomorrow afternoon. I feel really happy I'm actually branching back out and making more friends again outside of our tiny, safe, girly circle.

# Eighteen years old

David wants to tell my parents about the baby to their faces; he wants us to deliver the news together, as a couple. It isn't a choice: he hasn't asked what I want, and since we moved into this flat three weeks ago, his moods have been so up and down that I know I'll just go along with it to save another argument – despite knowing this is probably going to kill my mum off.

I was excited at first when he said he'd found the flat, especially so quickly – I was expecting it to be longer before we moved in together after him saying he was stuck in his tenancy. It's only ten minutes from my house share, so I know the area, and it's closer to his work, so I thought I'd see more of him – but he's working away loads more on family cases at courts all over London, meaning he stays away at least three nights a week. I feel since I moved in here I'm not only lost, I am now lonely and sad too, because I miss the girls I lived with. We got on so well, and there was always someone in at the house, whereas here, I am always alone. I feel frightened of the noises as it's a communal block of flats, and it often feels like someone is in our apartment. My rational brain knows there isn't, but when it's 2 a.m. and there's creaking and banging which I can't work out where it's coming from, my heart beats out of its chest and I feel genuinely terrified. I haven't told David. I know he will just do his usual scoff and call me pathetic.

I just have this sadness with me every minute of every day. Even when I'm at work serving hundreds of happy customers, surrounded by all my amazing colleagues, I feel like I am in the depths of depression. I refuse to allow myself to think about life before David, because I no longer recognise who I am now, and it would be impossible to ever go back to that life as I am now over three months pregnant and starting to show. I've also had the worst morning sickness every day since finding out – which has never just been in the morning. I don't know why it's called morning sickness because it's there all day and night; it just comes in waves and I am so exhausted trying to get through my shifts inhaling food smells that used to make me hungry, yet now smell repugnant . . .

I have a book, though, that David bought for me. It's called *What to Expect When You're Expecting*. I'm just in the second trimester now and it's crazy how things change each week. It's a nice book to read; the pictures fascinate me – it tells me about all the changes to my body and also a week-by-week guide on the baby's size, what body parts have formed, what new developments it's made. I really want to skip the pages to read it all but I force myself not to turn the page until the following week, and it keeps me excited to wait and see what comes next and what fruit or vegetable my baby now resembles . . .

When David works away he will always bring home flowers – huge, grand bouquets that he collects on his way home from the office. Some weeks he comes home happy and presents me with whatever blooms are in season – they're always wrapped so beautifully. He eats the dinner I spend all afternoon cooking and tells me it tastes amazing; he rubs my tummy in a loving way, then bends down, presses his lips to my belly button and says, 'Daddy's home,' to the baby. He drags both words out so they sound really long and slow, and he has a strange accent when he does it. He gives me a hug, a kiss on the cheek – but never the lips. Loving me since I've been pregnant looks like cuddles and cheek kisses at most – we stopped having sex the minute the test came back positive. David told me it would be weird whilst I have a baby in me. At first I protested, told him he was being silly. In another pregnancy book he bought me, it states that it is absolutely safe, natural and healthy to continue having sexual intercourse throughout pregnancy. I crave the attention of him wanting me in that way. At first I begged, and tried to do stuff to make him want me, but it just became embarrassing and awkward so I've given up now. I know it's pointless, and there was only so much rejection I could take.

Other times though, he will arrive home after being away on business with another glorious bouquet of flowers, but his smile will be different. There will be no real happy greeting – I mean, it looks as if it's there all the same, and to anyone on the outside looking in, they wouldn't see what's wrong, but I know it's false. I know what's coming. He will be scanning round our open-plan lounge and kitchen, his eyes darting everywhere. He will be opening doors to the bathroom, bedroom and cupboards, looking for the match to start the fire. He always finds something. It doesn't matter how clean the house is, I'll have always missed something – I will then be called a lazy, cheeky bitch. He dials 1471 on the landline to check who the last caller was, and begins interrogating me about who I've spoken to whilst he's been away, knowing full well I don't speak to anyone – even 1471 confirms that.

Other times, if he gets back and the house is immaculate, he will lose it that I'm not resting, and tell me it's unfair on the baby. I can't keep up. I feel like I live on my nerves and I have no idea what the rules are each day. He chops and changes them as often as his tie and socks. I feel like I'm walking on eggshells twenty-four hours a day – even when he is away on business, I spend my days in full preparation for his return. There is no downtime from feeling like this, even when he is absent. It is with me every hour of every day. I wonder if Aunt Peggy felt like this. I wonder if I'm now living her life?

David wants to tell my parents this weekend. We are going to drive down and announce the news. He wants to stay in a hotel. I didn't attempt to argue when he told me this. I called my mum early this morning to tell her we were coming over later, and she sounded super excited and said she would get the spare room ready for our visit. The guilt of having to tell her we had booked a hotel has consumed me ever since I hung up. I heard the rejection in her voice when I said it; the way she didn't have the time to hide her hurt when she said, 'Oh,' in response. She didn't question it, or plead for me to stay, or confirm she was upset, she just reassured me that she'd heard really good things about the hotel we'd booked and said, 'I'm sure it will be lovely for you, much nicer than staying here, anyway.'

I hate David, for making me do this to her. I wonder what she really thinks. I have been so cut off from her for such a long time now that I wonder if she believes that I would actually rather stay in a hotel – or does she know that this was David's decision? Or maybe she is relieved I will be staying in a hotel, because she doesn't want me to stay with her any more? I didn't want her to hear me upset, so I lied and said I had to go and get ready for work. She took a deep breath and said, 'Louise, darling, I want you to know that when you have children, you know them inside out, even when they don't know themselves any more, and even when you don't see them for a long time. I want you to know you don't have to come all the way here to tell me your news if it's going to make things harder for you.'

I thought I was going to be sick. I felt like I had been winded. 'I know, Mum,' I said, wiping away the tears that were falling silently from my eyes.

She followed up with, 'Remember this is your home, day or night, any time. Your father and I love you, we are always here for you, no matter what.'

I managed to say goodbye before I hung up, grabbed a pillow from my bed and hugged it until I felt like I was going to pass out.

I cried so hard, so loud and so much that my eyes still sting. It's a physical pain, that I thought I could let out of me by crying like that, but it's still here. I feel so pathetic, and as ashamed as I did to begin with.

And now we have to drive to Cornwall – I'm just waiting for David to pick me up, as he took his car to be valeted. He has a brand-new white BMW that we are driving down in. I no longer drive. The cost to do the work to my car after it failed its MOT three months ago was more than what it was worth, he said, so I scrapped it. David says I don't need another one because public transport is better where we live now, and we only have parking for one car at the apartment. I'm too young to be insured on his car, he said, so I walk and get the bus to work. I'm unsure how this will work when the baby arrives in autumn, but again, I know better than to raise any more issues or complaints. And at least it will keep me fit.

# WEDNESDAY

I feel pretty crap today. This flu thing has gone through us all, but I'm no worse than yesterday – which is a good thing. I was convinced I was going to become super poorly, but maybe someone out there knows I don't have the time for illness now because I have to reunite you and your baby. We've changed the Woody meeting to tomorrow, just to give me another day to be totally clear of this. I am keeping everything crossed that I can bring him up.

My mum called just before lunch. I'd fallen asleep on the sofa and her call woke me up. There's nothing I need more than a mid-morning siesta at the minute, I've decided. Mum asked if she and my dad could come and discuss something with me. I instantly felt sick – that dread of waiting for someone to speak to you about something you have no idea about instantly fills me with anxiety. It was a trick of David's throughout our entire relationship, where he would say, 'I need to discuss something with you when I get home,' or even worse, 'We need to talk when I return from my trip,' so I would spend days going out of my mind. When my mum said it today, I started panicking immediately – it was an instant reaction, not one I could help, and she immediately reassured me. She recognised immediately that I was spiralling and apologised for saying it over the phone without thinking what it might do to me. I told her I wasn't feeling great and didn't want to pass any germs on so asked her to tell me over the phone, but she said Dad wants to talk to me too – and it's a positive, nice thing, so I have nothing to worry about.

I feel better, but still slightly anxious as I have no clue what it could be. I worry now that my body is programmed to look out for danger and negative things. I rarely feel excitement or happiness without a constant feeling of anxiety in the background, waiting for something bad to happen. I really wish that would stop, but I suppose it's hard, because my entire adult life has been like this – and that doesn't just disappear, does it?

I've just sent you a load of videos of Woody trying pineapple before nursery this morning. We cut it together and I wasn't sure if he would like it, but oh my, he would have smashed the whole thing if he could! I packed some for him to take at snack time and when we arrived he was so excited, telling everyone he had 'anapple' in his lunchbox!

I met Dan at 2 p.m. We went to the farm shop café again. I figured it felt so easy and nice last time that we should probably stick to that – and it was just as easy and nice today, except for one thing. He's invited me to a reunion. It's this Saturday. He said he's been invited on Facebook. Dan keeps in touch with most of our friendship group from back then over Facebook, and they all went to his mum's and his dad's funerals.

I asked him honestly who knew what about me. I felt embarrassed, doing that – as if I'm the main character. But I know it's a small town and everyone knows each other's business. The reality, Dan reminded me, is that's only the case when you're in it. All of our friends live hours away from here now, in different cities or towns – countries, even. I mean, he's lived on the other side of the world for half of our lives! He promised me that people have their own stuff going on – jobs to work, kids to raise – they really weren't talking about little old me. That made me feel better.

He said he's told Rach and Jess that he met me, though, that they both asked for my number and were so excited that he'd bumped into me. I haven't seen them since I was seventeen – that's an entire lifetime. It's made me feel happy, that they are being nice and welcoming, and it makes me feel good when Dan and I reminisce about the life we led as teens, even though it was just a couple of short years. Even though I bolted before they all travelled the world and made more memories. Even though they're all still close friends . . . I feel included, welcomed, like I may have found my little community again. I might have some more friends to WhatsApp, chat to or visit . . . Maybe I am about to start living life again?

One thing's for sure, the thought of Dan collecting me on Saturday night at 7 p.m. to go to this reunion is making me feel like I'm about to shit my pants. I was about to google 'What to wear to a school reunion' before I gave my head a wobble and called Jo, knowing she will know how to make this situation better . . .

# Eighteen years old

We got to Cornwall around 3 p.m. after I said we would be there for midday. David didn't pick me up until mid-morning so we were much later arriving than I'd said.

Mum made a hot lunch that had gone cold – she asked if we wanted it heated up. David said no, and then told her we wouldn't be staying long as I was tired. I hadn't said I was tired – I'm unsure how he thinks I'm tired from sitting in the passenger seat of a car for five hours whilst he's done nothing but make calls on speakerphone to his colleagues and clients. It really annoys me that he is putting the blame on me for leaving, as if I somehow couldn't rest at my family home.

The house smelled of syrup and oats baking in the oven – Mum was baking my favourite biscuits. It made me feel so homesick. I was excited to just be in the house, peek in my bedroom and just be home. I also felt sad – my parents now have this whole new life I am no longer a part of. I could tell both Mum and Dad were struggling with my presence, or David's. They were so happy to see me, but there was also a sadness in their eyes that was present as soon as we arrived. I could see Mum was beyond anxious through her body movements alone, over the top with nerves, all twitchy and jerky.

Dad had just begun telling me about his new greenhouse, that he is in competition with our neighbour, Colin, to see who can grow the sweetest strawberries and tastiest tomatoes when David interrupted and said, 'Well, we've got some better news. Lou is pregnant.' Dad looked at Mum and Mum looked at me. Her eyes filled with tears. No one said anything.

'I'm due in six months, so we've already had the first scan,' I said excitedly, trying to fill the silence.

'Right, then . . .' Dad replied in his thick Yorkshire accent.

Mum now had tears rolling down her face, and her hand was clutching my dad's forearm as if she was steadying herself to keep standing. 'It's OK love, it'll be OK,' he soothed into her ear.

'Sorry, what will be OK?' David snapped. 'She doesn't have fucking cancer, Tony. She's having a baby.'

'We're very aware of that, and she's our baby and we want what's best for her,' Dad replied – as calm as a cucumber.

'I fucking knew it,' David spat. By this point, Mum was trying her hardest to stay calm, but I could see her hand on Dad was now trembling and the tears were pouring out of her face at such a rapid rate, no amount of wipes from the back of her hand could stem the flow of them for much longer.

'Knew what?' I bit back at David, angry because I knew he wanted to lose it with my parents due to a reaction we'd both known we were going to be met with.

'I knew that these two would put a dampener on our happy news.'

I immediately thought back to David pacing up and down outside his work after he was met with this 'happy news', when he wasn't sure if he wanted a baby or a termination. The rage inside me started to creep up because of what an absolute hypocrite he was being.

'They're just shocked,' I said. 'They'll be fine, it's just a shock.'

My dad moved my mum's hand off his and placed it on the counter so she could steady herself, then whispered, 'Wait there, pet.' I instantly recognised how sweet that was of him, and realised I'd missed watching how he loves my mum. Dad turned his back to David, faced me, held my hand in his and said, 'Sweetheart, can we just have some time alone to talk to you, the three of us. Please?'

It looked like his heart was snapping in front of me, and mine felt like it was too, with the pain I could feel pouring from him at where my life was going. Before I could even answer, David bellowed, 'Fuck you, Tony!' across the kitchen. My dad turned round to face him and before he could reply, David had grabbed me by the bicep, the same as he'd done the day I'd turned up to his work. He began marching me out the house towards the front door. I tried to yank my arm away from his grip whilst my dad was calling my name over and over and my mum was now fully hyperventilating. David pushed me out the front door and shut it behind him. Just as I was about to turn around, tell him to get fucked and walk back in to hug my mum and reassure my dad, Dan's mum appeared on the drive.

'Lou!' she shouted, excited to see me. 'Your mum said you were home, and you left this at ours when you stayed over with Dan a few months ago. I'm so pleased I caught you. Come here.' She grabbed me and hugged me a bit too tight. Then she handed me the cardigan and socks I hadn't missed and reached her hand out to greet David.

'Stayed over?' he asked her, with a smile that falsely suggested he was super happy about that.

'Oh yes, Dan loves a sleepover, and we love seeing the girls when they stay,' she said, making her son sound like he was Hugh Hefner and I was one of his many Playboy bunnies.

'Thanks, Ange,' I said, hugging her again.

'Yeah, thanks, Ange,' David repeated, with a tone that made me feel uneasy, but one Ange didn't even notice.

I gave her a kiss as she let herself into the house without knocking and said to me, 'Make sure you see me before you leave. Come to the house – Dan would love to see you before they all leave for the festival.'

She walked ahead, shutting the door behind her, and my heart sank at what she was about to walk into. I followed David down the drive to his car. I was reeling with anger over the way he'd spoken to my dad, but I was also panicking about what Ange had said about me sleeping over with Dan, even though I knew I'd done nothing wrong. David was already sat in the car when I began to climb in the passenger seat. I bent down to throw my belongings on the back seat. Before I'd even sat down – as I lifted my leg to get in – I flew backwards onto the road with such speed, the side of my head and face smashed onto the concrete pavement.

As I lifted my head to reach and feel the damage, I saw the blood pouring onto my T-shirt and jeans. I realised that it was coming from my nose, which was now throbbing as much as the side of my head. There was blood just pouring, but before I could even process that I'd just been punched in the face with that amount of force, David was leaning his whole body over the passenger seat and began picking me up off the pavement by my hair. I screamed. He tightened his grip, and through gritted teeth said, 'I fucking dare you to scream again.' I tried to clamber into the car, but I was so disorientated . . . My head and face were throbbing and there was blood everywhere. David reached into the back seat for a towel, threw it at my head and said, 'Don't get blood on my fucking car.' I was looking towards my parents' house, praying someone was watching – that one of them had heard my screams and would come out to help me. But there was no one there. I remember, in the midst of it all, seeing all the houses, the sun, realising he hadn't had the time to even assess if he would be spotted attacking me and yet he had just gone ahead and done it anyway, which made me not have the courage to run back in for fear of what he would have done.

It all just confirmed to me that I was in the exact same situation as Aunt Peggy. There was no difference here.

He sped off. I began to cry. In fact, I haven't stopped crying since. I think the longest I've gone is around ten minutes before I start welling up again. I think it's the shock at what he's done, but also the reality that this man is now in my life, forever. I am having his baby.

We didn't stay in the hotel, or in Cornwall. Instead, we drove back to London – and the entire journey back, he abused me. He repeatedly fired questions at me, but without giving me time to answer one question before he screamed at me to answer the next. So many disgusting, crude and vulgar questions about what I did with Dan when I stayed at his house. I soon learned I was safer staying quiet than trying to protest my innocence or defend myself. Any time I tried to say nothing happened or that we were just friends, he would get more wound up and hurt me again. He punched my leg so hard it went dead, he pulled my hair so hard and so quickly I would head-butt my own knee or smash the side of my face on the car centre console or dashboard. He backhanded me round the face four times, and on the last time, when I screamed, 'NOTHING HAPPENED!' he leant across whilst driving erratically up the M5 and spat in my face.

I've stayed silent since – the questions changed to accusations, then the accusations turned to insults. 'I bet you fucking loved it.' 'I bet you thought you were so fucking clever thinking you got away with it.' It's gone on and on, him continuing to slap, punch and grab me for the entire drive back to London.

I spent the entire journey panicking he would go for my stomach – and if I'm being totally honest, I still keep thinking maybe he will. In a way, I'm hoping he will. Maybe I'll lose the baby; then I can leave, and I won't be tied to him forever.

I feel so confused today. We got in last night and I didn't know what to expect. He ordered me to go to bed and he slept on the sofa. I didn't sleep. I heard him leave the house at 3 a.m., and so far he hasn't come back – it's now 4 p.m. on Sunday. I haven't eaten, my whole body's bruised and I've ignored umpteen calls and texts off my mum and dad because I just can't face them.

I cannot fathom how I closed my parents' front door, ready to lose my shit about the way he'd behaved towards them, yet within minutes he'd attacked me. And I never even got the chance to raise what he'd said and done in their home because *I* was the bad one – when I've done nothing wrong. Or have I done something wrong? I'm that confused I don't even know any more.

# THURSDAY

I loved bringing Woody up to see you this morning!

He was so excited, wasn't he? It was like he didn't see anything but you. He didn't feel weird about where you were, how you looked – he just was in awe of spending time with you and oh god, it's been the best day I've had in forever.

I really feel like it will give you the strength you need to keep fighting to get well enough to come home. I kept watching you study him, holding his cheeks and running your fingers through his hair as if you just couldn't believe he was yours. I remember those feelings . . .

It was so nice to take him into the gardens and have snacks on the blanket together. He was making the other patients and nurses laugh with his sense of humour – what a sense of humour he has, though!

The whole way to nursery afterwards, he was chatting about you – he barely drew breath. He was so happy and excited; the love he has for you was overflowing for the entire journey.

I dropped him off, and explained that I've arranged for my parents to collect him as I was then travelling to Devon to meet with Jo's mum. To me, the meeting feels rushed, to Jo, it doesn't. I think a day to her right now feels like a lifetime. She was so desperate to meet the woman who had brought her into the world. She has so much to try and grasp, both as a mother and a daughter – and actually just as a human being – to try and understand something that feels like such a head fuck.

The drive was approximately two hours. I was sick with nerves on the way up, so I had no idea how Jo was feeling. She drove. I'd said I would, but she was adamant – she needed to take her mind off the meeting, she said, and if she was a passenger it would mean she had nothing to concentrate on and she probably would talk herself out of going altogether.

We arrived in Devon just after 11 a.m. We were meeting Jo's mum at 11.30. I'd hired a pod in a local library – it had a café on site and was a private space. Jo hadn't been sure where to meet her mum; she didn't feel comfortable going to her house as she wasn't sure if anyone else would be there, or what state her house would be in. She also didn't want to meet in public because she had no idea how it would go, and chances were there would be visible emotions. I realised the library was public, but the pod was private – I'd called ahead and spoke to the loveliest librarian, who was massively supportive and said she would be working when we arrived, so to ask for her when we got there. We did that when we walked in at ten past eleven, and she showed us to the pod. It had a large white desk in the centre of the room and chairs all the way around it, neatly tucked in. I left Jo whilst I went and got us water and tea from the café and carried it back up. I was searching for anyone who could be her mum the whole time, but she could have been one of so many women in the library at that time that I quickly gave up, recognising that searching was making me way more anxious than I already was.

Jo was trembling when I got back, saying she thought this was a mistake. Her breathing was unregulated and I was worried she was going to go into a panic attack. I turned her chair to face me and leant forward to face her. I took her hands in mine and as I said, 'Copy my breathing: deep breath in . . .' there was a knock and her mum popped her head round the door.

Immediately, I felt emotional just at the sight of her. She was the spitting image of Jo, just an older version. She had a thick, natural grey bob, and her eyes twinkled the same way Jo's do, even though they were full of heartbreak and sadness. She had the same kind smile that made you feel instantly at ease in her company.

'Oh, sorry,' she said, in the softest-spoken voice I'd ever heard, as if she'd just interrupted something she shouldn't have walked into. I looked towards Jo to gauge her reaction, realising, as I spotted the tears falling down her cheeks, that I needed to wipe my own too. I let go of her hand and reached into my bag for my tissues.

'No, don't be sorry. Come in. Hi,' Jo replied through tears. She stood up and walked past me towards her mum and as I looked over, she embraced her in the tightest hug I'd ever seen.

Her mum instantly cupped Jo's face in her hands, like it was the most natural thing in the world to do, and kept saying, 'Just look at you,' over and over, like she was the most beautiful thing she had ever laid eyes on. There wasn't a dry eye between the three of us and we were all laughing then crying in turn.

Jo's mum looked nothing like I expected, and I hate myself a little for what I thought I'd be walking into. I convinced myself she would be nothing like Jo. Unclean, maybe; haggard looking, perhaps? A smell of stale alcohol or cigarette smoke surrounding her? Instead, she smelt lovely, her floral perfume filling the room within seconds. She wore navy trousers with gold ballet pumps and a navy and white striped jumper with a neck scarf. She had a large blue bucket bag which hung on her tiny forearm. She looked nice, clean, but she looked broken. Broken and lost, and as soon as Jo hugged her, the tears came for her too.

'I'm so sorry.' She must have whispered this a hundred times, with her head gently shaking.

I stayed seated at the back of the room and they sat together, facing me, in the seats on the opposite side of the table. There was just lots of crying for the first few minutes, and affection. I felt honoured to witness such an emotional, life-changing moment between a mother and daughter, even though I had no idea how things would go once they began to speak. They were studying each other's hands, faces, their features. Stroking the backs of their hands, sides of their faces. Jo felt her mum's hair. There were just noises of almost shock, I suppose, followed by more tears. The tears felt mostly happy, but I suppose, on reflection, they would have been repeatedly sad on Jo's mum's side.

I asked Jo's mum if I could get her a drink. She said water would be fine, and there was a jug on the table with three glasses, so it meant I didn't need to leave the room. I kind of wondered if I should, but I didn't feel out of place, and actually it soon became quite nice.

We started talking about the small stuff – the weather, how our journeys had been, getting there. Jo's mum lived half an hour away – she couldn't drive, so she had caught the bus into town. *Of course she can't drive*, my head said.

'Ask me anything,' Jo's mum said to her.

Jo let out a huge sigh, looked up to the ceiling then looked back down, took her mum's hand in hers, wiped her eyes with the soaked tissue, and said, 'Why were we adopted?'

*Fuck*, my brain went.

She just went in for it, hard and heavy.

That's what I admire about Jo – she just gets shit sorted, addresses situations everyone else skirts around. From what she's told me, she became this person after her first husband, Mark, left her, and almost broke her. She made a choice to fight after he ripped her heart out and left her with three tiny babies, and I don't think since then she's ever stopped fighting since – for herself, for anyone she loves. She fights when she doesn't have to. Almost fearless. Such a fucking inspiration.

'I tried to keep you. I begged, Josephine, honestly I did.'

I didn't even know that Josephine was her full name. I've only ever known her as Jo, and assumed at the most she was a Joanne or Joanna. As they sat there, breaking their hearts, my head was just trying to figure out if the name Josephine would ever suit her, because at that point, and as I'm writing this to you now, to my mind it still absolutely doesn't.

Jo's mum continued. 'I couldn't leave alone. When your dad first went to prison, I asked them to move us, I wanted us to leave, but they said we weren't at risk as he was in prison. I needed help because we had no money or anyone to help us. By the time he was out, it was too late again. From the minute your sister was born, they kept saying how good she and your brother would be for people looking to adopt – then when you came along, I knew I'd lose you. I managed to keep you for a year, but they made their minds up. It was my fault. It felt like no one was on my side, and in the end, I thought you'd be better with someone who could give you a life. I couldn't, with him . . .'

She started apologising again. There were more tears. It was clear to me she was taking full responsibility here. Although it was also clear that the reason Jo and her siblings were removed from her was because of Jo's biological father, from the reports we had seen. Her mum had made reference to that, but she was taking all the blame here. I know from so many women we've supported, many who were adopted, that the adoption processes and support available at that time were massively different, and in my opinion, wrong. Even in the early 00s we have some mums who had babies removed in domestic abuse cases who, with the correct support and care, could have absolutely kept their babies and been incredible mums. It's soul destroying, the amount of trauma and damage caused to so many families because of the way things were done in the past. What happened in front of me today between Jo and her birth mother was testament to that.

Jo asked about her dad. He left her mum long before he died – four years after her siblings and her were removed, in fact – for the landlady of the local pub. By all accounts, he made the years he was with her a living hell, too, Barbara told her. Barbara then moved to another town, to a one-bedroom flat. She never met anyone after him; her trust in men was gone forever, and she had no interest in having more children after losing her three babies. It was all so sad and heartbreaking – but what was worse was how much I recognised myself in Jo's mum. Everything she said, I resonated with. The desperation, the shame, the needing to run away and hide. Without the support I'd found in this woman's daughter and a few others, there was every chance I would have gone on to be just like her.

Barbara explained she worked as a cleaner, had done for years. She cleaned offices and schools for a company. It meant she worked in buildings when they were empty, so she saw no one. She had a few friends she said, but didn't elaborate – I couldn't help but think she wasn't being honest. She definitely wanted us to think she was fine, managing – happy, even – but she looked the opposite to all of that. Her entire being felt consumed with sadness and regret. Although she looked lovely, smelt good – the way she held herself, the look in her eyes, it felt nothing short of harrowing, and I knew Jo felt it as I did, without even having the conversation.

'OK, my turn,' Jo said. 'Ask me anything.'

And her mum did. She asked her so many questions – mostly about her childhood, what were her adoptive parents like. Did Joseph still love football? Did Kitty still have blonde hair? She asked if they were happy as children, and when Jo told her they were, I could see the joy she got from it – that immediately lessened her pain. The realisation I felt throughout this whole thing kept hitting me over and over – I could have been Barbara. If my boys had been born into poverty, if we'd had more eyes on us, more services probing . . . Of course, I could tell myself that if that had been the case I would have left, chosen to cut contact with David, flee out of the area to keep the boys safe . . . But I hadn't managed to do that with a pretty incredible amount of money in the bank, owned property, supportive, loving parents and a handful of amazing friends. When I was sat here listening to this woman, hearing her story – thinking of all the women living just like her – like you, Martha – I know that the reality is, I probably wouldn't have gone, or stayed away. I most likely would have crumbled, felt so low and worthless about what I couldn't give to the boys, and the pressure and guilt about the life they were living with me, that I may well have handed them over to an organisation who had adopters ready and waiting to give my babies a life I couldn't.

And that's what I was witnessing here. I didn't think for a minute Jo's mum didn't not love Jo, or her siblings – she didn't *not* want them. She just couldn't keep them in the life they were born into – and one I believe she didn't have enough support or care to safely get out of and stay away from.

I left the pod to go to the toilet, and popped outside to call my mum. I don't know why, I just needed to thank her. After seeing Jo and her mum together, I'd realised how loved I was, had always been. The pain my mum had endured when she lost her sister, then me . . . I have said sorry a thousand times, but today, I just wanted to thank her. I wanted her to realise how needed, loved and cared for she is.

We had a few tears, she reciprocated all her love for me, her pride in us for 'getting out', and thanked me for how her life looked now because of the boys and me. It took a minute for that to sink in – the fact that the best thing in my parents' lives, the thing that gives them purpose and happiness, is just the presence of my sons and me. That felt pretty special to me.

I went back in after I'd composed myself. Jo and Babs were still sitting facing each other, their hands clasped together – four hands, one on top of the other, entwined, embraced – like it was always meant to look, I imagine. Their faces less than twenty centimetres apart, both of them trying to take in as much as they could from the other – eyes wide, facial expressions crazy, trying to learn a whole lifetime in two hours.

Jo asked if Babs would like to see pictures of Kitty and Joe. She immediately clasped her hand over her mouth and nodded, welling up again. 'Would that be OK with them?' she checked, always being mindful of her position.

'Of course,' Jo confirmed, opening her phone to slide through an album she'd made called 'Us 3'.

She passed the phone over, and as Babs swiped the photos she repeatedly made an array of sounds such as 'Oh,' 'Ahhh,' and 'Oh, wow.' The whole time, the tears continued to flow that she kept wiping away with her ragged bit of tissue. I reached forward to give her a new one and she patted the back of my hand with hers, still trembling, and said, 'Thank you, for the tissue – but also for all of this, today.' She continued to look through the photos, stopping to bring the phone in closer, move it further away, study different parts by zooming in on most pictures, tapping with her finger. The emotion in the room was so high, but it felt good. It felt nice to even be a part of, to get a glimpse of.

I knew without speaking to Jo she was pleased this had happened. The outcome she got here couldn't have gone better, and I truly believe her and Babs will build bridges. I hope they go on to have the incredible relationship they both (I think) need and deserve. They were chatting about the future – Jo was talking about when Babs meets other family members and visits Cornwall, and I could see that Babs was totally blown away by that prospect – as if it was all a dream she didn't want to wake up from.

We left around 12.30 p.m. and walked into town to get lunch. We grabbed sandwiches from a little M&S and sat on a bench in the park. The sun was shining, and we were shaded from the heat under the trees close by. The polite conversation returned, with Babs asking Jo all about the baking that she does for the café. She was intrigued where she'd learned to bake, and was genuinely interested in how Jo had learned all her skills from her adoptive mum once upon a time. There was no animosity, no weird vibe or odd questions or remarks; it was all just feel-good chat where two people – one woman who had brought the other one into the world – were just getting to know each other, and getting high off the things they were learning as time went on.

I asked if they'd be OK if I made a few calls. Both happily said they'd be fine, so I went for a little walk. I didn't have any calls to make, and I was sure from the atmosphere that Jo was fine with me giving her some time alone.

I wandered round the large lake, which had three huge swans swimming across it. I stopped and tried to piece together their dynamic – three female friends, or sisters? A mum, dad and rather large baby? Three brothers? Did they even know each other? I caught myself studying the swan trio and wondered why I have to pick everything to pieces and question things. I wonder if one day I'll ever just think, *Cute swans*, and walk by like everyone else seems to do, without questioning every part of a swan's life, how they are feeling, whether they're happy or sad, lonely or fulfilled, the same as when I see so many things in life, be it human, animals, insects or even pieces of fruit and veg.

I just want to not overthink if a potato is in pain because I peeled its skin off. Honestly.

I left them for almost half an hour, and when I returned, they were still chatting away, really trying their hardest to cram a lifetime of conversation in just a few hours.

We had to leave. I had to get back, as I'd promised I would collect Woody from Mum and Dad this afternoon.

We left. I gave Babs a huge hug and thanked her for coming. She felt fragile, as if she would snap if I squeezed her too tight. She was still shaking, but not as much. She thanked me for arranging everything and sorting it out. I offered her a lift home, but she said she wanted to catch the bus, as the ride would help her to calm down and process the day.

She turned to face Jo. They hugged, and she whispered, 'I'm truly sorry. I wish I did things differently, but I'm so pleased you are who you are. You're perfect, Josephine.'

Jo reminded her she didn't need to say sorry. She asked if she could text her later, when she got home, and Babs replied with, 'Any time, any time at all.'

They squeezed hands and then I linked Jo's left arm into my right and rubbed the back of her hand with the palm of mine. 'OK?' I asked her as we began to walk.

'OK,' she confirmed, smiling up to the sky and letting out a huge sigh.

The drive home was intense. Jo repeated everything they'd spoken about, mainly, I think, because if she told me it was another person who knew, in case she forgot stuff. Part of me thinks they should have both taken pens and paper, made notes about everything they spoke about. They had so much to remember, to process and make sense of, that I honestly think Jo was terrified about forgetting stuff. She was repeating as much as possible to me in the hope that saying it all would somehow make it soak into her brain better.

She told me they spoken about her biological dad when I'd left them to walk around the lake. Babs hadn't been forthcoming in chatting about him, but this made Jo feel better – it showed what kind of person her mum was more, I think. Jo had asked her about the reports which had stated she got beaten, that he beat Joseph.

Her mum admitted all of this was true. She said she would spend days in bed from her injuries, but also because her mental health was so bad that some days she just couldn't function. This, she said, was what in the end made her know her children needed more, needed better than what they had right then and there. It was never about whether they were loved; she was battling against something at that time she felt she couldn't win. It wasn't about giving up her kids, it was about allowing them to have what they deserved and needed. I got that. I got it so badly that my heart wrecked for her, for my boys, and for me. For the first time, I grieved me, and what life could and should have looked like for my children and me. I cried.

I'm crying now, writing this to you, knowing you will understand exactly what I mean.

Goodnight, Martha. I can't wait to see you again.

# Eighteen years old

Harry was born at 7.21 p.m. last night. He has bright blue eyes and a mop of red hair.

I went into labour around 4 p.m. I called David on his mobile, but it was off, and he has told me under no circumstances to call the office as he is at court this week and calling would be pointless. When the pain began to worsen, I thought about ringing them, just because I feel there must be some way they'd have been able to contact the court to inform him I was in labour, but I remembered his warning, and knew it wouldn't be worth the possible outcome.

My waters went.

I called the hospital and they told me to get to the labour suite as soon as possible.

I called David again – his phone was still off.

I called a taxi. It arrived, and I managed to hobble to it with one of my bags.

Alone.

That word feels like it explains my entire personality.

*Alone.*

I climbed in the back seat and began trying to regulate my breathing, but I couldn't. I should have been in an ambulance. I couldn't work out which form of transport I would be in more trouble with David for using – I thought he would accuse me of being dramatic and trying to make him look bad if I called an ambulance, but now I was worrying he would go mad that I hadn't called an ambulance and hadn't thought of the risk if this all went to shit. I had all of these thoughts darting round my head whilst my baby was desperately trying to exit my vagina.

The driver was panicking. He kept asking if he should pull over, call someone. The only person I wanted to call was my mum. I wanted to cry to her, tell her I was scared . . . I needed her to know that I wanted her, I needed her. But I couldn't. I knew it's not allowed. I knew that, despite the fact David was uncontactable during the time our baby was making his way into the world, two days past his due date, the 'unspoken rules' were that I would give birth alone – which is exactly what I did.

The sun was still beaming through the labour suite window as the baby's perfect 7 lb 6 oz body was placed on mine. He started rooting around on my chest with his mouth within seconds of being placed on me. The midwife told me he was looking to feed and she helped lift his head to latch him onto my nipple, where he stayed, on and off, in and out of sleep, happy and content, until David burst into the room hours later.

He looked emotional at first, but as he leant forward to look, the first thing he said was, 'He's ginger.' He hadn't even lowered his tone, so the midwife heard. I felt like I'd been punched.

'He is,' I replied with a smile, trying to pretend to the listening ears in the room that he was having a joke. I wasn't sure what he was expecting, considering he had chosen to procreate with me. I have a full head of red hair and seventy-four million freckles dotted over my face, and both of those things I had assumed, until yesterday, David loved about me.

The midwife didn't hang around. As soon as she left, David asked what I was doing. I knew he was livid, though I had no idea why – but that's normal by now. My life is a total guessing game.

The feeling of euphoria at meeting my new baby, the pride I felt at my body for working so hard to deliver this perfect miracle, disappeared in less than a minute of David's arrival and it hasn't returned since. It was replaced with a fear of the unknown. In this case, genuine terror at how I should answer his question.

Before I could speak, he said, 'Why are you fucking breastfeeding?' He began ranting about all the bottles that he'd bought, sterilised and packed in the hospital bag. I told him there were three hospital bags and I was only able to carry one of them into the taxi as I was already in labour. 'You should have asked for fucking help, then,' he spat, his face so close to mine that his nose was pressed into my cheek. He started pacing the room and I began apologising. Apologising for breastfeeding our baby, for not bringing all the bags. I feel sick, remembering that vision of us now.

He started ranting about needing to have his sleep, that he wouldn't be able to focus on his career if I was encouraging 'my fucking kid' to continually wake through the night.

He disappeared out the door. The midwife came in and asked if I was OK. I said I was. I was crying; it was clear to both of us I was anything other than OK. She asked where David had gone and I said to collect the rest of my belongings. She didn't comment. I couldn't tell if she could see what was happening or not, and I was totally overwhelmed with all these thoughts, feelings and hormones.

David returned forty minutes later with the two other hospital bags and began unpacking the bottles and box of formula. I could see he was seething, so I edged myself out of the bed and placed Harry in the see-through plastic crib next to me. I was unsteady on my feet. I felt dizzy and exhausted, and as I fumbled to hold on to the table to steady myself he said, 'Don't make a fucking meal out of it, Louise,' through gritted teeth, as he was scooping heaped spoonfuls of powder into a plastic bottle.

I'm not sure I'll ever forget how he said that.

When I look back at yesterday, and as I write this now, I feel so angry at myself. I feel raging that I'm not screaming for help, that I didn't tell him to get the fuck out, latch my baby back onto my breast and just fall asleep together . . . But I didn't. I can't.

Instead, I apologised again. I waited for the kettle to boil and poured in the water to complete the bottle of milk our baby hated drinking. He fussed and whinged and struggled with the teat and David said, 'He's probably not hungry because you've pumped him full of the breast milk we agreed he wasn't having,' before he walked out again.

Another midwife appeared. She was older, I'd say in her sixties. She had a strong Irish accent and a natural grey pristine bob. 'Hello, my darling,' she said to me before removing my notes from the bottom of my bed and reading through them. 'Oh,' she continued. 'It says here that you're breastfeeding and baby latched on well?'

'Yes,' I replied, trying to think of what excuse I could come up with that I was currently trying to force a bottle into my baby's mouth that he absolutely didn't want or need. Instead, I just rolled with what I thought was the truth. 'My husband works long hours, he has a busy career and we've decided bottle feeding will be best as we can get him into a proper routine.'

She smiled at me and perched on the end of my bed, my notes splayed out across her thighs. 'My lovely, there is no such thing as a routine in newborns. It doesn't matter how they're fed, they'll likely wake at all the inconvenient hours because they don't understand those hours are inconvenient. This baby wants his mummy's milk, he's shown that. Now, if you decide you don't want him to have it, that's OK, but just promise me it's you making that decision, no one else.'

My eyes filled up, which she saw. She stroked my ankle and whispered, 'There's help if you want it.'

The door swung open and David appeared. 'Has he drunk it yet?' he asked, looking at the full bottle of formula I'd replaced on the bedside cabinet.

'I'll leave you to it,' said the midwife, letting go of my ankle. I wanted to beg her not to leave, I wanted to grab her hand and drag her back and get her to convince David to allow me to keep feeding my baby. I didn't want her to go out of the room, because I was frightened of what might happen afterwards . . . But she did.

David told me I'd be leaving with him within the next hour. He had spoken to the doctor, who had agreed I was fit and well with no complications, and could go home.

I felt devastated, and scared. God, I felt so unbelievably scared.

I asked if I could call my mum. David scoffed. Again. He said I could send her a text, which he wanted to check the content of before I sent it. He checks all the texts I send to my mum because he says he doesn't trust her – I don't even understand what that means.

Mum replied immediately:

**Congratulations to you all. Dad and I can't wait to meet your precious boy. We can't wait hear more from you.**

I felt hurt that she didn't try to call, which David took great pleasure in pointing out. He said it was the reason he only wanted to send her a text with our news, because it was all she was worthy of, as a text was all she sent back.

I don't know what to think. I can't help wonder why she didn't call me straight away and ask to see us. It's what I would have expected . . . I wish she would just turn up at the house unannounced, on a bad day – and take me and Harry back to Cornwall with her. I wish she could see what was happening without me having to tell her.

I didn't reply to her, because I knew I'd have to ask permission to do so and I wouldn't get it, and also because I did truly feel hurt that she'd only responded by text. I mean, I absolutely don't want her to call – in fact, I was petrified of her calling as I didn't know how David would react if she did, then I wouldn't know what I should or shouldn't say. I worry she will ask to come and visit . . . But the reality is, these are all of the things I was gearing up for as soon as I pressed 'Send' with my original message. I expected the calls, the questions, the intrigue. My heart was pumping with adrenaline, waiting for that kind of response from her, so when I was met with a twenty-one-word text back, I felt rejected.

David carried on ripping her apart for all the things she hasn't done, such as immediately calling us, asking to visit us, asking his name, his weight. He just went on this mad rampage, shouting about how awful my parents are, how infuriating I am that I can't see their true colours, and that I still bother with them. He continued to rant until I asked him to calm down in case he woke the baby – and to my surprise, he immediately became emotional. He perched on the end of the bed and began crying. It was the first time I'd ever seen him cry. He was looking up to the ceiling whilst the fattest tears were streaming down his cheeks. He kept saying, 'I'm just so sorry that they are what you got given as parents,' whilst I scooted down the bed to comfort him. I felt so confused and tired.

As soon as we got home, David went to the office, and I am lying here working out what the fuck has happened since I gave birth. Picturing that last hour in the hospital, mainly – how I sat there, in masses of pain from giving birth, stroking David's back, consoling him, in the hope I can make him feel better about how terrible my parents are. My head feels like mashed potato or rice pudding, like someone is lifting off the top of my head and just stirring inside my whole mind with a wooden spoon. I have no idea who is right or wrong, who cares about and loves me and who doesn't. I feel so overwhelmingly confused and sad. But even though I am on the verge of tears with it all, I know I can't cry, in case David comes back unexpectedly from the office and sees me. I know without doubt crying wouldn't be allowed. I would be accused of crying for the wrong reasons – and I no longer know what is right and wrong in terms of my reasons to cry, so I have learned to clench my jaw so hard my entire skull shakes, and hold it together.

My boobs are so huge and sore and are just dripping milk constantly. I desperately want Harry to take the milk, but instead I'm making bottles of formula he hates that I will continue to give him against his will.

I feel like such a fucking failure.

# FRIDAY

I went shopping this morning and bought the bits for Woody you asked for, which I'll bring up tomorrow. The police have called Mags as they want to come and speak with you about the charges against Craig and next steps.

It makes me feel sick.

Meg said she came to see you today. She said Tabby was with you when she arrived. Tabby is the kindest support worker at the unit and really spiritual – I feel like she's really helping you stay positive and focused at the minute. She was giving you a hand massage, meditating with you in the garden, when Meg got there, and Meg said you were proper chilled and calm.

She said you were buzzing about seeing Woody yesterday and were so positive, which makes my heart feel so happy. I am excited to bring him again tomorrow. He has made a Duplo dragon, which he can't wait to show you. It's basically a tower of bricks that I stuck some red and yellow crêpe paper on for fire, and Sharpied some eyes on the top brick, but to him it's a work of art and he has put it next to the front door ready to bring you when he wakes up tomorrow. I know you're going to love it. I can't wait for him to see how super excited and impressed you will be when he presents it to you!

## Rachaele Hambleton

I really want to cancel going to the reunion tomorrow night, but I also know that Dan is expecting me to come. And maybe it will be nice to see everyone after all these years.

# Eighteen years old

I saw my parents today.

We met them halfway, at a park. Harry is exactly three weeks old.

They offered to come to us, but David refused, saying we would like to make the effort to join them.

We met at lunchtime. It was warm, perfect weather to be out all day. The heat wasn't overbearing and there was a gentle breeze in the air.

Mum brought a picnic blanket and some fold-out chairs, and Dad carried the big wicker hamper across to us. I felt consumed with emotion when I saw them, but knew I had to hold it together. Mum hugged me so tight. I breathed in her familiar scent, then went to Dad. He pulled me into him. He felt so safe, he smelt safe . . . Everything about Dad has always been safe. The clean, fresh scent of his aftershave, mixed with the warmth of his hug. I don't think there have ever been nicer, safer smells than the scent of my parents.

They both cooed over Harry, overcome with emotion and telling each other about all his features like I wasn't there. 'Look at his button nose.' 'Look at his long lashes.' 'Look at his red hair, just like our Lou.' They went on and on. David nodded at them both to greet them, then stood with his back to them and began unstrapping sleeping Harry from his pram (something he had never done before) and rocking him in his arms. Harry woke instantly and began fussing before he started full-blown screaming. I could tell from Mum's face what she was thinking – exactly the same as me, that David didn't have a clue what he was doing and was upsetting Harry for no reason – all whilst Dad busied himself shaking the picnic blanket out on the grass and opening the hamper to sort the food and drinks.

As usual, Mum had put on the most incredible spread. God, I miss her food. Homemade gammon ham, pickles and cheeses, with a crusty loaf and local fresh apple juice from her friends' farm. She pulled out the plates and glasses, napkins and cutlery, and said, 'Help yourselves,' before she held her arms out to me to take the baby. I was hesitant. Harry was still crying and I wasn't sure he would settle for her – although he never settled for me either. 'Eat,' she said. 'And you, David – help yourself, love,' she added, as if she didn't secretly want him to be struck by lightning on the spot.

I could sense David wasn't happy with the situation, but in less than a minute Mum was rocking, shhh-ing and singing whilst she walked around the picnic blanket. Lullabies I faintly remembered and nursery rhymes that brought back strong memories of being small. Mum settled back into her camping chair and snuggled Harry into her chest. Dad reached over to her, breathed in Harry's baby scent and said to us, 'He's absolutely perfect.'

Mum nodded and confirmed, 'He really is. A miracle,' before I caught her head turn away in the hope I wouldn't see her wipe away the tear which fell down onto her cheek.

David spent the majority of the time talking business, covering the cases he'd succeeded in and all of the events he was due to speak at – all of which my parents lapped up and appeared impressed with. Their acting skills were pretty impressive, I thought. He didn't eat or drink, and I wondered whether he would be annoyed I was scoffing my face.

Harry lay on Mum for the next hour, fast asleep and more content than he had been in the entire twenty-one days he's spent on the planet so far. Eventually, he began fussing, so I started getting a bottle ready. Mum said, 'How is he feeding?'

David interrupted, on the defence, saying, 'We decided on bottle over breastfeeding so I can support Lou and we can get him in more of a routine.'

Mum replied with a far too long, 'Rigghhht . . .' whilst I wondered how David felt about the fact both he and I knew he was lying – as, to date, he hasn't fed Harry one bottle or changed any of his nappies. At most he will 'watch him' whilst I quickly shower, and most times that has resulted in him shouting at me to hurry up as Harry was crying.

'Well, then, we best make a move,' David said, after we'd been in my parents' company for an hour and forty minutes.

'Oh,' Dad said, before he thought to hide his upset. 'I thought we could have a walk and feed the ducks?'

'Gotta get back, unfortunately – don't want to hit the traffic. And I have so much work to get through,' David shot back.

'Well, it's been lovely to see the three of you,' Mum cut in. 'Perhaps next time we could come to you, and then we could stay for a bit longer?'

'I'd love that, Mum,' I said, my voice cracking with the pain I felt at them going so soon and knowing deep down that David would never allow them to visit us.

'Well, that's settled then,' she soothed, rubbing the back of my hand to let me know she knew. I wanted to squeeze her hand back, so she could feel my love, but I sensed David's eyes penetrating through me so I stopped myself.

I handed Harry to Dad after his bottle, as David was on a phone call, not far enough away for me to speak freely, but far enough to know I could get away with allowing my dad a quick cuddle. Dad put Harry over his shoulder whilst he rubbed and patted his back until Harry gave a ginormous belch that made us laugh, before he fell back into a deep sleep. Lying on Dad's chest with his little mouth open and his eyelids moving frantically, dreaming about the unknown.

David returned and politely ordered me to get Harry back in his pram. None of us protested. It was like we all knew better. Instead, we just all followed the rules, me pretending I was happy, David fully embracing my act, and my parents, I imagine, experiencing déjà vu from Aunt Peggy.

They followed us to the car and as David bent into the car to slot the car seat in, Mum mouthed silently to me, 'We love you and we're here,' and I couldn't stop the tears. I would have given anything at that point to have climbed in the back of their car with Harry and gone home with them, where I would have felt safe and loved and cared for – all the things I hadn't felt since being with David and leaving them. But I also know that I made this choice, that Harry is also David's baby, that my emotions are chaotic right now, and that going with my parents is just not even an option.

'Bloody hormones,' David snapped. 'I can't wait for you to get back to normal!'

'Sorry!' I laughed, wiping my tears and hugging my dad.

'We mean it,' Dad whispered into my ear. I was terrified David would have heard that, but part of me also hoped he did. Part of me hoped he lost it in front of them so they could see what a monster he can be, and so they would take me and Harry back with them. Instead, he outstretched his hand for my dad to shake, and gave my mum a five-second awkward hug before waiting for me to climb in the car. Then he shut the door behind me and walked round to the driver's side. As he sped off in a rage, my parents – stood on the pavement, waving to me – went from wearing fake smiles to shocked expressions . . . and then they were out of sight.

I heard the smack before I felt it. And I saw the blood before I recognised which part of my face was injured. He had elbowed me with such force, he had split my ear.

'I saw her fucking fake tears!' he began screaming. 'Stupid slag that can't cook, having to sit there and eat her shit food!'

He hadn't even tried the food. He refused to eat anything, making the whole situation feel so awkward.

I got Harry's muslin square out of the changing bag at my feet and held it to my ear to try and stop the blood flow, but it just kept soaking more up. I knew if I messed up the car interior with my injuries it would wind David up even more. I was crying – but quietly. I was so worried about the baby waking that I didn't say anything. David then grabbed a handful of my curls with his left fist and smashed my face into the dashboard, screaming, 'Fucking answer me!' The pain seared through my nose, which was also now pumping blood all over my white linen trousers. I scrambled for the wet wipes from the changing bag, petrified about the blood staining David's car seats, whilst repeatedly whispering, 'I'm sorry.'

'You'd best be sorry. You three, thinking you can make me look like a fucking mug. Clean your mess up,' was his response.

We drove the remainder of the car journey in silence, our newborn baby blissfully sleeping through another savage attack.

All I could feel was some kind of hope that Harry would get to have a relationship with my parents, and be loved by two safe people, if David killed me.

Maybe one day he will . . .

# SATURDAY

How lush was today? For you to spend four whole hours with Woody. It was so heartwarming to see. Watching you mum that boy is mesmerising, Martha. I took some videos without you seeing, of you building more Duplo and chatting about all the big and small stuff. He asked so many questions that you answered with ease. I can just tell what an honour you find it to be his mum. I brought him a packed lunch and the staff brought your lunch out to the garden, and you had a picnic together on the blanket. It was the most wholesome thing to watch. I feel like parts of me I didn't know still needed healing are doing so because of you. I'm watching you be this determined mum whilst you're living in turmoil, and it just brings back so many memories. The stuff we have to get through and manage when we come out of abusive relationships is just shit.

I hope you loved the videos of you both that I sent you when I got home this afternoon. I hope it made you see what an amazing mum you are. I can really feel things getting better for you. The positive days are happening, and although you're still having to work hard every day to get well, you're putting in everything you have to do it so you can get home with Woody. I am so proud of you.

Mum and Dad picked the boys up at 2 p.m. Turns out, they've come up with a plan. They asked if I would like to house swap, with the intention that you could then come and stay with us in their house when you leave the rehab unit. I immediately said no, but then we chatted – and they said their house is so big, they're rattling round in it most days, and other than George staying over, they feel it's pointless having so much space. If I'm there, the boys will all have their own rooms, plus there's another spare you can have when you come out. They will also be right on the beach if they're in the apartment, and it's much smaller, so Mum can keep on top of the cleaning more easily. I don't know how you'll feel about it – maybe it will be something you absolutely don't want to do. I imagine you will want to get back to your house and routine with Woody ASAP once you leave the centre. But I will speak to you about it and see what you think.

Jo and I went to get our nails done this afternoon, when the boys left. They're both sleeping at my parents' tonight as I have the reunion. I did worry about Woody staying there, but since he's been with me he's seen my parents every day and idolises them, so he will be so excited to stay there with George.

I feel so sick about it. Jo helped me pick some outfits. It's so weird, dressing up. I never go anywhere that requires me to wear anything other than comfies and trainers, so it feels so odd to know I'm going to be in a dress and heels tonight with make-up on . . . and the thought of who might be there is making my tummy flip. Jo is going to help me get ready tonight – she's brought a bottle of wine – and Dan's collecting me at 7 p.m. It starts at eight, but we're going to go and get a drink first to calm my nerves, which are worsening by the second.

Anyway, I'd better go . . . Wish me luck!

# Thirty years old

This hospital feels different to the ones I am used to in London. It was easy to move between hospitals up there, and whenever I had to go, they just had a quick chat, believed all the lies I told them, then they'd repair me and send me on my way. But now we're back in Cornwall, I think it will be different. I had a doctor come and speak to me and it was like he could see into my soul. He was the kindest, most genuine doctor I have ever met, and is the only person to date I've almost disclosed the truth to.

I have a broken wrist, and bruising to the entire top half of my body. I need an operation to pin my arm.

The social worker arrived shortly after the doctor called her, and asked David to leave the room for the second time so she could speak to me alone. The panic in me was on par with the panic I saw in David for the first time ever. I was aware he would know he hadn't prepped me for this happening. The doctor had already spoken to me alone, which hadn't really bothered him, but we'd never got to this point before, where things had led to a social worker rocking up. David had assumed that, like always, the hospital staff would buy our story and we'd be on our way. The story this time was that I had lost my balance on a ladder, whilst watering the hanging baskets we didn't even have.

I thought David might refuse to leave, become argumentative ... but instead, like a pro, he said, 'Of course, absolutely,' then gave me a kiss on the forehead and said, 'I've got some work calls to make, darling, so I'll go and grab a coffee. Just call me when you're done.'

The social worker had been called by a member of staff at the hospital who was concerned my injuries didn't match my story. Of course I played the game and reassured her that I had absolutely fallen from the ladder, and I was happily married, and my husband would never hurt me or my children.

Throughout our chat she stood towering over me with her bag on her shoulder and her pen and pad in hand. She continued to check her watch every few minutes, and her mobile phone pinged continuously, which she huffed at every time. She let me convince her, with total ease, that my amazing, well-respected solicitor husband was just that. She lapped it all up and apologised to me for having been called to come in. And then she left. Case closed, before it was even opened.

When she left, I sent a message to David to tell him, and he was back in the room within thirty seconds – coffee and work calls, my arse.

He quizzed me on what she'd asked. I am confident he didn't actually hear what she'd said, or how I responded. Even though I have a bed on a ward, and the woman hadn't bothered to pull the curtains closed to give me the privacy I probably would have wanted, should I have confessed that these injuries were actually caused by my husband sexually assaulting me while I lay face down on the kitchen floor. That my wrist was broken by him smashing it with the wrought-iron fire poker and, as I managed to push myself up off the floor with my other hand and tried to run, him grabbing me from behind and dragging me back to the floor, meaning I landed on the already broken wrist and broke it some more. I am confident he didn't hear, because as the woman towered over me and began asking me her tick-box questions, I watched him walk out of the heavy glass-framed fire door on the opposite side of the room, quite far away, and I gauged that even if he was stood on the other side, listening, he wouldn't have been able to hear over the business of all the people on the ward and the buzzes and bleeps of the machinery everywhere.

I told David someone at the hospital had reported my injuries to the authorities and had concerns I was lying about how I got them. That was the truth. He then asked if the social worker had believed me when I told her I was telling the truth. I told him I wasn't sure. I mean, I was absolutely sure she believed me – I'd put my life on the fact she most probably won't ever give me a second thought ever again. So that was a lie. The first lie I have ever told in our thirteen-year relationship.

But it was a lie that I am praying may make things better – because it was the first time I have seen him panic, properly panic, about people knowing who he really is. About people talking, and about me maybe gaining the strength to speak up. Part of me was concerned about the doctor, though. I know he thinks there's something more to it, and I can't help but feel guilt for that – because he knows I'm lying, he thinks I am a liar. Does that make me a bad person?

I just need to ensure I do whatever it takes so I don't come back to this hospital again.

# SUNDAY

I'm so sorry we missed seeing you this morning. Woody has a fever (he seems fine, although I don't want to risk making you unwell!), but I have so much to tell you! I don't even know where to start. I feel like I haven't felt in almost twenty years . . . but I can't quite work out what I feel. Happy? Excited? Anxious? (But a good anxious, if that makes sense?)

So, Dan arrived to pick me up at 6.40 p.m. last night, far too early – I wasn't ready, so he came in for a drink. Jamie had arrived to pick up Jo, so the guys sat in the lounge together whilst Jo finished curling my hair in the bedroom. Jo was so excited for me to be going out. It feels so lush to have a friend who totally roots for you doing the simplest of things because she knows how huge they feel to you.

I wore an emerald-green dress. It went well with my skin tone and red hair. I teamed it with some heels I'd ordered from Zara in a tan colour with clear Perspex straps. Sounds gross, but they looked good, I thought. I felt nice when I looked in the mirror – pretty, even. I haven't felt pretty in so long.

Woody forgot his muslin, which he can't sleep without, so Mum called in to grab it. She came into the bedroom and started crying when she saw me. That made me feel sad, and special.

To be honest, I felt a bit overwhelmed with her reaction, but then I realised she's never seen me dress up as an adult. In fact, I've never really dressed up like this as an adult – except for my wedding. But Mum wasn't at our wedding. David decided he wanted us to do it alone. No family. Even if Mum had attended, I doubt her tears would have been from happiness. And since then, I've raised kids just wearing clothes that keep me invisible, making as little effort as possible with my appearance. I'd forgotten how it feels to look pretty.

Mum went in the lounge and spoke to Dan for ages – about him, his mum. I could tell from their conversation she still misses Ange. That's the thing with life, isn't it? None of us know what's coming next, or how long we have left of the situation we're in. When it was time to leave, Mum gave us all kisses and I walked her down through the café to say goodbye. She started welling up at the door, held my cheeks in her palms and said, 'If only Peg could have made the choice you did. I am so proud of you, my darling.'

My mum has only ever had two girls in her life who she's adored – her sister and me. And she lost us both to abusive men. I am just thankful one of us escaped – and she has me back for good again. I am so lucky, to be loved by her like I am. I wish Aunt Peggy could be here too.

Jo was tipsy as we were leaving the flat. She called home, and Belle and her boyfriend said they were fine to babysit the younger ones, so she and Jamie walked into town with me and Dan for a drink. We went to Gloria's bar for cocktails – we all chose espresso martinis. I've never tried one before, but I felt like if you had more than one, you'd be awake with the caffeine for days. I felt ridiculously nervous by this point, and I was enjoying the four of us hanging out so much that I wanted to stay. But just before 8.30, Dan reminded me we had a reunion to attend . . .

Jo gave me the 'You are worthy' pep talk I didn't know I needed; Jamie gave me the best big-brother-feeling hug and forehead kiss; and I linked arms with one of my oldest best friends and tottered to the function room of the local pub, home to so many of our younger memories.

I felt like I was going to hurl, walking in. It was busier than I'd expected, and there were faces I didn't recognise. I wasn't sure if it was because two decades had passed and everyone had aged, or because there were a load of people here who had joined the group after I'd left. The first person I recognised was Rachel – the ex-girlfriend of my first boyfriend, Jason, who once upon a time was a total bitch to me at school, but who became a close friend in college when we realised a boy isn't worth falling out over – especially the boy *we* had fallen out over. Rachel came running over and literally picked me up in excitement. It felt genuine, like she was super happy to see me. She didn't ask me any awkward questions – in fact, as the evening went on, no one asked me any awkward questions about David or the trial – despite what I'd set myself up for.

Within minutes, more people had come over to chat to Rachel, and me, and it felt nice. My anxiety lessened, because I quickly realised that all these people had simply been living their lives for years and years, and there was so much to talk about and catch up on that actually, it was really easy to divert the conversations to someone else and not talk about myself at all.

And then it happened. I heard him before I saw him, and although it has been almost twenty years since I last spoke to him, as soon as I heard the words, 'Hey, Lou,' I knew. My heart plummeted to my knees, and I looked up and felt like I was about to faint. I reached forward to steady myself on the edge of the bar, overwhelmed with emotion.

It was Tom. Tom, who had broken my heart; Tom, who had given me the most memorable summer I'd ever had in my life.

'It's good to see you. How are you?' he asked.

I was so shocked, I couldn't find my voice. Why hadn't Dan told me he was coming? He wasn't even a long-term member of the group – it hadn't even entered my brain that he might show up. Yet here he was, still as beautiful as the last time I saw him – the same perfect olive skin, just with new fine lines round his eyes when he smiled at me. His cheeks were stubbled, and his dark hair was woven with grey, which made him seem even more attractive. He looked so cool, like he'd made no effort and a shitload all at the same time, if that's possible. He smelt like nothing I've ever smelt before . . . I wanted to rip his shirt off and take it home, and spend forever inhaling it. My entire body was buzzing, and I wasn't sure if it was the wine and espresso martini, or seeing him again.

I finally managed to find my voice and assured him I was good, even though I was anything but good. My hands began to shake, my legs felt weak and my brain couldn't process what was happening. As I steadied myself against the bar with a fake smile, I scanned the room for his stunning wife, feeling like at that point I could have been Alanis Morrisette singing 'Ironic'. But I mean, the room was full of beautiful women, many of whom I didn't recognise, so I just bit the bullet with my first word:

'Married?' I asked, still smiling like a twat.

He giggled – *god*, I thought, *he's so fucking good-looking*.

'No, not married,' he replied – still smirking.

I wasn't sure where to steer the conversation at that point, or how to slow my heart rate down, so when Dan appeared I simply said, 'You didn't mention Tom was coming.'

'Thought I'd keep it a surprise,' he said, as if that was somehow a good idea.

Dan bought a round of drinks and I remember wondering how Dan would just know what Tom drinks, considering he hadn't had a drink in his hand when Dan ordered. I realised they must be friends. And then I realised that by this point, I'd told Dan everything about my situation – and I'd gone pretty deep about everything that happened with David. Despite us not seeing each other for almost twenty years, Dan's still one of my favourite people to talk to. He makes it easy to say what you feel, what you truly feel, without the worry of any judgement. But at that point, I started panicking about everything I'd said, and wondered if he'd told Tom about it . . .

But I didn't have time to panic further because immediately, it became chaos, with so many of my friends from my teenage years coming up to me, giving me massive hugs and cheek kisses. I genuinely felt that they were happy I was there. I felt that they knew what had happened to me. I mean, I knew that everyone must know, because they were all asking about the boys – their ages, names – all of that – so I figured if they knew about the boys, they knew about their dad, and my situation. And although no one mentioned anything, I got the feeling they were all rooting for me, the way they smiled at me, gave me hand squeezes, or ensured I felt included the whole time I was there.

Being in Tom's company made me feel like fireworks were going off inside my body. As much as I was joining in with the reunion and chatting to everyone, I was also trying to process how I had ended up here – and how he had, too, after all these years.

I stopped drinking by 9.30 p.m. as I was pretty pissed and didn't want to make a dick of myself. When the event ended around 11 p.m. I felt a little tipsy still. We all walked to the shop in town – I'd never been there before, but apparently it's the only takeaway that stays open until late. I didn't know what to order – kebabs hadn't been a thing in our tiny Cornish town back when I was young enough to rock up to takeaways at close to midnight, pissed. Tom recommended the chicken shish kebab so I went with that. He ordered the same, with a side of cheesy chips. When it came, it was all in one bag, together, and he scooped it off the side. Weirdly, Tom and I hugged and kissed everyone goodbye together, as if we were a married couple. Everyone was drunkenly making dates to meet again, and we were all promising that this would be a regular thing. Dan gave me a huge drunk hug and told me he loved me, then pointed at Tom and said, 'Get her home safely, buddy.'

Tom replied, 'Roger that,' and we left them awaiting their kebabs.

We strolled the five-minute walk back to my flat, without either of us mentioning that was what we were doing. I asked him all about his family. I'd loved his family when we'd spent that summer together. He told me that they all still live in London – on the north side. Both his parents are still alive – his dad's in his eighties, but still really fit and well. His mum is sixty-five and he says she's got the most amazing life. His sisters are doing well, both married with kids, and he clearly loves being an uncle. He told me that he'd never married, or had kids. I think he married his job, by the sounds of it. He's a heart surgeon, like his dad was – of course he is. I mean, I say he married his job, because he made it sound that way, but everything in me is still wondering if he has a wife and kids hidden away.

He came in – again, we didn't talk about it. I just opened the door and we walked through the café and up to the flat. In hindsight, I wonder why I wasn't panicking about how he'd behave – I mean, I've spent just eight weeks of my whole life on this planet with this guy – a very, very long time ago – yet here I was, just casually bringing him back to my home . . . I went to get plates for the food, and Tom just grinned and said to save the washing up, because he reckons kebabs taste better from the paper. We sat in the window seat, looking over the harbour at all the pretty lights in the dark, and watching the few people strolling back to their hotels and holiday apartments from the incredible restaurants and bars we have dotted around the marina.

'He called me,' he said.

'Who, Dan?' I asked, thinking he was talking about Dan having invited him to reunite us.

'David.'

'What?' I gasped, unable to process what I knew was coming next.

'I called you a few times, I left a voicemail after a couple of weeks on your landline after I didn't hear back from you. And then David called me to tell me he was seeing you, and he warned me not to contact you again, as you didn't want to hear from me. It weirded me out, because I didn't know how he'd got my number. But you hadn't returned my call, so I did what I was told and I left you alone – I'm so sorry.'

It was like I'd been shot. I was so confused: on the one hand, I was raging at my parents for not telling me about that message – but back then, the answerphone would get so many messages, and they wouldn't have known I was desperate for a call from Tom. They probably just cleared it and forgot, but I can't imagine them doing that – they would always make notes on the pad next to the phone of who had called. They were at work all the time then as it was summer, and I can't help but think that David would have played it and deleted it as he was at the house with me all the time – we would be in the garden sunbathing and he would forever be popping inside to the toilet, for a drink . . . I started picturing how things would have looked for me if I had got Tom's message, and he and I had stayed in touch. I felt sick – my life could have been completely different.

So I told Tom the full story – all of it. I know he would have heard parts, but the truth is, I've never told anyone out loud. My friends know bits because they were there, but in a small town like ours, rumours circulate and things get spread around that often aren't completely true. I didn't feel uncomfortable, I didn't worry he would judge me or think badly of me, which has always happened before with anyone I've told, even my closest friends. I just talked, and he listened, and at times we paused for me to catch my breath or for him to wipe away the tears that he didn't try to hide from me. And then when I was done, I said, 'So now you know.'

'So now I know,' he said, and scooted over towards me, pulling me into his chest. I let the whole weight of my head be held against his chest. And as he stroked my hair and I inhaled his scent, I began to cry, then sob. I felt so . . . relieved. The pressure of him holding me felt so good, and I realised in that moment it was the first time as an adult woman that I have ever felt safe, and myself, around a man other than my dad. I wanted to stay there, like that, being held and seen and heard, forever.

We changed position once I'd gathered myself, and I sat with my back resting into his chest, both of us looking out to sea and talking. We talked for three hours about everything and nothing – and we laughed, fuck me, we laughed so hard! I kept thinking of the times I've spent with Jo and Jamie, and how often I've thought how lucky they are to make each other laugh – like it's so unusual to have that kind of relationship . . . But perhaps it's not; perhaps couples laugh all the time, I've just never seen it.

At 2 a.m., Tom said he would leave. I felt disappointed, but I was also terrified that I felt disappointed. I've done so well alone, and the reality is that I don't ever want to put myself in a position where a man can hurt me again. So I stood up to see him out. He picked up the takeaway remnants off the table and walked them to the kitchen. 'I'll do that,' I said.

'No, you won't,' he laughed, as he put everything back in the carrier bag and tied a knot in the top. 'I'll take this with me and put it in an outside bin; you won't want to wake up to the smell of kebab in the morning.'

I giggled, realising this was the first man other than my dad who had ever done something like this for me. And then we hugged again – another huge hug, where Tom's broad shoulders and massive arms just enveloped my whole body. He kissed my forehead and said, 'I don't want to put any pressure on you, but I wrote my number on your calendar and I'll happily wait forever for you to call.'

I laughed again, and then just kept smiling.

'You are amazing, Lou, and I am so sorry I listened to him and didn't call you again.' As the words left his mouth, it felt like he was looking into my soul to see what I felt.

It floored me. I burst into tears – I don't know how I had any left. Tom held me again and just kept shushing me, the same way I did to my boys so many times when things were bad, the same way my dad did to my mum when Aunt Peggy died. It was the first time any man has ever held me and shushed me to help me heal. I was buried into his whole body, my weight resting into him, and we were stood rocking side to side and I just let it all out. Nothing about it felt wrong or weird, not at the time and not now reflecting back. It was like he was meant to be there – even if nothing ever came of it, I feel like it helped me to heal.

I composed myself for the third time and Tom picked up the takeaway. He opened the door to leave, and squeezed my hand in his. 'I have had the best night,' he said.

'Me too,' I replied.

And then he walked up the street, swinging the takeaway bag in his hand.

I double locked the door and set the alarm, then went back up to the flat. I crossed to the calendar and saw the note that said *'Please call'* with his number. Every part of me wanted to call him right then, and ask him to come back and never leave . . . But he is a surgeon. In London. And this will never work. I have two damaged kids and he's never been married . . . I talked myself out of it all before I finally fell asleep, but even as I drifted off – and even as I'm writing this now – I knew that the only time I have felt a high like this over anyone was when I spent a summer with him as a teenage girl.

That feeling is back, and I don't know how to make it stop.

And I don't know if I want to.

I woke up around 7 a.m. this morning and called my mum. She asked me how the night had been, and kept telling me she was proud of me for going. I told her I would walk up to get the boys, but she said Woody was sleeping and Dad had taken George to see the boats. She told me to rest and that she would call me when Woody woke, so I made a cup of tea then got back into bed.

I had seven messages from the girls at the party – my old friends. All of them made me emotional. All of them acknowledged, in the messages, what they had chosen not to speak about at the party, telling me how amazing I am or how proud they are of me – and all of them asked me to see them again.

And just like that, I feel accepted again – like I have a little bit of me back, and people actually like me. I sipped my tea and sent a message to Tom.

**Fancy a dog walk?**

He replied: **I do . . . see you in half an hour.**

FUCK . . .

# Thirty-two years old

David has been bad lately. He was really good at keeping his temper for so long after I went to hospital. I genuinely thought for a long time that he might never hurt me again. After the hospital incident, he let me reopen my parents' café. They had closed it indefinitely when they left, wanting to be sure that they loved Spain before advertising the lease.

I was so devastated when they left, but I got it, they had nothing to stay here for because we never really saw them and the plan was always for them to retire in the sun when I was grown up. It was always Dad's dream and Mum would always say she wouldn't do it as she wanted to be around for her grandkids, but the reality was that she had no relationship with them other than a few supervised hours every few months under David's watch. As heartbroken as I was inside, I was accepting of their decision. Actually, the pressure it's taken off me by not having to see them under these circumstances, and the freedom from the hurt I have when I watch them with the boys, feeling like I am at fault on both sides from stopping so much love, have been a relief, which fills me with shame.

When I asked them if I could take on the café, they were so happy. And I was happy. I have felt like I've had a purpose since I opened, and word has got round that the food is incredible and that we're child and dog friendly . . . Of course, there isn't a part of David that's happy about this, especially because all of his colleagues pop in most mornings for takeaway coffee. Rather than be proud of me, or happy, he has been accusing me that I'm getting too big for my boots, and he is off the scale with his mood swings again.

It all happened yesterday afternoon at home. David sat on the sofa in the orangery with a beer in hand and the newspaper spread over his lap, rested back against the cushions with his legs out in front of him, crossed at the ankles. A stance he does when he wants to remind us he is in charge. He didn't look up when we walked in. Just that alone – his complete ignoring of the three of us, as if we were completely invisible – was enough for me to know it was going to be a bad day. The violence has definitely got worse since I've had both boys, I feel like he struggles to love them. In fact, he almost hates them at times for different things depending on his moods and chooses to pick fights. Both boys knew too, I could tell. They didn't even react when he didn't greet them, they just said, 'Hi Dad,' as normal, knowing they wouldn't get a reply. Then they cleaned their muddy boots in the utility sink, stripped their kits and tracksuits off, put their water bottles in the dishwasher and headed up to their en-suites to shower, get in PJs and hide in their rooms. By this point, we all knew the drill of what these Sunday afternoons looked like.

David ignored me all day. When I served roast beef at 5 p.m. on the dot, he took his to eat at the other side of the house in the sun lounge, away from the boys and me. I knew at that point that things were spiralling. Harry did too; I knew from the constant eye contact he was making with me. It's weird, when you're in an abusive relationship, how you can sense how bad it's going to be without any words. Just David's body language alone, and the atmosphere he created, always tell me when he is about to blow. It's like a missile that has already been let off. There's nothing you can do to stop it: you just have to wait for the explosion, and pray you recover from it.

As David stormed out of the dining room with his plate of dinner, he pushed Harry out the way, I realised Harry was almost the same height now as David – but broader. He plays rugby every weekend and trains most days; he goes to the school gym every morning with his mates, and what with the other sports he does, he is very fit and muscular for a lad of his age. He looks years older than he is.

We finished eating. The boys put their plates, cutlery and glasses in the dishwasher. Both of them asked me what they could do to help, but I reassured them I was happy to clean up, the three of us all silently knowing I wanted them out the way as quickly as possible. I cleaned everywhere, popped the dishwasher on, then sat back at the dining table with my laptop. I placed an order online for the café with our catering supplier for the next day, and then began arranging the fresh flowers for the reception table in our hallway. David likes the flowers to be changed every Sunday. I often wonder why he wants flowers placed there – as if he is Elton John, greeting the rich and famous – because we never have any visitors or guests other than the postman and delivery drivers to our front door.

I then hoovered, mopped and dusted. As I did all of this, I was just waiting for the start of it to happen. Living on my nerves every single second because I knew what was coming . . .

I went and tucked the boys into bed. They have to get up each day at 6.30 a.m. to be in school early. Private schools mean long days, and we have to leave each day by 7.20 a.m.

David went upstairs and showered, leaving his dirty clothes and towel on our en-suite floor for me to pick up. He left his toothbrush next to the sink rather than back in the cupboard, and the paste on the side with the lid off. He'd spat his gargled mouthwash into the sink, on top of the foam from the toothpaste he'd also spat out, and hadn't bothered to wash either of them away, knowing it would be a job for me to do. I think he does that to remind me of my place and the hierarchy within our home.

I went back downstairs and started cleaning the already immaculately clean fridge . . . and it then happened.

'Louise, here!' he called from the lounge.

I knew then it was coming. It was like the missile had about twenty seconds to land, as if I could see it in the distance hurtling towards me at a speed of light, but I had no time to run, to get out of the way, to hide or make it stop.

I braced myself as I headed into the lounge from the kitchen, ready to have an answer for anything he was going to accuse me of having purposely done to make him mad, or anything I hadn't done which I should have known to do, which had also made him mad . . . I was still hopeful, at this point, that I could keep him calm.

'Why is my bag still sitting by the front door when you know I leave for another trip tomorrow?'

'Sorry,' I replied. 'I'll sort it now.' As I turned around to empty the dirty washing from his bag, he grabbed a fistful of my hair from behind and pulled me to the floor. The move took no more than two seconds and the pain was immediate. I didn't make a sound. I knew the boys would most likely still be awake – Harry definitely would – awaiting this moment. This moment he and I had known was coming. I stayed where I'd landed on the floor, face down, on my stomach, with his whole body weight lying on top of me so I struggled to breathe, the left-hand side of my face rammed into the woven rug, which felt like sandpaper against my cheek. David whisper-shouted, 'It's no wonder I fucking hate you, you lazy fucking cunt,' into my ear canal. His breath felt so hot against my skin, it made me shiver.

I knew that any second now Harry would hear, because my not reacting would worsen David, and he would begin shouting and smashing things. But reacting would also mean Harry would hear me. I never know which is worse. Whenever I reflect on the violent incidents, the amount of things that run through my mind in literally a few seconds blows me away. I don't know how I manage to think about so many things, how I ask myself so many questions and try and analyse the situation to stay as safe as possible – and at times, alive – in such an unbelievably tiny amount of time.

As my mind was still racing over which decision to make, I felt David's teeth sink into the top of my scalp. The pain seared through me and I let out a noise. Not a scream – more a wail. I was still trying to be as quiet as possible, praying the boys wouldn't hear.

'Fucking cunt,' he repeated over and over, emphasising the 'F' each time, whilst deciding on where to inflict the next hidden injury to my body – his all-time favourite game. He climbed off and pulled me by my arm so I was lying on my back facing him, and then he said, 'One day I will leave you.'

'Leave her, then! Just fucking leave her!'

I looked to my left. Harry was stood in the entrance to the lounge, his face bright red, with tears streaming down his cheeks.

*Fuck.* My brain just screamed that word, over and over. As I scrambled up off the floor, I felt relieved the only injury I had was on my head, hidden by my crazy mane of hair – again, thinking about so many things again in just a few seconds.

'Tell her,' Harry said to David, in a firm but quiet voice. I imagine, like me, he was trying to ensure his younger brother didn't hear.

'Go to fucking bed,' David scoffed with a smirk as he calmly stood up off the floor.

'Fucking tell her!' Harry screamed, losing his awareness – or concern – about George waking.

'Honey, let's get you back to bed,' I soothed. Whatever the secret was that Harry wanted to come out, I knew I definitely did not want to know it.

'He's having an affair,' Harry spat. 'He's shagging another solicitor who he takes away on his business trips. I've heard him on the phone to her.'

By this point I knew David was shagging someone – or multiple people – from the clues she continued to leave me. The lipstick on his shirts, and the smell of her expensive perfume coating everything from his suit jacket to his underwear every time he had returned from a work trip for the past year and a half.

'Baby, let's get you to bed,' I said again, walking towards Harry.

'Who would fucking blame me?' David muttered with a disgusting giggle.

'I FUCKING HATE YOU!' Harry screamed, lunging at his dad.

*Fuck, fuck, fuck.* That word was back again.

I was totally out of my depth, with no idea what to do whilst my son rugby tackled his father to the ground.

'STOP!' I yelled, trying to intervene, but the punches they both threw were so quick I couldn't even get between them

– Harry's coming from years of built-up rage; David's coming from years of experience of throwing punches at me.

'Please, Harry, stop!' I cried as he managed to take full control of the fight, sitting on top of his father and raining punches to any part of his body he could physically hit – his face, shoulders, arms – even arching his body backwards to hit him in his kidneys and legs.

David went from fighting back to trying to protect himself, using his arms and hands to fend off the strong, sharp blows, whilst screaming, 'GET THE FUCK OFF ME!'

David was on the carpet, his back on the floor, looking into his son's eyes – the exact same position I'd been in just moments before. He looked up at me and pleaded, 'Make him stop.'

I was frantic, crying and screaming for Harry to get off him. All of a sudden, Harry stopped the punches. I ran behind him to pull him off David backwards . . . but he leant forwards, still sat on his dad's stomach, and put both hands round his throat.

'Harry, for fuck's sake, stop. Please stop,' I begged, genuinely terrified where this was going to end. It was like I was invisible, powerless. I was using my entire body weight and strength to drag him off his dad, but it was like an ant on a lion's back, as if he couldn't even feel me.

As David spluttered for breath and began turning purple, Harry let go and said, 'Touch my mum again and I will fucking kill you.' He then stood up and turned to face me, a tear falling down his cheek as he said, 'I'm sorry, Mum,' then walked out the room.

*Fuck fuck fuck.* My brain felt as battered as my body had so many times over the years.

David was still rolling round the floor, gasping for breath. I went to the kitchen to grab a couple of things, then followed

Harry upstairs – petrified that if I stayed downstairs, David would kill me, but also petrified he would try and seek immediate revenge on Harry.

I opened Harry's bedroom door, handed him the glass of water I'd poured – then put the huge carving knife under the side of the mattress. He finished gulping the water and said, 'We're using that if we need to. Agreed?'

'Agreed,' I whispered, climbing in beside him wondering what David's revenge was going to look like. I wondered whether to bring George in, but I knew he wouldn't settle. Plus, tonight we were the ones who had enraged David – George wouldn't even have been in his thoughts.

I heard David leave just before 6 a.m., his usual time to leave. I hadn't slept. I felt wired. I wondered what his injuries looked like this morning. I peered over at Harry. He was facing me, sleeping. He'd been sound asleep for the past few hours, which amazed me – but I suppose he's been listening to David do this to me for years. For his whole life. He must be so used to falling asleep, not knowing whether, in the morning, I'd be OK. Or alive. I feel like I'm actually starting to admit to myself what Harry living in that house, hearing what he's heard, has done to him for so long.

I crept out of bed and looked outside. The sun was shining as I watched David roar out the electric gates onto the road.

I went to the toilet and threw up last night's dinner.

I walked downstairs. The woven rug had splatters of blood across it, so I rolled it up, ready to clean it or throw it out – I'd decide later. Then I picked up my phone.

A message from David.

My stomach flipped. He had sent it at 5 a.m. – that would have been as soon as he woke.

**I am back on Wednesday. Find that entitled little cunt**

**somewhere else to stay. He is not living in my home whilst he behaves like a fucking animal.**

*Fuck, fuck, fuck* – that word again, chiming repeatedly in my brain.

I woke Harry. He took ages to come round – he was probably trying his hardest to stay asleep, as I imagine life in his dreams felt safer than the real world he has to wake up to.

When I was sure he was coherent enough to have a two-way conversation, I asked him how he was feeling. He looked up to the ceiling, rolled his eyes, let out a huge sigh, and said, 'How are *you* feeling?'

I tried not to cry again. I am pretty good at holding it together usually, but I soon realised today was not a day where I was going to be able to do that. So I gave up pretty quickly and let the tears flow freely down my cheeks, joining my son in looking up towards the ceiling in despair at how our life looked.

'We need to leave,' he said. 'We *have* to leave, Mum.'

'Don't ever do that again,' I said. 'Don't put yourself in danger like that.'

He looked at me and said, 'He is going to fucking kill you.'

'He won't,' I replied, trying to convince him of a truth I didn't believe.

'Look at you,' he said, walking towards me. He took my hands, drew my arms outstretched, and lifted the sleeves on my dressing gown. As we both looked at all the scars, burns and bruises, Harry began to cry and said, 'Fucking look at you, Mum.' His voice broke and I began to sob. We clung to each other and cried together, knowing everything had changed forever.

I know. I know it is no longer an option to stay, but I need time to prepare so much to leave properly. I have promised Harry that we will leave before Christmas, which is just a few months away. I need to sort money, my things, their things, a home. I am not just leaving on whim with nothing – he will destroy me.

I asked Harry to stay at his friend Charlie's this week – Charlie's parents are super wealthy and rarely in the country. He is mainly raised by nannies, and can have a friend to stay over whenever he pleases. Harry is always desperate to stay there but is rarely allowed to by David, who I am hoping will be OK with it. Well, he's the one who told me to get Harry out of the house.

I could see Harry was torn. He absolutely wanted to be out of the house and as far away as possible, but was terrified of not being around for me when David gets back. I begged him to go, and to stay a few days beyond Wednesday when his dad returns, to allow David to calm down. Harry agreed, on the provision we would start prepping to leave tonight when he returns from school. I promised we will, then kissed his forehead and asked him to get ready for school as normal. The lump in my throat hurt, and I wanted to curl up and cry, but I knew I needed to keep things normal for George. I had the café to get to and I needed to keep my head focused to stick to the plan, for the three of us to be able to leave as safely as possible.

I dropped the boys off at school. George must have fallen asleep last night and not heard anything, as he chatted away like normal during the journey, all about what Pokémon cards he has ready to swap with his friends, and how excited he is for the holiday we have booked to America in a few months' time. He didn't seem anxious or worried, and he didn't make any matter-of-fact statements about what he had seen or heard like he sometimes does, which I was also terrified about him doing at school, so I took that as a win. Harry, on the other hand, stared out of the window for the entire twenty-five-minute journey, rubbing his left palm with his right thumb to the point it looked painful. The stabbing pain in my throat returned, and I repeatedly tried to swallow away the tennis-ball-sized lump of devastation.

They got out of the car, both reaching forward and giving me a kiss. George's kiss hurt my heart because of the innocence still within him, and Harry's because of the way he was already so broken at the age of just fourteen.

I drove to the café, tears running down my face the entire way, the desperation of my life consuming my entire being.

How the hell am I ever going to be free from it all?

# SUNDAY

I spoke to Mags earlier. She went to visit and said you're not so good today. I think you must have what Woody has got – it's everywhere.

I really hope you feel better tomorrow, so we can come up. I've just sent you a message saying I have so much to tell you, but it hasn't delivered, so I guess you must be sleeping and have your phone switched off.

This weekend has been beyond weird. Mum called me back yesterday when I was on my dog walk to tell me Dad and George had bumped into Dan on the harbour and invited him for a barbecue. She said they'd invited Jen, Jo, Meg and their families over. I was worried about Woody and whether he was well enough, but Mum said he had woken and perked up, and reminded me there was enough of us there to snuggle him if he needed it. And their house is huge, so I knew if he needed to sleep it off he would have the space and quiet to do that.

As soon as I hung up, Tom's mobile began ringing. After he answered, I heard him say, 'A barbecue where?' My tummy flipped, and then Tom laughed and said, 'I'll need to speak with Lou, mate,' and I knew it must be Dan on the phone, ordering him to come.

I'm not going to lie – I felt massively overwhelmed by the idea of Tom coming to a barbecue with my sons, parents and a load of my friends. I tried to put him off. He told me if it felt weird or uncomfortable for me, he wouldn't come. But the truth was, I wanted him there – and I was also a little frightened by how much I wanted it. I reminded myself that Tom was coming as Dan's friend, and it would be busy – as Mum and Dad's place often is. My boys are used to this, and have never questioned anyone new turning up before – and they wouldn't now.

We walked the dog all around the coastal path, then got brunch at another seaside café a little way up from ours, and sat outside in the sun. It all felt so good, and so natural to be with him. Like when I'm with Dan, but totally different. I get the impression that Tom also feels something when he's with me, but then I also know he's never settled, and I don't want to get my heart ripped out if he decides I'm too complex or my situation isn't for him. I annoy myself when I think like this, because I remind the women I work with every day not to settle for less than they deserve, and do so much work to point out their worth – and yet here I am, tearing myself to shreds that I'm not good enough for this guy.

Urgh.

Tom and I went home, and then Dan came over. It was so nice just to hang with them both. It was like old times – except that now we're in our thirties, and two of us have teenage kids. They both told me so many stories about things that have happened over the years. Tom has spent time with Dan in Australia, he's godfather to Dan's daughter, and Dan has stayed at Tom's when he's come over. It's clear they are best friends. I was crying with laughter at some of their stories. They told me about a time in their mid-twenties when Tom was staying in Australia, and they decided to do some magic mushrooms. Only, they never got round to doing them, and when Tom left to fly home and was going through security, he found them in his pocket . . . So he panicked, and ate them. As soon as he got on the plane, he started hallucinating. Honestly, the way he described the entire journey home made me cry with laughter. But at the same time, I was realising what a chunk of my life I've lived apart from them, which makes me so sad.

We left my house about 2 p.m. to make the short walk up to my parents, stopping on the way at the local deli. Mum's friend, Joan, runs it with her daughter Lily; they moved here from Wales a few years ago and are so lovely. I saw Joan double-take when I walked in with two handsome men, so I explained they are childhood friends. It made me wonder, though, if other people will look twice if ever they see me with a man, given how small this town is, and how everyone knows my past. Dan bought some beers and a bottle of wine for the barbecue, and Tom bought some cheeses, breads and olives, despite me telling both of them that they didn't need to do that.

We arrived at my parents' to an empty house except for them and the two boys. I only realised I hadn't returned Jo's three missed calls as she was walking up the drive with her tribe, carrying more food and drinks. I walked down the drive to greet them and apologised for not having been in touch – then muttered, 'There's another friend here, I'll tell you about it tomorrow. Don't ask, and act normal, OK?' She squealed and skipped at the same time.

Jamie rolled his eyes and said to me, 'You look happy; it's good to see.' Those words made me want to sob.

Next, Pat arrived, and then Jaclyn, with Harry and Molly. Meg and John came with their kids, too.

By 4 p.m. the barbecue was started, music was blasting, and the kids were playing with all the toys on the lawn that Mum had got out of her shed. Tom, Dan, John and Jamie were playing football against all the kids at the bottom of the garden, and us women were all sat around the table with a huge jug of sangria that Mum had made. Dad was tossing sausages on the barbecue far enough away not to hear us, so Pat went first.

'Who are your friends?'

My cheeks went crimson as I explained they were childhood friends I'd known years ago. I caught Mum's eye, and she gave me a smile that let me know she knew I wasn't telling the whole truth.

Jo chirped in with, 'Have you shagged Tom before?'

Mum and Pat almost choked on the air, and everyone started laughing out loud and screaming, 'JO!!!!'

'What?' she replied, stuffing more crisps in her face and smiling at me.

'No,' I laughed. 'I haven't shagged either of them!'

'Well, do you want to shag him?' Jaclyn chirped in.

Once again, the half-cut women round the table started laughing, and as soon as I replied, 'Yeah, I think I do,' they were roaring. Roaring to the point the entire garden looked over, and I was the only one not roaring, so it was clear the joke was on me. Tom gave me a smile that made every part of me throb and I stood up and mouthed, 'Fuck off!' to Jo and Jaclyn before giggling and walking in the house to check Woody. He'd perked up, but had just been chilling on the sofa for most of the day – sleeping for a few hours and occasionally playing with the toys in Mum's basket.

George was in the lounge, too, sorting his Pokémon cards. He's happier alone, lining up, stacking and sorting his cards, or watching YouTube videos about boats or people's rare Pokémon collections. As I sat opposite him at the dining table, Tom appeared. 'Ah, Pokémon,' he said to George.

'Yeah,' George responded, without looking up.

Tom sat next to me, directly opposite George, and asked what his favourite character is. Within minutes, it became apparent that Tom knows as much about Pokémon as George, thanks to his nephew. He began showing him Pokémon events the two of them had been to, like showcase collectors' days and other things. George was mesmerised – and then Tom FaceTimed his nephew, Rupert, who is a year older than George. Rupert began showing George all of his cards, and George was jumping around with excitement as he was looking at the rare ones. I didn't know whether to explain he was autistic, or if that wasn't necessary, or if it would make him seem weird, but as I was overthinking it, Tom said, 'You're a happy boy, mate – that's good to see, you having a hobby that makes you so excited.' Everything inside of me wanted to cry with happiness, that George was on actual FaceTime to a lad in London, and they were both obsessing over the same thing, that was making them beyond happy!

I looked over and Woody had fallen back to sleep. It was 5.30 p.m. and Dad was dishing up the first round of food. George said bye to Rupert, and we went into the garden to eat. As I followed George, Tom followed me and gave my hand another squeeze as we made our way through the house. I squeezed it back, wondering where on earth this was heading.

We spent the evening in the garden. I carried Woody up to bed at 8 p.m. and gave him another dose of Calpol. Around 9 p.m. all of Jo and Meg's big ones took their little ones back to Jo's – they live a few doors down from Meg and John. Dad lit the firepit, and Mum and Pat brought out three bottles of champagne. 'What's the special occasion?' Jo asked, smirking at me.

'We have some news,' Meg said, and I knew immediately what she was going to say. 'We're having another baby.'

I was so happy for them. After all they've been through, losing their first baby. It took me back to the day we sat on the beach and she was so broken, and it reminded me once again that 'happy-ever-afters' do exist.

Wow. What a way to end the weekend. We were all beyond buzzing for them. It turned out that Meg's sixteen weeks, almost halfway. She is terrified, clearly – but they're monitoring her regularly, and we reminded her of the incredible babies she already has, that are here and healthy. What a blessing.

Most people had left by 10 p.m., and I was sitting in the garden with my parents, Jaclyn, Dan and Tom. Molly and Harry arrived back from Jo's and we all chatted about how life had been when we were young, back when Dan's parents were here – and how weird it felt that so much has changed. Harry asked questions about what I was like when I was young, and Dan said he wasn't sure what he was allowed to say infront of my parents and son. I laughed. 'Tell them what you want; it will be nice for them to know once upon a time I was someone who was fun.'

'You've always been fun, Mum,' Harry said. 'It was him that ruined that for you, but you were still fun with me and George.'

Everyone shot me a look of sadness, and my eyes filled.

'Right then, shall we start with the time Tom gave you that bong when we camped and you went on a whitey and threw up on Rachel's burger?'

'Fuck's sake,' I answered, realising I haven't ever really sworn in front of anyone round this table other than the two men I hadn't seen for almost twenty years. 'Yeah, go on then, do your worst.'

We sat up until midnight, sharing stories which made us all cry with laughter. Both Tom and Dan remembered so many things I'd forgotten, or maybe blocked out. I felt a happiness, talking about who I used to be, how I used to act, that I hadn't felt since I was that person. I am determined to get back to being her.

We said goodnight as the taxi turned up to take Jaclyn, Molly, Tom and Dan home, and we all hugged our goodbyes. As I hugged Tom, he whispered in my ear, 'I've had a better night than last night, and I thought that was impossible,' then squeezed my hand. He was heading back to London first thing, and I felt sick at that thought.

As they drove away, I walked to the kitchen to pour a glass of water, and Harry came over to kiss me goodnight. 'I've had the best night, Mum. I've never seen you laugh like that before.'

My mum, stacking dishes at the kitchen table with my dad, put her hand over her mouth, but that didn't stop her tears.

'Oh, Grandma, don't be sad,' Harry said.

'No, no, I'm not sad, darling,' she replied. 'I'm happy that your mum's happy – it's all we've ever wanted, isn't it, Tony?'

'It is,' Dad said. 'It bloody well is.' He walked over and hugged me, and it felt so good.

Later, after I got into bed, I checked my messages. The first one was from Tom:

**Call me if you can't sleep, but if you can, call me next time you can't. Had the best weekend with you.**

The second was from a very drunk Dan:

**I think Tom wants to marry you, and he doesn't believe in marriage.**

And the third was from Jo:

**You have to shag Tom!!**

I snuggled up, and decided I couldn't sleep, so I called Tom . . .

# Thirty-two years old

Whilst I was at home today, Jo turned up. That's never happened before. Not in all the years I've lived in this house has anyone ever turned up unannounced to see me. I called in sick to the café because the bruising to my cheek isn't ideal, and I don't think I can hold it together at the minute – I've never been 'here' with one of my sons before.

I was sorting Harry's stuff, hiding anything away of sentimental value in case David smashed it up on his return. I didn't see Jo coming. The gate buzzed twice, but I ignored it. Unless it is a safe time to allow delivery people up the drive, I always ignore the buzzer. They just deposit the parcels through the slot in the main gate which drops into a secure box on our side. I wasn't expecting anything, so assumed it would be a delivery for David and continued sorting through Harry's things.

And then I heard Jo shouting through my letterbox. I wanted to be sick. My mind instantly went to panic. This wasn't allowed. David would lose his shit if he thought I'd allowed someone enough access to me to think they could just rock up to our house without warning – especially given the current climate between us.

*Fuck.* I held my breath, leaning against Harry's bed, out of sight of the window I'd spent the last fifteen minutes with my back to – and through which I knew Jo most likely would have seen me. I exhaled.

'Lou?' she called again.

I remained still, breathing as quietly as humanly possible.

I must have stayed there for an hour, unsure whether Jo was still there or if she'd left, terrified of getting up and her instantly spotting me. Eventually, I crept to the hallway, where my mobile was sat on the landing, and saw a message from Jo. It read:

**Hey sweetie, called over to check on you, but think you were sleeping. Left you some flowers. Call me when you can chat. Lots of love xx**

I deleted the text, then ran down the stairs to collect the flowers. A beautiful bouquet filled with sunflowers and asters. I wouldn't be able to explain these to David, and he would spot them immediately upon his return. He would know they were a gift – I never buy flowers for myself – and the questions wouldn't be worth the potential outcome. I went to the wheelie bin and lifted out a black bag, placed the flowers on top of the bag underneath, then replaced the original bag to cover them.

*Phew.*

The school called me just before lunchtime. My tummy did a flip when I heard the ringtone, because my mobile phone never rings for good reasons. It's only ever really David that calls, or someone to do with the café. They said Harry was complaining of stomach ache and had asked to be picked up. He was never usually sick, never asked to come home, so it was clear they'd believed him. I told them I'd be there within the hour – but then panicked, because Harry had agreed to stay at Charlie's for the week and it was only Monday. David was due back in two days.

I arrived at the school and Harry was in the medical room. I went in and saw him alone, sat on the chair next to the bed, with his chin in his hands and his elbows on his knees. When he saw me, he stood up and wrapped his arms round me. I hugged him back and swallowed away my tears. It wasn't safe for us to do that there in case someone walked in. David is on the school board, and every female member of staff here lives up his arsehole.

The nurse came in after a few minutes and explained there were lots of children off right now with a bug that's contagious, so she thought Harry may be in the early stages of that, although he didn't have a fever. I wanted to tell her it couldn't be contagious as it wasn't a physical illness, it was the effects of having threatened to kill his own father, who he's witnessed assaulting his mother several times over the years.

Instead, I replied, 'Hopefully he won't get too poorly,' before helping Harry stand up and putting his bag over my shoulder ready to leave, feeling massively paranoid she knew I was lying.

I signed Harry out at reception and we drove home. He looked the same as he had done on the journey into school, his hands fidgeting, but this time the tears ran off his chin and splashed onto his blazer. I passed him a tissue, squeezed his hand, and said, 'I promise I'll sort it. For good.'

We got home and we sat in the sun lounge together.

I know we have to go. I reiterate that to Harry. It isn't an option to stay any more. It is about how we leave, not if. I need to do it properly, to plan it well, cover every angle. I need to plan all of this, because I know if I don't do this properly, he will ruin all three of us.

We packed bags, four in total. I knew I had to show Harry I'm serious, and this would give him hope and keep him strong. Harry helped me pack George's, as we didn't want him to know the plan – as he's only just turned nine, it's too risky to tell him, in case he slips up to his dad – or worse still, in case he doesn't want to leave. He also cannot lie: George has to be truthful about everything, and I just knew informing him of this would be disastrous.

We packed clothes David wouldn't notice disappearing, and things that held sentimental value to us. Harry wanted to take the Zhu Zhu Pet he'd named Ziggy. I'd bought him this when he was tiny. I asked why he wanted to pack it, and he said, 'Because every time Dad hurt you or got angry, I would ask Ziggy to keep us safe and let us escape one day. And now we're finally going, I want to take him with me to say thanks for making our dreams come true.'

Hearing that sentence felt like I'd taken a bullet. I imagined him, for all those years, that tiny little boy, up in his bedroom, whispering into his toy's ear every time things were bad. He was being subjected to the most devastating things, hearing David abuse me in the worst possible ways, and now truly believes, at his age, as we are packing to flee, that one of the reasons we are escaping is because he begged a battery-operated toy that cost me a tenner to help us. And he wants to thank that Zhu Zhu Pet by letting him come along with us. Devastating.

For George, Harry packed his first football cup – he's kicked a ball since the second he could walk, and this trophy is the one that he won when he was just five, which sits by his bed. As we pack it, I realise that David doesn't even know his sons well enough to know what's sentimental and what isn't – or even their likes or dislikes. It enrages me that he has spent so many years being a parent to my boys without ever actually being a parent. George has many other cups and trophies, but Harry told me that one is George's favourite. That made my heart break – and beam – that amongst this chaos, my boys knew each other better than anyone else in the world. I will tell George I've sent it off to be polished, if he asks.

In my bag, I packed old clothes I knew David wouldn't notice as missing, and also because if he found the extremely well-hidden bags, I could point out these were 'old clothes' I'd stored away ready to take to a charity shop.

The fourth bag I filled with more sentimental stuff. All of the boys' hospital stuff from when they were born, their name bands. I inspected the anklets, remembering how tiny their little ankles were, wondering again how their dad could have caused so much pain to two such innocent little babies by the way he treated me when they were that small. The rules he put in place, where they weren't allowed to be breastfed or picked up too much; the way he made me leave them to cry at times, telling me I was spoiling them by fussing them too much and encouraging them to be needy. I realised again, whilst packing that sentimental bag, that I was married to a monster. I could truly see it now.

Harry and I talked the whole time we were packing the bags. Harry pulled a picture out of a huge wooden hamper of old photos of me as a little girl sat on a rock next to my dad at the beach. I had a mass of wild red hair and a navy-and-white bikini on. I'd loved that bikini so much, and now I saw how good it looked with my hair, which I'd hated when I was little. Harry smiled as he studied me, and asked about my parents. 'Why don't we see them, Mum?' he asked. I was going to tell him because they lived abroad now, because they didn't come back much, but then I realised I would be lying to him again, and in order for things to change I had to stop lying.

'Because your dad doesn't let us,' I started. 'Your grandparents were the most incredible parents to me and they would have been the best grandparents to you . . . in fact, they will be. Very soon, you will have the best grandparents in the world, who you will see whenever you want to, baby.'

'I can't wait, Mum,' he replied.

Me neither . . .

We decided that Harry would stay at home with me that night, then tomorrow he'd go back to Charlie's before David gets back, so I can sort things at home and get a plan in place.

We agreed a code word that we would use together to reassure each other things were OK and still on track for us to leave.

We chose the word 'grass'. Random, I know, but it was something I felt we could use in so many contexts without David becoming suspicious.

It was a word we would use to reassure each other that we had a plan, that we were playing a game and that we would be free by Christmas.

Christmas.

Only a tiny space of time to gather evidence of David's abuse, along with enough money to flee – but I know David, and the incidents may now become more regular, in order for him to regain control. I have to promise myself that this time, if the violence becomes unmanageable, four months is too long to continue living this way. If that happens, we will leave sooner.

Harry was super emotional this evening about David returning on Wednesday and him not being in the house, but I gave him the go ahead to WhatsApp video call my mum and dad, which made him happy. I reminded him to delete all calls, just in case.

Harry knows George will be at home, which I know makes him feel better, and also me. I constantly reassure myself that Aunt Peggy wasn't murdered when I was in the house with her. Sometimes I hate myself because of my thought patterns, which I know are just excuses.

# MONDAY

I worked in the café this morning.

I really loved working today. I think we're all enjoying covering for you until you're back. I didn't realise I'd missed it until I started working back there, but I have. I have really missed the café. It has meant such a lot to me.

I opened up and put the cakes out.

The usual customers called in for their morning takeaway coffees and bakes. Weirdly, I can still remember the orders of the most loyal clientele off by heart, but I still waited for their instruction as if I didn't.

Marcus came in first. Do you know Marcus? He owns the florist on the outskirts of town with his husband, James. They also rent fields where they grow wild flowers to create the most stunning bouquets. I wonder if he chats to you when he comes in? He's always happy and positive. He used to chat to me about mundane stuff, like the weather, weekend plans, which flowers are doing well – and he did just that today, three years on from when I last served him a flat white.

Next in was Kate. She's a producer for the BBC and was grabbing her usual latte with a caramel shot on her way to get the train to London. She works in the city half the time, and from home for the rest. Her life seems nice. She doesn't have children and she's not married – or she wasn't when I last served her, thirty-six months ago. She held my hand across the counter as she left and said, 'Bloody lovely to see you, Lou, you look incredible.' That made me feel special.

Jen arrived next, grabbing two takeaway teas for her and Megan. I first met Jen in the café – I'm not sure if I ever told you that. She once told me over a coffee in here how her first partner had just left one day. He went to work, leaving her at home with their son, and just never returned. She wasn't bitter or angry by the time she told me about it – it was like she didn't care enough to even have an opinion on it any more. It was refreshing, to meet someone who had healed. She was working last night, so she missed the barbecue. She told me she delivered two babies and I smiled, knowing she was about to go on a beach walk with Megan and would find out her news.

Next up, Tom walked in. God. My whole body felt like it was on fire, and I knew he'd noticed I was blushing. He'd told me he was leaving first thing, and it was now 8.45 a.m. and here he was.

I called Pat out of the kitchen and asked if she'd cover the till for ten minutes whilst we were quiet, then began making him the latte he'd ordered.

'Can I have a go?' he asked.

'What?' I laughed.

'I've always wanted to learn how to be a barista.'

'Right,' I answered. I lifted the hatch and opened the gate for him to come behind the till. I made mine first, so he could copy. I did a leaf coffee art (it's what I'm best at) and I could tell he was impressed. Next, I guided him through how to make his coffee, how to steam his milk, and I asked what coffee art he wanted.

'A heart,' he smiled. I got him to hold the jug of milk and I put my hand over his to create a heart. We almost got there . . . but it resembled more of an onion, mainly because my hands were trembling from the feeling I got, touching his. I asked if he wanted any breakfast but he said he would eat on the train, so we went to sit outside.

I told him I feel sad that he's leaving. He said he feels sad too. I wondered if this was mental – we hadn't even kissed. It kind of reminded me of when we were young, when we'd never even had sex, but the connection we had to one another was like nothing I've ever felt since.

Harry arrived as we were chatting, to say goodbye, as he was going back to Bath to do some shifts at the new bar. He has a rugby tournament tomorrow and he also has therapy booked, which I'm proud of him for not wanting to miss. I went in and made him a flat white and brought out a croissant, and he sat with us. It was lovely to see him and Tom chatting. Tom seemed genuinely interested in the answers to his questions about uni and rugby. In return, Harry asked him questions about his work – it's clear Tom really loves his job. Harry gave me a kiss and a huge hug and asked the same question he asks every time he leaves: 'Will you be OK without me? You know I can stay?' I assured him I would be absolutely fine, as I always am, and told him to FaceTime me when he could.

When he left, Tom said what amazing lads he and George were, and that I should be proud of what I protected them from, for them to turn out as they have. I got emotional – only a bit, but we had another hand squeeze over the table, and I asked if he would be coming back any time soon. He AirDropped me his shift pattern and said, 'You tell me when you're free and I'll come and visit.' He works a mixture of early and late shifts, and he's on-call at various times, but he also gets a good few days off in chunks. 'I have a ton of holiday to use, too,' he added, 'so I can be here more.'

Oh, God.

I saw that he's off next weekend again, for three days, from Saturday to Monday. 'Then?' I asked, pointing to the days on the rota. 'Or is that too soon?'

'Then,' he replied, smiling. 'Nothing is too soon.' He kissed my forehead, said I make good coffee, and gently pulled me upwards off my seat, linking my hands in his. As he hugged me into him, I didn't feel worried or stressed about cuddling him in public. I leaned up to kiss him on the lips. JESUS CHRIST, my entire body felt like it was on fire. Just from two five-second lip kisses, with no tongues! This guy! He left to catch his train, jogging towards the station so he didn't miss it, and I walked back into the café as high as a kite.

It was so lovely to see you this afternoon. You seemed happy, and upbeat – which was nice. I feel like I know you well enough to know if you're putting it on, and I really believe you're not.

I'm glad we were finally able to talk about us moving into my parents' home. I'm not going to lie, I panicked when you got emotional, but I'm so glad you love the idea. You said it was a huge relief. I had no idea that you were behind on the rent for your flat. It feels like it could be a godsend for you to give your notice in on a home that has so many bad memories. I hope you'll be able to save some pennies, be supported, have company, then start afresh in a new place.

I never returned to our family home after the last attack, not even to collect my things. I sent Jo and Jen, which was good, because they ended up taking no notice of my instruction to just bring the bare minimum. A blessing, as I would have left all my jewellery and money. I'm thankful that they took it from the safe, because David dragged out the financial hearings and divorce and I would have been absolutely shafted without it. I'm so grateful to have friends like them.

I called Mum when we left you and she was so excited that I've agreed to house swap. I think she and Dad are relieved to downsize. I had the flat fully refurnished last year when I got my settlement through, so it's really beautiful.

We'd emailed the letting agents together from the unit to give notice on your flat. The girls have set up a GoFundMe – I am not on any social media, but they've said lots of people locally have donated, and so far it's raised £8,000 to help you. People know you won't be able to work and will be financially struggling, so we can pay off the £1,200 you owe on rent, and you will still have money to start afresh.

We are going to arrange the move in around three weeks. That way I can get Woody in and settled and get everything sorted before you come home. I'm excited for you, but I am excited for me too. I often get lonely at night when George is in bed, and even though I'm years down the line, I often sit with my own thoughts in the evenings. I'm aware it's most people's downtime so I don't want to intrude with phone calls, but it's the heaviest time for me. I know if I just had someone – not even to chat to, but just another adult present around me – things would feel lighter, safer.

I'm excited for us, Martha – for you and me and our boys, together.

# Thirty-two years old

I think David knows we are leaving. Since Harry intervened, his behaviour just gets worse and worse.

He arrived back two nights ago just after 6 p.m., dumping his new Louis Vuitton bag just inside the front door as he strolled in.

I'd made sure George was fed, showered and watching a film in his room, out of the way. Safe. That's what I told myself, anyway.

David opened the cutlery drawer, took out a spoon, lifted the top of the slow cooker and tasted the gravy from the sausage casserole that I'd spent all day slow-cooking. He walked to the sink and spat it out. 'Needs seasoning,' he snapped. 'Get it ready for half past; I'm going to shower.'

I wanted to spit in the casserole, to take a piss in it. The rage that consumed me from my toes to my scalp made my whole body tingle. I ground some more salt and pepper in, that I knew the casserole didn't need, and popped the peeled potatoes on the hob to boil.

I heard David open George's bedroom door. 'Hi, champ, where's your brother?' he asked.

'At Charlie's,' George replied, and David shut the door without any further conversation. He'd opened it just to get his question answered, not to check up on the wellbeing of either of his sons.

I bit the tiny bit of remaining skin left around my nails whilst I waited for the potatoes to become soft enough to mash, and at 6.30 p.m. I plated them up with the 'tasteless' sausage casserole that I knew was delicious, and a handful of cabbage I prayed he would choke to death on. I placed it on the dining table with a beer and left the room as David entered.

'Eat with me,' he said. The tone threw me; it wasn't a command or an order, it was a soft, gentle voice that I hadn't heard for a long while, and it made me feel sick. I knew this night could only go one of two ways. And if it went bad, it would be going really bad – and I knew deep down that was the only way it was heading . . .

'OK,' I replied, and walked to the kitchen to plate myself up a dinner that the thought of eating made me heave. 'Where shall I sit?' I asked, as I walked back in the dining room.

'Next to me,' he said, pulling out the seat to the left of him as he headed up the huge oak table that had never sat more than four people. I sat down and began chewing on my sausage. I just couldn't swallow it. Every time I tried, I just chewed again and again and again, wondering how I was going to digest this plate of food without vomiting everywhere. I gulped my water and swallowed it down like I do when I accidentally buy those huge round paracetamol tablets instead of capsules.

'How have you been?' he asked.

'OK,' I replied. 'How have you been?'

He then began to reel off a load of shit about how he's closed a huge deal with a wealthy client and everyone at his firm was buzzing because it was the biggest achievement in a long time. I smiled along, nodding as he boasted about how amazing he was. I struggled to listen, couldn't have even repeated the details of the deal back to him if he'd asked me, which was pretty unbelievable considering the risk that put me in. I knew at that point he was on a high. This wasn't about sharing his success with a wife that he loved, it was about needing everyone possible around him to know what an absolute legend he was.

When he'd finished talking about himself, I cleared the plates and began cleaning the kitchen. I went upstairs, tucked George in and wondered how best to play the situation. It's a constant guessing game; the rules change daily – hourly. I went back downstairs. David was sat in the lounge in his grey Dior tracksuit bottoms, with no top on.

*Crazy*, I thought when I looked at him, *how beautiful a man can look but be so ugly inside.* He had one leg tucked under his bum and the other stretched out in front of him. I wondered if he'd noticed the footstool no longer sat on top of the expensive designer rug that I had had to throw out – after an hour attempting to scrub my blood out of it – or if he just chose not to mention it. I wondered if he was perhaps saving the question for later.

'What have you said to Harry?' he asked.

*Here we go*, I thought.

'I told him he was to stay out because of his behaviour.'

'Yes, but did you tell him that *you* felt like that, or did you pin that decision all on me?'

I wanted to scream at the top of my lungs, to tell him I wished Harry had killed him, that it should be David that was the one kicked out of the house. Instead, I played the game, remembered my promise to my son, and assured David I had told Harry how unhappy I was with the way he'd treated his father.

'Good,' David replied. 'I'm off to bed,' he said, as he placed his wine glass on the coffee table. 'Join me.' And just like that, I knew it was going to be the worst night ever. My tummy did the flip. I knew what was coming.

I checked on George on my way up as I went past his room. He was definitely asleep – mouth open, deep sleep-breathing and too warm from where he'd wrapped himself in his duvet. I pulled it back, kissed his brow and felt my stomach do another flip as I left his room to walk into hell.

And hell it was. That night was one of the worst incidents I've ever endured – I knew it was coming, because of Harry standing up to his dad. I knew in my bones this was all about David regaining control over me, showing me what would happen if I didn't control our son and keep him in his place.

The attack lasted over four hours. Longer than some, but shorter than most. Forever trying to turn a negative into a positive . . .

He finally stopped just after 1 a.m. and was fast asleep shortly after, breathing heavily next to me like the most rested man in the world, whilst I lay next to him wondering if my jaw was badly bruised or actually broken, and how I would go about finding that out.

I still haven't done anything as of yet.

The following morning went ahead as normal. I remained in the bedroom and David told George I had a migraine. The boys know not to come in to me during these times. I've often wondered, over the years, if they've really believed I've had a migraine for up to a week whilst my injuries disappeared, or if they knew what was going on. David was usually far too careful to injure my neck and face – always starting at the collarbone down. I knew he would be livid that I had visible facial injuries this time; in his mind, that would be my fault. It always was.

I heard him walking down the stairs on the phone to Jo. I felt sick and didn't hear whether he had called her or she had called him. He opened the front door as he was chatting to her, then called George out to the car to take him to school. I heard him end the call, then shortly afterwards, he was sprinting back up the stairs. Before I could even process what emotion I was feeling, he had opened the door, turned on the main light in the pitch-black room and launched the battered flowers at me. 'Lying fucking whore,' he spat. 'You fucking ask for it.'

Brilliant. Jo had told him about the flowers.

He walked back down the stairs, slammed the front door and roared down the drive with one of my precious babies as cargo.

I dragged myself out of bed and stripped down to my knickers.

The bruising isn't fully out yet. I know it will get worse before it will get better – I've been here a thousand times before – but fuck, this is the worst one I've had for a while. I don't know whether this will be healed by the time Harry gets back. I could cover the yellow brushing, but the swelling and state of my eye mean it will take at least a week to heal.

I got the secret mobile phone I'd recently bought from the café's takings from its hiding place inside an old puffa jacket. It's an Android, no sim, but it has the best camera I could find. I set it up in selfie mode on video recording, and stood in front of it. As I turned around from back to front, I saw my knickers were stained with dried blood from the sexual assault. I was throbbing all over and I crumpled in a heap on the bedroom floor, wailing like an injured animal while the video continued to record. After ten minutes, I reminded myself I have a plan. I need to sort myself out and stay focused, no matter how much pain I am in or how desperate things feel. I took selfies of my facial injuries, and of the ones on my body I could get to. I turned the phone off and hid it back in its safe place, then checked my mobile phone. I still hadn't replied to Jo's message from Monday, or thanked her for the flowers, but now I had no clue about how the conversation she'd just had with David had gone. And if I *was* in bed with a severe migraine, as I had heard him tell her, she would find it odd to get a text from me anyway.

I ran the shower. I dread getting in when I have these kinds of injuries because I know the pain of the water hitting my open wounds will feel excruciating, but I needed to wash myself – especially the bites, to prevent any infection from the bacteria.

I stepped into the shower, clenching my teeth. The pain of the damage to my jaw seared through me.

I showered as quickly as I could, but it still took much longer than normal because I couldn't move very well, or fast.

I got out and drip-dried, because attempting to use a towel felt like I was drying myself with sandpaper.

I wanted to climb back into bed, but the sheets were a state, covered in blood, so I stripped them and remade the bed. It took me over an hour, and I had to keep stopping to cope with the pain.

I put the sheets in the wash, threw the flowers in the wheelie bin for the second time, took two paracetamol and two diazepam and went back to bed. I checked my phone and saw a message from Harry.

**Hi Mum, had a nice night at Charlies, we're gonna play football on the grass today. Let me know when is good to come back, love you.**

I turned the phone to Do Not Disturb, half hoping David would try and call, get so angry that he couldn't get through and come home and kill me . . . Then I realised how life would look for my two boys, living with him without me, so I switched the phone back on. I began to message Harry back to tell him I was good, when he began calling. I didn't answer the first time because

I knew I'd sound slurry with the jaw pain I had – I could hardly open my mouth – so he called again, and again. I knew I had to answer, because his mind would be in overdrive, not knowing if I was dead or alive. I prayed I didn't sound different because of my jaw as I answered the phone and, in my cheeriest voice, asked him how he'd got on at Charlie's. He said it was good, lied and told me he was good. He asked me how it was at home; I said good. He asked how I was; I lied and said I was good. I could tell he was trying to convince me he felt OK with the situation, so I played along and continually reassured him everything was fine and that I was working on him coming home as soon as possible.

'Did you play on the grass yesterday?' I asked.

I felt his smirk in the way he replied with a 'Hmmp' noise, where I know the apples of his cheeks would have stuck out and his lips would have widened as he smiled. 'I did! Love you, Mum!' he replied.

I ended the call, saying, 'I can't wait for us to hang out on the grass again. Love you, baby.'

I put down the phone, rolled onto my right-hand side as it had less injuries than the left, and felt the tears fall from both eyes before I went into a deep, drug-fuelled sleep.

# WEDNESDAY

I loved our day at the beach. Were you annoyed that the carers wanted us to stay on the promenade? You'll soon be well enough to not need carers, but for now I need to have my full attention on Woody when we're out. Sorry, Martha! Even though we couldn't get you onto the sand, it was still lush, sitting by the café. Like me, the beach makes your soul happy, and I know you just being there, breathing it in and people watching, made you feel so good. Your mood when I first saw you to when I left was totally different. We need to do more of this, so that you get glimmers of how life is going to look for you again, hopefully in the near future.

It was nice to see Jo and Pat too. So kind of them to bring coffee and brownies, and as we sat there, chatting and laughing, watching Woody build sandcastles with your two carers – who are just the loveliest guy and girl possible – it made me feel really lucky.

Lucky might feel weird, but coming from where both you and I have come from, I know it's a miracle we got to sit on that beach today, together. We got to put the world to rights and slag our old lives off together, and I feel so very grateful for that.

I loved that you instantly told Jo about the house plans. I haven't mentioned it to anyone yet, only because I haven't seen anyone — but it's lovely for me to hear you telling people, to watch your excitement at the thought of us having a safe home together where we can support each other, where we'll have company and won't feel alone. To hear you are as enthusiastic as me about this makes me so happy. Pat and Jo feel the same about the idea, I can tell. Jo got really emotional, and Pat stroked your hand, then came over and gave me a hug. There's something so powerful about women supporting women. If only we'd learned that before we met the monsters . . . I loved Jo's suggestion of a moving-in party. It wasn't something I was thinking of, but I think it would be lovely for all of us to have a barbecue or get-together to celebrate your new start!

# Thirty-two years old

Every time I think things are at their worst, they just get worse.

I know what happened today is a good thing – although I can't tell Jo that's what I think, and although it's taken me the whole day to convince myself it's a good thing, and although she doesn't think I think it's a good thing, I can't allow her to think that – it puts her at too much risk. I don't want anyone knowing or being in on my plan.

It's been three days since David attacked me. I was still in the 'I am strong' mindset yesterday, when I was pottering about very slowly downstairs. I sent Harry a morning message, then turned my phone off in case anyone tried to get hold of me from work. David had told them I wouldn't be in for a while as I was really poorly with migraines and had an urgent referral to the hospital.

My injuries and bruising are now fully developed and as I was washing the crystal vase to shine it up, I heard a knock at the window directly in front of me. I jumped backwards and looked up to see Jo stood there. The reaction on her face made me feel like throwing up. Her eyes filled with tears; she went white with shock. She pointed to the front door. So many feelings ran through me in so few seconds. Mostly panic, in case David returned – although he never returned unannounced because I was always at the café usually. The only time I was ever at home during the day was when he'd hurt me, and he always wanted to avoid me when that had happened. Mainly I thought, *Fuck*. Like, *Fuck fuck fuck, this is going to totally mess the plan up.*

I started shaking my head to say no. I needed her to leave. I pointed towards the drive to tell her to go. She shook her head and told me to open the door or she would call the police. I wanted to be sick.

I opened the door. As she came in, I went into meltdown. I just kept thinking, *This wasn't part of the plan.* Her turning up like this was ruining everything.

I begged her to go again. It felt like a total blur, until I saw her run to the door. I thought she was running to call the police, but as I went after her, she threw up all over the porch.

Projectile. A shitload of projectile vomit everywhere. I think it was at that point I realised how fucked up all of this is. I realised that this situation I have normalised is so bad that when faced with my truth, it made my friend throw up from shock.

She begged me to call the police, but I refused. I know her partner, Jamie, is a client of David's, and I instantly panicked that Jo would tell him, and that he might not believe me and might mention it to David . . . Or, if he did believe me, what if he challenged David?

Jo promised me she wouldn't tell a soul, or call the police, on the condition she could take pictures of my injuries.

I agreed. I had no option.

I think her being in my home and me seeing another person's reaction to my situation has made me realise there is a real chance here that David could kill me. And I needed someone to have evidence in case that happens, so at the very least my boys will be saved.

I trusted she wouldn't use the pictures without my permission. And part of me thinks, if she does, it will be clear I can't leave bite marks on my own shoulders, back, genitals and boobs. When I stripped off, the shame flooded me – more so when I braved myself to look up and clock her reaction. Then I begged her to leave.

I think that's what's broken me the most in the last few days: my friend's reaction to my life, and how dire it is, how hidden it is.

She hugged me, and although this situation is the worst thing possible, although the shame of how my life looks is overwhelming my entire being, I felt loved, and supported. For the first time, someone knows what I live like, how life is for me and the boys. In the past I have always overthought having to tell people, and what David's reaction would be to that – I've always convinced myself I'd never be believed, but now Jo has walked into it. I didn't confide in her or reach out – it's like a bomb went off in both our worlds that neither of us was expecting. And although for her, it's nothing but negative, I suppose, for me – I have a support network. The hugs she gave me felt like hugs I haven't had in years – the hugs I used to get from friends and family before David came into my life and stopped them, along with everything else. The hugs that I need right now, to get me through until I get out – and I am getting out.

# THURSDAY

I went up to Mum and Dad's today and videoed a walk-through of the house, with all the rooms and the garden. I inherited a love for making a house a home from both my parents, I think. Our houses have always been beautiful, something they take great pride in. It gives them pleasure to redecorate and keep their gardens amazing. Their place already feels like home to me, and I really hope it will for you and Woody too. I am going to come up tomorrow and show you the videos.

I told George the news this evening. He had a million questions about it, but appeared calm. He just wanted to understand when he would be staying where, what both houses would look like and what things would mean for him. As soon as I gave him the answers he needed, he said, 'OK, let's do it,' then returned to sorting through his new rare vintage Pokémon cards my dad had found for him on eBay.

Mum has got keys cut and we've arranged to take you to the house on Saturday with one of the carers. I can't wait for you to see your new home and what it looks like; I'm so excited to show you, and Mum is too. We're going to pick you up at 9 a.m., take a look with Woody, then go for brunch at the café with all the girls. You seem super excited for it all – I hope you are – and I really hope this will help to keep you motivated to get well.

I've spoken to Tom every day, by text and on the phone. We speak at different times, depending on his shifts. It feels nice to chat to him. I'm trying to take it slow, not to fall too hard or fast – or at all, for now. I'm not sure it'll work – he's in London and I'm here, so at the most it will be a long-distance thing. But I'm OK with that – I want to give everything I have to my boys and you and Woody, and Tom would need to fit into that mix for it to work, you know?

Things feel good, better – no, actually, things feel the best they've felt in a long time, which is strange given you're still in a rehab unit working hard to recover, and I'm not working because I'm caring for your son . . . But the future excites me now. I've realised that I haven't been so excited about anything in forever. I haven't had butterflies of excitement for anything for as long as I can remember, and I imagine it's the same for you too . . .

I've just plodded, got through each day – if anything, I haven't even planned towards the future because the thought of it terrifies me. That's changed now. I'm excited for how it looks, for us to raise our boys together and get each other through the hard days. I am excited for us, for you and I.

# Thirty-two years old

I woke to the sound of David coming home with George. I looked at my phone. It was 6 p.m.; I had slept all day without waking once. I'd had several missed calls and messages from Harry. He'd sent the last one at 5 p.m.:

**Gonna stay at Charlie's again if that's OK, Mum? We're going to play tennis and make tacos. Let me know you're OK.**

The paracetamol had worn off, so had the diazepam, so I quickly dosed myself back up with both as the pain was now excruciating. There was fresh blood on the pillow from the cut on my cheek. David came up with a plate of burnt toast with jam and a cup of tea. I wondered if I'd be in trouble for having the side lamp on. I was supposed to be in total darkness in case one of the boys came in – that's what the rules had been for years every time we pretended I had a migraine after he'd beaten the shit out of me. I never knew what his moods would be like after incidents, and neither did he – it fluctuated. Usually, when it was really bad like this, he would be nice, remorseful, but I knew this time he was pinning this all on me. Using the hidden flowers as an excuse . . .

He sneaked into the bedroom, closing the door behind him. To my surprise, I could tell instantly he wasn't annoyed. He passed me the toast and placed the tea on the coaster on the bedside table and asked how I was feeling. 'OK,' I lied.

'If there's anything else you want, let me know. I'm not the best at making toast,' he laughed, as if he was a loving husband, supporting me as best he could to recover from a tragic accident he'd had nothing to do with. As he was chatting, he casually picked up my phone and began scrolling, investigating my messages on iMessage and WhatsApp like it was the most normal thing in the world to do. Weirdly, by that point, it was. 'Reply that you're fine, and tell him to stay at Charlie's for the rest of the week,' he said in regard to Harry's message.

'OK,' I replied in a whisper.

'I hate when it gets to this point,' he said, as if we were both at equal fault. I looked down, not knowing what to respond, even though we'd been here so many times before. 'This doesn't make me feel good,' he said, placing his hand on top of my newly damaged wrist. I immediately winced in pain and he took my hand to his mouth and kissed the wounds softly. 'Let's try and be better. We've done it before . . . Let's get there again, Louise.' These promises used to feel like glimmers, they used to give me hope, back when I'd thought perhaps he meant it – now, they disgusted me.

I despise him.

'OK,' I replied, a tear falling down my cheek.

Mistaking it for genuine sadness, David smiled and stood up. 'Right,' he clapped. 'I'd better sort George out. I'm not very good at this single dad malarkey,' he joked, before sauntering back out the bedroom. I felt suddenly . . . smug. Smug at how I knew his life would look in a few months. I knew the violence would not be a thing for a while now, because of this huge outburst and my injuries – it was always the way when he had a release as big as this one.

As long as I can keep Harry in check, I will be left alone until Christmas, and then we'll be gone.

I feel strong, which is odd. I am black and blue, bruised and battered, but for the first time I feel a massive 'fuck you' in my brain because for the first time ever I have the control. I have a plan in place and he knows nothing about it.

I picked up my phone and messaged Harry back:

**Babe, I'm good, but Dad is still upset with your behaviour so if you can stay at Charlie's this week, we will get you home next week. Remember if you're playing on the grass, check your shoes in case they're muddy. Love you.**

**OK cool, plz tell him I'm sorry and it won't happen again. Yeah I've been on the grass loads so will check my shoes. Love you Mum.**

# FRIDAY

It was nice to visit today without Woody. I was really proud of how well you held it together, chatting to the social worker. I think it helps because she's lovely, so you don't feel judged or at fault. It's lovely to listen to you chat about the future – our plans for the house and the support you know is in place from us all. Hearing you tell her that you've decided you want to study to become an IDVA (an Independent Domestic Violence Advisor) to support more victims and survivors of domestic abuse made me want to sob. If I'd had you to support me, my goodness, it would have felt like a lottery win.

I keep thinking about what you said about me and Tom. I loved how buzzing you are for me that I've met him again, and I've thought about you saying that you can watch George some weekends or in the week, so that I can visit him in London. I hadn't even thought of that until you said it. I just imagined him coming here when he's off work, but you're right, I can absolutely get on the train to London and spend time with him up there. It makes me feel nervous, but also excited – so excited that I get to have a life again, where I can do things that I like, for me, not for anyone else. I've actually never done that as an adult. Crazy really, isn't it? But neither have you – and I can do that for you. I don't know why all single friends don't just live together with their kids. They say it takes a village, and I'm so excited to start ours together.

# Thirty-two years old

David, the boys and I went to Jo's last night. Weird, I know, after she found out about the situation, but she's stuck to her promise and kept my secret – so her husband Jamie had invited us for a barbecue on Saturday evening. I didn't want to go, but David did, which was odd considering we'd never done anything like this with anyone ever.

The boys wanted to go, but when we arrived, David got pissed quickly, and I could tell Harry in particular was worried about what would likely be coming when we got home.

Harry is David's preferred target out of the boys, but I imagine he's thought better of it now he knows Harry could now kick the shit out of him, so he went for George last night instead, nagging him about what he was eating in front of everyone. George instantly withdrew from everything and became stuck to me. Because of this I tried even harder to act normal, chatting and smiling and pretending the situation Jo was definitely aware was happening wasn't.

David was spiralling, at a rapid pace. Downing alcoholic drinks where he was free-pouring the spirits, becoming more arrogant and loud, and swaying as he walked. I wanted to die, but I also knew that the boys and I would definitely be in for it when we got home if I didn't play this game properly. The sickness swirled in the pit of my stomach. Jo's eldest daughter, Belle, returned with two of her friends, Meg's stepson Jacob, and their friend Molly. Shortly after they arrived back, there was an incident outside the front of the house. I knew, without question, that David would be involved – and if I'm honest, part of me prayed he was, because I had that gut feeling something bad was going to happen, and I'd rather it happened there than back at home.

I think somehow I knew that one way or another, whatever was about to unfold would end my marriage. All I could think was, *Please don't let him kill me or the boys.* So I opened the front door and walked straight into it.

He lost it – big time. For some reason he was gunning for Molly and her mum, who had just arrived to pick her up. I put it down to the amount of alcohol he'd consumed, and before I had time to even process the incident I was in the back of an ambulance with a broken jaw.

And now I'm lying here, in a hospital bed, and they are treating new breaks to my body – and old ones. He has broken my jaw on top of breaking my jaw previously, and I have to have a similar operation to the one my Aunt Peggy had years ago, when she was attacked by the man who claimed to love her . . . But I am going to change the story here. I refuse to copy hers. Aunt Peggy would want better for me. I feel like she is guiding me to stay strong right now.

This is the last time David Metcalfe will hurt me. The last time I will lie in a space with him where I feel terrified for my life. That is it. I have made the choice. I am done; it is over. I choose me, I choose my sons and I choose freedom.

Although I've been injured and am in horrible pain, I also believe this is the best way for it to have happened. If I'd just left, he would have found us, he would have made out I was crazy – he probably would have sent me crazy.

No, now my boys and I get to live in peace, and once I am in a place to do so, I am going to make it my mission to create awareness of domestic violence and to do more work to save the lives of more women and children. Because I want our lives to be waking in the morning without that pit of worry in our bellies, without walking on eggshells, without thinking ahead, having to watch everything we say, where we go, who we talk to. I have realised peace is a lottery win, and I feel fortunate that as soon as I'm healed, that when I am out of here, I will have a whole team around me to ensure that is how my life and my sons' lives will look.

# SATURDAY

I don't even know how to write this.

It doesn't feel real.

I was about to end this letter – I was going to bring it up with me to give to you to read after we viewed the house this morning – but then Mags called.

The nurse from the rehab centre called her today. At 7.50 this morning, you died in your sleep.

You had a severe acute brain haemorrhage.

I've never even heard of that before.

You wouldn't have been in pain, they said. You didn't cry out. They just tried to wake you, and couldn't.

I don't understand. I don't know how you worked so hard to get to here, and now this . . .

Woody thinks we're going to see the house today with you. He's so excited. I don't know what to do or say to him. I don't know what Woody's future looks like now. Except that I promised you that I would ensure he was loved and cared for. That's my duty. I told Mags I promised you that. I have it in legal documents. She's reassured me that will happen, that he will be OK and safe with me.

I'm heartbroken. I'm so angry. I don't think my heart has ever been this damaged before.

How am I going to I tell the girls?

How am I going to tell your beautiful boy?

Why is life so unexplainably cruel and hard and unfair?

This isn't what was supposed to happen.

I had this plan. I was going to print this letter off, pop it in a cute envelope – that I was going to decorate with Woody, knowing how much it would make you smile. I was hoping somehow it would make you feel better about the situation, that maybe you'd learn something from my story – but more than anything, I hoped you would never feel alone again. Because that's what I can't bear, couldn't bear – the thought of you feeling alone. Because I've been there, and I hated you feeling that.

I'm devastated I never got to give this to you.

I cannot believe that instead of placing this letter in your dinky little palm, I'll be putting it in your coffin.

How are we here? It's like a bad dream. A nightmare I can't wake from.

Fuck, I'm so sorry, Martha.

I promise, because of you I will resolve to continue to support other amazing women and their babies. I will scream about domestic abuse until my voice gives up ... and more than anything, I will stick to my last promise to you. I will ensure your baby boy is loved, looked after and protected every single day for the rest of his life, no matter what it takes.

Martha, thank you for teaching me so much without even knowing that's what you were doing.

I love you more than you will ever know and I am so, so sorry that this is goodbye.

Louise xx

# Acknowledgements

To my incredible literary agent, Jo, who keeps me sane and makes me cry with laughter on every project we do together: I'm so grateful to you.

To Gina and my whole publishing team: thank you for everything you do and for supporting all that I write. You're all lush humans!

To my friends and family: thanks for being my biggest supporters and for loving me like you do.

To you reading this: thank you for taking the time to read my work, I hope you enjoy it. It's because of you that I have written five books – I never forget that.

To my children, all six of you: I love you so much, no matter where we are, what's going on or how life looks. You are my reason for everything, and I adore you all.

To every woman that my women's centre and team have had the honour of supporting since we opened our doors in 2021: I hope this book does some justice to what you've been through and how utterly unfair and cruel life can be. You are all so strong, so brave and so incredible, and I am in awe of you all. x

To Kaceylee: I am in awe of you, I'm so excited for what your future looks like, and I can't wait to read your book one day.

Linda, thanks – for everything. I love you more than words could ever explain . . .

. . . And to all the women reading this living with abuse: there is a whole world out there, full of love and kindness and humans who calm your nervous system instead of terrorising it. It's never too late to leave and you're never too old to start over. x